MURDER GONE MAD

MURDER GONE MAD
Philip MacDonald

VINTAGE BOOKS
A DIVISION OF RANDOM HOUSE
NEW YORK

First Vintage Books Edition, June 1984

Copyright 1931 by Philip MacDonald
Copyright renewed 1958 by Philip MacDonald

Library of Congress Cataloging in Publication Data

MacDonald, Philip.
Murder gone mad.

Originally published: London: Published for
the Crime Club by Collins, 1951.
I. Title.
PR6025.A2218M8 1984   823'.912   83-40370
ISBN 0-394-72437-2

Manufactured in the United States of America

MURDER GONE MAD

CHAPTER ONE

I

THERE had been a fall of snow in the afternoon. A light, white mantle still covered the fields upon either side of the line. The gaunt hedges which crowned the walls of the cutting before Holmdale station were traceries of white and black.

The station-master came out on to the platform from his little overheated room. He shivered and blew upon his hands. The ringing click-clock of the "down" signal arm dropping came hard to his ears on the cold air.

"Harris!" called the station-master. "Six-thirty's coming!"

A porter came out from behind the bookstall. He was thrusting behind a large and crimson ear a recently pinched-out end of a cigarette.

The six-thirty came in with much hissing of steam and a whistling grind of brakes. The six-thirty reached the whole length of Holmdale's long platform. The six-thirty looked like a row of gaily-lighted, densely-populated little houses. The six-thirty's engine, for some reason known only to itself and its attendants, let off steam in a continuous and teeth-grating shriek. The doors of the six-thirty all along the six-thirty's flank began to swing open. Holmdale was the six-thirty's first stop since leaving St. Pancras, now forty miles and forty-five minutes behind it.

The station-master stood by the foot of the steps leading up to the bridge. He opened a square and bearded mouth and chanted his nightly chant, quite

5

unintelligibly, of what was going to happen to the train
He should properly have walked up and down the train
with his chant, but he knew only too well that to walk
at all against this tide which now covered the platform
like a moving carpet of black, huge locusts, was im
possible.

The six-thirty's engine ceased its hissing There was
a great slamming of doors which sounded under the
station's iron roof like big guns heard in the distance.
There were indistinguishable cries from one end of the
train to the other. The guard held up his lantern,
green-shaded. The six-thirty settled down to her work.
The little lighted houses, most of them now untenanted,
began once more their rolling march. . . . The six-
thirty was gone.

But, as yet, only the very first trickles of the black
flood were over the bridge and outside Holmdale station.
They were so tight packed, the units which went to the
making of this flood, that speed, however passionately
each unit undoubtedly desired it, was impossible. They
surged up the stairs. At the head of the stairs they split
into two streams, one flowing right and east and the
other left and west. Two streams flowed across the
bridge and down other stairs. At the foot of each
staircase stood a harassed porter snatching such tickets
as offered themselves and glancing, like a distracted
nursemaid, at hundreds of green, square pieces of paste-
board marked "Season."

The left-hand staircase leads into the main booking
hall of Holmdale station and this hall is lighted. As
the flood, after the first trickling, really surges into the
hall, it is possible for the first time fully to realise that
not only are the component parts of the flood human,
but that these humans are not uniform. Look, and you
will see that there are women where at first you would
have been prepared to take oath that there had been

nothing save men. Look again, and you will see that
all the hats are not, as you first supposed, bowler hats
and from the same mould, but that every here and there
a rebellious head flaunts cap or soft hat. Look again,
and you will see that the men and the women are of
different height, different feature and perhaps, even,
different habit. But you will look in vain for man or
woman who does not carry a small, square, flat case.

The flood pours through the booking hall and out
through the double doors into the clear, cold night.
In the gravelled, white-fenced, semi-circular forecourt
to the station, wait, softly chugging, two bright-lighted
omnibuses looking like distorted caravans. Each of
these omnibuses is meant to hold—as he who peers
may read—twenty-seven passengers. Each, not less
than two minutes after the flood has begun to break
about their wheels, grinds off through the night with
fifty at least. The rest of the flood, thinning gradually
into trickles and then, at last, into units, goes off walking
and talking. Their voices carry a little shrill on the
cold, dark air and the sound of their boot-soles rings
on the smooth iron road. Between the forecourt and the
station is a dark expanse edged at its far sides by little
squares of yellow light where the houses begin.

2

"Coo!" said Mr. Colby. "Sorry we couldn't get
the bus, ol' man!"

"Not a bit. Not a bit," mumbled Mr. Colby's friend,
turning up the rather worn velvet collar of his black
coat.

"Not," said Mr. Colby, "that I mind myself.
Personally, Harvey, I rather look forward to a nice,

crisp trudge. Seems somehow to blow away the cobwebs."

"Yes," said Mr. Harvey. "Quite."

Mr. Colby, having shifted his umbrella and attache-case to his right hand, took Mr. Harvey's arm with his left.

"It's only a matter," said Mr. Colby, "of a mile and a bit. Give us all the more appetite for our supper, eh?"

"Quite," said Mr. Harvey.

"I wish," said Mr. Colby, "that it wasn't so dark. I'd have liked you to have seen the place a bit. However, you will to-morrow morning."

Mr. Harvey grunted.

"There are two ways to get to my little place," said Mr. Colby. "One's across the fields and the other's up here through Collingwood Road. Personally, I always go over the fields but I think we'll go by Colling-wood Road to-night. The field's a bit rough for a stranger if he doesn't know the ground." Mr. Colby broke off to sniff the cold air with much and rather noisy appreciation. "Marvellously bracing air here," said he. "Didn't you feel it as you got out of the train? You know we're nearly five hundred feet up and really right in the middle of the country. Yes, Harvey, five hundred feet!"

"Is that," said Mr. Harvey, "so?"

"Yes, five hundred feet. Why, since we've been here, my boy's a different lad. When we came, a year ago, his mother—and his old dad too, I can tell you—were very worried about Lionel. You know what I mean, Harvey, he was sort of sickly and a bit under-sized and now he's a great big lad. Well, you'll see him yourself. . . . . Here we are at Collingwood Road."

"Collingwood Road, eh?" said Mr. Harvey.

Mr. Colby nodded emphatically. In the darkness, his round, bowler-hatted head looked like a goblin's.

"We don't live in Collingwood Road, of course.
We're right at the other side of the place. More on the
edge of the country. Our bedroom and the room you're
sleeping in to-night, ol' man, look out right across the
fields and woods. In the spring, as Mrs. Colby was saying to me only the other day, it's as pretty as a picture."

Mr. Harvey unburdened himself of a remark. "A
good idea," said Mr. Harvey approvingly, "these
Garden Cities."

"Holmdale," said Mr. Colby with some sternness,
"is not a Garden City. You don't find any long-haired
artists and such in Holmdale. Not, of course, that we
don't have a lot of journalists and authors live here,
but if you see what I mean, they're not the cranky sort.
People don't walk about in bath-gowns and slippers the
way I've seen them at Letchworth. No, sir, Holmdale
is Holmdale."

Perhaps the unwonted exercise—they were walking
at nearly four miles an hour—coupled with the cold
and bracing air of Holmdale—had induced an unusual
belligerence in Mr. Harvey. "I always understood,"
said Mr. Harvey argumentatively, "that the place's
name was Holmdale Garden City."

"When you said *was*," said Mr. Colby, "you are
right. The place's name is Holmdale, Harvey. Holmdale pure and Holmdale simple. At the semi-annual
general meeting of the shareholders—Mrs. Colby and
I have got a bit tucked away in this and go to all the
meetings—the one held last July, it was decided that
the words Garden City should be done away with. I
supported the motion strongly ; very, very strongly !
And fortunately it was carried." Mr. Colby laughed
a reassuring, friendly laugh and once more put his left
hand upon Mr. Harvey's right arm. "So you see,
Harvey," said Mr. Colby, "that if you want to get on
in Holmdale you mustn't call it Holmdale Garden City."

"I see," said Mr. Harvey. "Quite."

They were now at the end of Collingwood Road—a long sweep, flanked by small, neat, undivided gardens and small, neat-seeming, shadowy houses.' Beneath a street lamp—a curious and most ingeniously un-street-lamplike lamp—which was only the third that they had passed in the whole of their three-quarter mile walk, Mr. Colby stopped to look at his watch.

"Very good time," said Mr. Colby. "Harvey, you're a bit of a walker! I always take my time here and I find I've beaten last night's walk by fully half a minute. Now we haven't far to go. We shall soon be toasting our toes and perhaps having a drop of something."

"That," said Mr. Harvey warmly, "will be very nice."

They crossed the narrow, suddenly rural width of Marrowbone Lane and so came to the beginning of Heathcote Rise.

"At the top here," said Mr. Colby, "we turn off to the right and then we're home."

"Ah!" said Mr. Harvey.

"The only thing about this walk," said Mr. Colby glancing about him in the darkness with the air of one who knows the place so well that clear vision is not required, "the only thing about this walk that I don't like, is this bit. Of course you can't see it, Harvey, but I assure you Heathcote Rise isn't—well—isn't, as you might say, worthy of the rest of Holmdale. I don't think any one could call me snobbish, but I must say that I think it rather extraordinary of the authorities to let this row of labourers' cottages go up here. They ought to have kept that sort of thing for The Other side."

"The other side," said Mr. Harvey, "of what?"

"The railway, of course," said Mr. Colby. "You see, the idea is to have what you might call an Industrial quarter one side of the railway and a—well—a superior residential quarter on this side of the railway. Very good notion, don't you think, ol' man ? "

" Splendid ! " said Mr. Harvey.

" Round here. Round here," Mr. Colby, with increasing jocularity, swung Mr. Harvey to his left. They entered the dark and box-hedged mouth of what seemed to be a narrow passage. They came out after ten yards of this into a small rectangle. So far as Mr. Harvey was able to see, this rectangle was composed of small and uniform houses all " attached " and all looking out upon a lawn dotted with raised flower beds. Round the lawn were small white posts having a small white chain swung between them. All the square ground-floor windows showed pinkly glowing lights. Mr. Harvey wondered for a moment whether all the housewives of The Keep—he knew his friend's address to be No. 4, The Keep—had chosen their curtains together.

" Here we are ! Here we are ! Here we are ! " said Mr. Colby in a sudden orgy of exuberance. He had stopped before a small and crimson door over which hung by a bracket a very shiny brass lantern. He released the arm of Mr. Harvey and fumbled for his key chain, but before the keys were out the small red door opened.

" Come in, do ! " said Mrs. Colby. " You must both be starved ! "

They came in. The small hall was suddenly packed with human bodies.

" This," said Mr. Colby looking at his wife and somehow edging clear, " is Mr. Harvey. Harvey, this is Mrs. Colby."

" Very pleased," said Mr. Harvey, " to meet you."

" So am I, I'm sure," said Mrs. Colby. She was a plump and pleasant and bustling little person who yet gave an impression of placidity. Her age might have been anywhere between twenty-eight and forty. She was pretty and had been prettier. She stood looking from her husband to her husband's friend and back again.

Mr. Colby, whose christian name was George, was forty-five years of age, five feet five and a half inches in height, forty-one and a half inches round the belly and weighed approximately ten stone and seven pounds. He had pleasing and kindly blue eyes, a good forehead and a moustache which seemed, although really it was not out of hand, too big for his face.

Mr. Harvey was forty years old, six feet two inches in height, thirty inches round the chest and weighed, stripped, nine stone and eleven pounds. Mr. Harvey was clean-shaven. He was also bald. His face, at first sight rather a stern, harsh, hatchet-like face, was furrowed with a myopic frown and two deep-graven lines running from the base of his nose to the corners of his mouth. When Mr. Harvey smiled, however, which was quite frequently, one saw, as just now Mrs. Colby had seen, that he was a man as pleasant and even milder natured than his host.

"This," said Mr. Colby throwing open the second door in the right-hand wall, "is the sitting-room. Come in, Harvey, ol' man."

Mr. Harvey squeezed his narrowness first past his hostess and then his host.

"You coming in, dear?" said Mr. Colby.

His wife shook her head. "Not just now, father. I must help Rose with the supper."

"Where's the boy?" said Mr. Colby.

"Upstairs," said the boy's mother, "finishing his home lessons. It's the Boys' Club Meeting after supper and he wants to get the work done first."

"If we might," said Mr. Colby with something of an air, "have a couple of glasses. . . ."

Mrs. Colby bustled away. Mr. Colby went into the sitting-room with his friend. Mr. Colby impressively opened a cupboard in the bottom of the writing desk and took from the cupboard a black bottle and a syphon of soda water. Mrs. Colby entered with a tray upon which were two tumblers. She set the tray down upon the side table. She raised the forefinger of her right hand ; shook it once in the direction of her husband and once, a little less roguishly, at Mr. Harvey.

"You men !" said Mrs. Colby.

Mr. Colby and his guest lay back in their chairs, their feet stretched before the fire. In each man's hand was a tumbler. They were very comfortable, a little pompous and entirely happy. To them, when the glasses were nearly empty, entered Master Lionel Colby ; a boy of eleven years, well-built and holding himself well ; a boy with an engaging round face and slightly mischievous, wondering blue eyes which looked straight into the eyes of any one to whom he spoke. Lionel obviously combined in his person, and also probably in his mind, the best qualities of his parents. He shook hands politely with Mr. Harvey. He reported, with some camaraderie but equal politeness, his day's doing to his father.

"Homework done ? " said Mr. Colby.

Lionel shook his head. "Not quite all, daddy. I came down because mother told me to come and say how-do-you-do to Mr. Harvey."

Mr. Colby surveyed his son with pride. "Better run up and finish it, son. Then come down again. What are you going to do at the Boys' Club to-night ? '

The round cheeks of Lionel flushed slightly. Lionel's blue eyes glistened. "Boxing," said Lionel.

The door closed gently behind Lionel.

"That," said Mr. Harvey with genuine feeling, "is a fine boy, Colby !"

Mr. Colby made those stammering, slightly throaty noises which are the middle-class Englishman's way when praised for some quality or property of his own.

" A fine boy ! " said Mr. Harvey again.

" A good enough lad," said Mr. Colby. His tone was almost offensively casual. " Did I happen to tell you, Harvey, that he was top of his class for the last three terms and that the headmaster, Dr. Farrow, told me himself that Lionel is one of the best scholars he'd had in the last twenty years ? Not, mind you, Harvey, that he isn't good at games. He's captain of the second eleven and they tell me he's going to be a very good boxer. I must say—although it isn't really for me to say it—that a better, quieter, more loving lad it'd be difficult to find in the length and breadth of Holmdale."

" A fine boy ! " said Mr. Harvey once more.

3

At nine o'clock in the Trumpington Hall, Master Lionel Colby had the immense satisfaction of having proved himself so immeasurably superior to his opponent, a boy three years older and a full stone heavier than himself, that Sergeant Stubbs had stopped the bout.

" I only wish," said Lionel to himself, " that dad and mum had been there." " I'm sorry," said Lionel aloud to his cronies, with a self-condemnatory swagger quite delicious, " I didn't realise I was hitting so hard."

At nine o'clock in the Holmdale Theatre—a building so modern in conception, so efficient in arrangement, and so pleasantly strange in decoration that earnest Germans made special trips to England to see it—the curtain was going down upon the first act of the *Yeomen of the Guard* as performed by the Holmdale Mummers.

With supers, the cast of the *Yeomen of the Guard*, as performed by the Holmdale Mummers, amounted to seventy-four. There were in the theatre somewhere between two hundred and fifty and three hundred people, two hundred and twenty-two of whom were relatives of the cast.

At nine o'clock in the library of The Hospice, which was the large house of Sir Montague Flushing, K.B.E., the chairman of the Holmdale Company Limited, Sir Montague himself, was concluding a small and informal speech to those six of his fellow directors who had, that night, dined with him. Sir Montague was saying :

" . . . . and so I think that we may, gentlemen, very fairly congratulate ourselves upon drawing near to the conclusion of a very successful year. It is true that this year, as in the past, we have been unable to pay any dividend upon Ordinary Shares. It is also true that we have had to mortgage a thousand acres of building land on the Collingwood site, but, in opposition to these two facts, we have the increased and ever increasing influx of citizens. We have the success of our (*a*), (*b*) and (*d*) building schemes and we have the satisfaction of knowing that before many more months are out we shall be a fully self-contained borough with an Urban District Council of its own.

" I am sure you will join with me, gentlemen, in giving thanks to Mr. Dartmouth for his untiring efforts towards this very desirable end. When I tell you that Mr. Dartmouth is to be the Clerk to the new Urban District Council, nominally giving up his position as Secretary to the Company, I am sure that you will appreciate how very helpful the new situation may prove."

Sir Montague sits down. There is no clapping because this is an informal meeting, but there is a hearty and hive-like bumble of appreciation. Sir Montague's

manservant—the only manservant in Holmdale as this
is the only library—makes slow and steady round. The
glasses of Sir Montague, the Managing Director, Mr.
Dartmouth the Company's Secretary who is soon to
be Clerk to the Council, and the six Directors—Mr.
Archibald Barley, Colonel Fairfax, Mr. Cuthbert Mellon,
Mr. Ernest May and Mr. Charles E, Lordly—are filled.
A prosperous enough gathering of men who have, in the
manner of all big fish in small ponds, persuaded themselves that their pond is the world.

At nine o'clock in the Maxton Hall, which is on the
Other Side, Mr. James Wildman is concluding a speech
to an earnest audience. Mr. Wildman is saying :

" . . . . And now to come to the peroration of my
remarks. I can only hope that I have done some little
service to the cause, by making certain-sure that all
of my audience to-night will be fighting heart and soul,
tooth and nail for the Silk Workers. (Applause.)

" Before I sit down I should like to add to my final
and concluding remarks the final statement that before
I sit down I should like to say that, in conclusion, and
quite apart from my proper subject, it would give me
great pleasure to add that I consider Holmdale Garden
City (What's that, Mr. Chairman ?). I beg your
pardon, ladies and gentlemen, I should have said
Holmdale, that I consider Holmdale to be a proper
move in the right direction. It has not been my
pleasure and privilege to visit this salubrious spot
before this occasion of this, my auspicious visit to-night,
but now that I have paid a visit to Holmdale Gar . . .
I beg your pardon, Mr. Chairman, to Holmdale, I feel
that it would not be right for me to conclude my remarks
and to sit down without expressing my appreciation of
the very salubrious qualities of this . . . . er . . . .
Holmdale. It seems to me that here you have pleasant
homes for jaded workers ; pleasant homes set in

delightfully rusticating surroundings. It seems to me, in fact, that here you have the beginning of what some of our more educated friends would call the millennium. When I looked about me on my pleasant walk here with Mr. Todd here up from the station to this hall where I was to address you to-night I took the opportunity of keeping—as I always do—my eyes open. What I saw was a very pleasant, clean and delightful town set down in the heart of England's fair green countryside. It has been my painful lot, Mr. Chairman, ladies and gentlemen, to have most of my life's work laid down in the paths of the great cities, and I cannot tell you, I cannot even hope to properly or even with any degree of truthfulness tell you how much I opened my eyes at this very aptly named Holmdale of yours. It is, if I may coin the phrase, Holmdale by name and Holmdale by nature. It is a home town of little, clean, nice, decent, orderly homes ; homes for that backbone of England, the working man . . . . God bless him ! "

At nine o'clock in the Baden-Powell Drill Hall, Mr. William Farthingale had amassed so many points in the Progressive Whist Drive, organised by the Holmdale Mothers' Protective Aid Society, that it seemed almost certain that he would run away with the first prize of a massive pair of ebony and silver-backed hair brushes. At nine o'clock in No. 3, Pettifers Lane, Mrs. Sterling was, not without grumbling, cooking the late supper of her husband who worked at the Holmdale Electricity Supply Company. At nine o'clock in No. 14, Prester Avenue, Mrs. Tildesly-Marshall was announcing to the guests in her drawing-room that Mr. Giles Freshwater would now sing—Miss Sophie May accompanying—Gounod's " Ave Maria," after which we will have a little bridge. At nine o'clock in Claypits Road, Miss Ursula Finch, the part proprietor and sole editor of the *Holmdale Clarion*, locked up the *Clarion's* office.

At nine o'clock in the surgery of No. 10 Broad Walk, Dr. Arthur Reade was assuring the wife of Mr. Fox-Powell, the solicitor, that there would be no addition to the family. At nine o'clock in Links Lane, Albert Rogers was kissing Mary Fillimore. At nine o'clock in the parlour of The Cottage in High Collings, Mr. Julius Wetherby was having his nightly quarrel with Mrs. Julius Wetherby. At nine o'clock in The Laurels Nursing Home, which was on the corner of Collingwood Road and Minters Avenue, Mrs. Walter Stilson, wife of the Reverend Walter Stilson, was being delivered of a son. At nine o'clock in the drawing-room of No. 4 Tall Elms Road, Mrs. Rudolph Sharp, having been assailed three times that day by an inner agony, was drafting, for the eye of her solicitors, a codicil to her will. And at nine o'clock down by the station, Percy Godly, the black sheep son of Emanuel Godly, the tea-broker, whose house, just outside the bounds of the town at Links Corner, was the envy of all Holmdale, was missing the last train to London.

It was at ten-fifteen that Mrs. George Colby first evinced signs of more than normal perturbation. She and her husband and the long and saturnine-seeming Mr. Harvey had finished their last rubber of wagerless dummy.

Mrs. Colby got suddenly to her feet. Her chair fell with a soft crash to lie asprawl upon the blue carpeted floor. In a voice which sounded somehow as if she were having difficulty with her breath, Mrs. Colby said :

" George ! I—I—don't like it ! What can 've happened to him ? George, it's a quarter past ten ! "

Mr. Colby looked at his watch. Mr. Colby looked at the clock upon the mantelpiece. Mr. Colby consulted Mr. Harvey. Mr. Colby, after two minutes, came to the conclusion that a quarter past ten was irrevocably the time.

"Don't you remember, dear," said Mr. Colby, "that time when he didn't come back until just before ten. The boxing had gone on rather longer than usual. You remember I wrote a stiff P.C. to that Mr. Maclellon about it——"

"I know. I know," said Mrs. Colby, stooping down and picking up her chair. "I know, but it isn't a few minutes to ten now, George. It's a quarter *past*!" She suddenly left off fumbling with her chair and as suddenly was gone from the room. The door slammed to behind her.

"I expect," said Mr. Harvey, looking at his host, "that the lad's up to some devilment. A fine lad that and, personally, Colby, I've no use for a boy that hasn't a bit of the devil in him. I remember when *I* was a lad——"

"Clara," said Mr. Colby, "gets that worked up." He looked at his watch again. "All the same, Harvey, ol' man, it's late for the nipper. Have a drink? I'd go out only I expect that's where Clara's gone. She'll find him all right playing Tig at the end of the street or something."

"Yes," said Mr. Harvey, and laughed with due heartiness.

The door opened again. A small rush of air blew cool upon the back of Mr. Colby's neck. Mr. Colby turned. He saw Mrs. Colby. She wore a coat about her plump and admirable shape and a hat pulled anyhow upon her head. But she did not go out. Instead, she dropped in the chair which just now she had left, and, gripping her hands with tightly interlocked fingers one about the other, sat breathlessly still and said:

"I don't feel up to it, George. You go and see."

George looked at his Clara. "Tired, my dear?" said George. "We'll go instead, eh, Harvey?"

" A breath of fresh," said Mr. Harvey facetiously, " is just what the doctor ordered."

There was a hard, black frost. After the warmth of the little parlour, the cold air outside caught at their breath. They both coughed.

" A snorter of a night ! " said Mr. Colby.

" It is," agreed Mr. Harvey, " that ! "

They turned left out of the little red door. They turned up the path to the narrow passage which joins The Keep to Heathcote Rise. Out of the passage Mr. Colby turned to his right.

" The Trumpington Hall," said Mr. Colby, " is just up here. Matter of three or four hundred yards."

" Ah ! " said Mr. Harvey. " Quite."

They did not get so far as the Trumpington Hall. There are two street lamps in the quarter mile length of Heathcote Rise. The first was behind Mr. Colby and Mr. Harvey as they left the mouth of The Keep. The second was about two hundred yards from the mouth of The Keep. They were walking upon the raised side path and as they came abreast this lamp, Mr. Colby, as seemed his habit when passing street lamps, paused to take out the great silver watch. Mr. Harvey, halting too, happened to glance over Mr. Colby's plump shoulder and down into the road.

" My—*God* ! " said Mr. Harvey.

" What's that ! " said his companion sharply. " What's that ! "

But Mr. Harvey was gone. With an agility which would at any other time have been impossible to him, he had dropped down into the road and was now half-way out into the broad thoroughfare. Mr. Colby, despite the cold, bony fingers of fear clutching at his vitals, scrambled after.

Mr. Harvey was on his knees in the middle of the road,

but he was within the soft, yellow radiance cast by the lamp. He was bending over something.

Mr. Colby came trotting. Mr. Colby halted by Mr. Harvey's shoulder.

Mr. Harvey looked up sharply. " Get away ! " he said. " Get away ! "

But Mr. Colby did not get away. He was standing like a little, plump statue staring down at the thing beside which Mr. Harvey knelt.

" *Oh !* " said Mr. Colby in a whisper which seemed torn from him. And then again : " *Oh !* "

What he looked at—what Mr. Harvey was looking at—was Lionel.

And Lionel lay an odd, twisted, sturdy little heap on the black road and where Lionel's waistcoat should have been was something else. Mr. Harvey picked up one of Lionel's hands. It was cold like the road upon which it was lying.

CHAPTER TWO

I

THE next day—Saturday—was a windless day of hard frost and bright sunshine. The sort of day, in fact, which had been used to fill the placid heart of Mr. Colby with boyish joy. But now Mr. Colby's heart was black.

Mr. Colby sat, a huddled and shrunken little figure, at the table in his tiny dining-room. The chair upon the other side of the table was occupied by Miss Ursula Finch, the editor and owner of the *Holmdale Clarion*. Miss Finch was small and neat and brisk. Miss Finch's age might have been thirty-three but probably was ten years more than this. Miss Finch was severely smart in a tweedy-well-tailored manner. Miss Finch's pencil was busy among the rustling pages of her notebook, for Miss Finch was her own star reporter. But the eager, piquant face of Miss Finch was clouded with most unbusinesslike sympathy. And although her questions rattled on and on and her pencil flew, the eyes of Miss Finch were suspiciously bright.

It seemed suddenly to Mr. Colby that he could not stand any more. Miss Finch had asked him a question. He did not answer it. He sat staring across the little room at the yellow distempered wall. First, all those policemen asking questions. *What time did he leave? What time did you expect him back? Where was he going? What was he doing? Why was he doing it? What time did you start to look for him? Did any one go with you to look for him? Where did you find him? How did you find him? Do you know any one who bears enmity against yourself or him? If so, why? If not, why not? How?*

Who? Where? What? When? And now, this woman —although she was nicer than the policemen—now this woman, asking *her* questions. The same questions really, only put differently and more, as a man might say, intimate . . .

Mr. Colby thought of the bedroom immediately above this room where he sat ; the bedroom where, on the double bed, Mrs. Colby lay a huddled and vacantly staring heap. . . .

Mr. Colby got to his feet. His chair slid back along the boards with a grating clatter. He said :

" I'm sorry, miss. I can't tell you any more. I want— I want——" Mr. Colby shut his mouth suddenly. He sat down again with something of a bump and remained sitting, his folded hands squeezed between his knees. He looked at the floor.

Miss Finch shut her note-book with a decisive snap and put round it its elastic band. She rose from her chair. Automatically Mr. Colby, a well-mannered little person, got to his feet. Miss Finch came round the table in an impulsive rush. " I ought," said Miss Finch, " to have something awful done to me for worrying you, Mr. Colby, upon such a dreadful day as this must be for you. But I *would* like you to understand, Mr. Colby, that however much of a ghoulish nuisance I may seem, I may really be doing *something* to help. It may not seem like that to you at the moment. But it really is. You see, Mr. Colby, nowadays the Press, by throwing what you might call a public light on things, helps authorities to . . . to . . . to find the monsters responsible for——"

" Oh, *please* ! " said Mr. Colby, holding out his hand as if to protect himself from a blow.

Miss Finch, with an impulsive gesture, seized the hand in both of hers and pressed it. " You *poor* man ! " she said.

Mr. Colby withdrew his hand. Mr. Colby opened the door for Miss Finch. In the hall Miss Finch halted and collected her stubby umbrella and tucked it martially beneath her left arm. She said:

"If there *is* anything I can do for you or Mrs. Colby—in a purely private capacity, I mean, Mr. Colby—I *do* hope you will let me know . . . You wouldn't like me, I suppose, to run up and sit with Mrs. Colby for a little while? It would only be a little, because I'm so busy . . ."

Mr. Colby shook his head dumbly. He opened the street door and shut it, a second later, upon the well-tailored back of Miss Finch. He wandered back to his dining-room and sat down once more at his dining-table and sighed and swallowed very hard and put his head in his hands.

2

"Do they," asked Sir Montague Flushing of his man-servant, "insist upon seeing me personally?"

Spender bowed gravely. "Yes, sir."

"And you have put them in . . .?" said Sir Montague.

"In the library, sir."

Sir Montague blew out his cheeks and frowned. Sir Montague paced up and down the carpet. He said at last, half to himself:

"These newspaper men are a public nuisance!"

"Should I, sir," suggested Spender, "tell them that you are too busy to see them?"

"No," said Sir Montague. "No. No. No. I suppose I must see 'em. What papers did you say they came from?"

"One of the—er—gentlemen, sir," said Spender, "stated that he represented *The Evening Mercury*. The other was from *The Wire*."

" I see. I see," said Sir Montague.

(Extract from *The Evening Mercury*, dated Saturday,
24th November, 193 .)

" THE HOLMDALE MURDER
etc., etc.

" (From our Special Correspondent.)

" *Holmdale, Saturday.*

" Stranger and stranger grows the mystery of the
murdered schoolboy, whose body was found at 10
o'clock last night in the middle of a peaceful roadway
in Holmdale Garden City. The problem that faces the
police is no small one. The boy—Lionel Frederick
Colby, of 4 The Keep, Holmdale—had left home at
about 7.30 p.m. to visit the Boys' Club, whose meetings
are held in the Trumpington Hall. He had been in good
spirits when he left home and had arrived at twenty-
five minutes to eight at the Boys' Club. Here he had
spent the evening in the usual way, and had notably
distinguished himself in the boxing competition which
was held that night. He left the Hall with a number of
companions when the Club meeting closed at 9.20.
Half-way back towards his home—The Keep, which
is off Heathcote Rise, is not more than five or six minutes'
walk from the Hall—Lionel remembered, according to
two of his friends who have been interviewed by the
Police, that he had left his gymnasium shoes and sweater
behind. His companions had tried to dissuade him from
going back, telling him that he would not find the place
open. Lionel, who was a boy of great determination,
stated that he had promised his mother not to forget
the sweater as she wanted to wash it the next day.
One of the boys, Charles Coburn (13) of 28 Lochers

Avenue, Holmdale, stated to the police that he remembered Lionel saying that he would be able to climb in at a window. He left Coburn and the other boys in the middle of Heathcote Rise at approximately 9.25. At about a quarter past ten, Mr. Colby, the boy's father, together with a guest (Mr. Harvey) went out to see whether they could find Lionel. They walked down Heathcote Rise towards Trumpington Hall, but halfway on this journey—beside a street lamp—they made the appalling discovery.

" Police Theories :

"As was reported in earlier editions, the wound which caused Lionel Colby's death had apparently been made by a very sharp implement, probably a long knife. The stomach had been slit open from bottom to top. Death must have been instantaneous. The night was hard and frosty, and it was not possible therefore to find any trace such as footmarks, etc. The police are certain, however, that the murder was done on the spot where the body was found, as all traces of blood, etc., point to this conclusion.

"People resident in the houses which line both sides of Heathcote Rise have, of course, been questioned, but none of them can testify to having heard any disturbance. Dr. F. W. Billington of Holmdale, who acts as Police Surgeon to the Holmdale and Leewood district, examined the body at 11.30 p.m. last night. Dr. Billington gives it as his opinion that life had not then been extinct for more than two hours. The police are of the opinion that Lionel was killed on his return from the gymnasium whence, as all windows were locked, he had been unable to fetch the shoes and sweater. The police are completely puzzled by the absence of a motive for such a terrible crime.

"Mr. and Mrs. Colby are extremely popular in their

own circle and have no enemies. Lionel, too, was a very well liked boy. He had no enemies at school, and was a prominent and popular member of the local Boys' Club and also of the Holmdale troop of Sea Scouts. At present the police theory is that the crime was committed by a pervert, or homicidal lunatic.

" They have, of course, several clues which they are following up.

" Mrs. Colby, Lionel's mother, is prostrate from shock, but I managed to secure an interview with Mr. George Colby, the father. He could give me no help, but stated that all he lived for now was to see the capture of the wretch who had robbed him of his only child."

"Grave Concern in Holmdale.

" Sir Montague Flushing, K.B.E., the prominent Managing Director of the Holmdale Company Limited, stated in an interview to-day that he was himself deeply and terribly shocked by the tragedy.

" ' How such a thing,' said Sir Montague, ' could take place in this happy little town of ours is utterly beyond my imagination ! '

" Sir Montague added that he would be only too grateful if the London Press would give full publicity to his statement, ' that not only the citizens of Holmdale, but mothers and fathers throughout England could rest assured that the Holmdale Company (who are, of course, the proprietors of the whole Garden City) would do everything in their power to aid and assist the regular authorities in tracking down the author of the outrage.' "

3

That was in *The Evening Mercury* late afternoon edition. Similar writings were in the other evening papers. The station, usually deserted upon a Saturday afternoon, was besieged at the time of the paper-train's arrival by a crowd fully a third as big as that which upon week-days left the six-thirty. Within four minutes of the arrival of the papers, the book-stall had not one left.

There was, in Holmdale to-day, only one topic of conversation. Holmdale was duly horrified. Holmdale was duly sympathetic. Holmdale was inevitably a town in which every third inhabitant was satisfied that, given the job, he could lay his hands upon the criminal in half the time which it would take the police. Holmdale was also, though it would have vilified you for making the allegation, very delightfully excited. It was not every day that Holmdale came into the public eye. Holmdale looked forward to Monday morning when once more ' up in town ' it would be the centre of a hundred interested groups all asking—" I say, don't you live in that place where that boy's been killed ? "

Something, in short, had happened in Holmdale. Holmdale was News. Holmdale was on the Front Page.

The papers came down on Saturdays by the train arriving at Holmdale at 6.20. By 6.45 all Holmdale knew what London was saying of it. But all Holmdale did not know that at 6.45, Holmdale's postman was carrying in his bag three letters for which the London Press would have given the heads of any of their reporters. The first of these letters was delivered at The Hospice. The second at The White Cottage, Heathcote Rise, which was Holmdale's Police Station, and the third at the office of the *Clarion* in Claypits Road. In that order—because that was the way the postman went round—they were delivered, and in that order they were read.

Sir Montague Flushing, going through his evening's

post, came suddenly across a yellow linen paper envelope. He was a man who always speculated about a letter before he opened it, and this letter he turned that way and the other between his fingers. He did not know the paper. He did not know the minute, backward-sloping writing. He had never seen ink so shinily black. He slipped an ivory paper knife under the flap of the envelope. . . . .

He found himself staring, with wide and startled eyes, at a single sheet of paper of the same texture and colour as the envelope. Upon this sheet was written, in the same ink and writing, but with larger characters :—

" My Reference ONE
R.I.P.
Lionel Frederick Colby,
died Friday, 23rd November, 193 . . .
THE BUTCHER."

CHAPTER THREE

I

THE Chief Constable looked at Inspector Davis, then from that unreadable face down again to his blotting pad where there lay, side by side, three quarto sheets of yellow paper, each bearing in its centre a few words written in a dead black and shining ink.

The Chief Constable cleared his throat; shifted uneasily in his chair.

"What do you think, Davis?" said the Chief Constable, "Hoax?"

Inspector Davis shrugged. "May be, sir, may be not. One can't tell with these things."

The Chief Constable thumped the desk with his fist so that the glass ink-bottles rattled in their mahogany stand. He said:

"But damn it, man, if it isn't a hoax, it's . . . ."

"Exactly, sir." The Inspector's voice and manner were unchanged. His cold blue eyes met the frowning puzzled stare of his superior.

The Chief Constable picked up the centre sheet and read aloud to himself, for perhaps the twentieth time this morning: "*My reference One. R.I.P. Lionel Frederick Colby, died Friday, November 23rd. The Butcher.*"

"Oh, *hell!*" said the Chief Constable, "I never did like that damn Garden City place."

Inspector Davis shrugged. "So far it hasn't been any trouble to us, sir," he said.

"But," said the Chief Constable interpreting the Inspector's tone, "you think it's going to be."

30

" May be," said Davis. " May be not."

The Chief Constable exploded. " I wish to God you'd be less careful ! .... Now, let's get down to business. I suppose you've tried to trace this paper."

Davis nodded. " This paper is what they call Basilica Linen Bank, sir. It's purchasable at any reputable stationers. It's expensive and it's only made in that yellow colour for Christmas gift boxes. The number of Christmas gift boxes of the yellow variety sold since the first Christmas display about three weeks ago is so large that we can't get any help that way."

The Chief Constable held up a hand. " One moment, Davis, one moment. Is this stuff on sale at the Holmdale shop ? What do they call it ? "

" The Market, sir," said Davis. " Yes, it is. But not the yellow variety, therefore this paper was bought somewhere outside Holmdale."

The Chief Constable scratched his head. " Post mark ? " he suggested without hope.

" The letters were post-marked 10.30 a.m. Holmdale."

" So that," said the Chief Constable, " they were posted actually in the place itself, on the morning after the crime was committed and were delivered that same evening ? "

" That, sir," said Inspector Davis, " is correct."

" And," said the Chief Constable, " we've no more idea of who cut this boy up than the man in the moon ! "

Inspector Davis shook his head. " None, sir. In fact, so far as we can see, the man in the moon's about the most likely person."

" I can't," said the Chief Constable, " give you a warrant for *him*." He dropped his elbows on his desk and his face into his hands. He said after a moment,

" Damn it, Davis. We can't sit here *joking* about this ! "

" No, sir," said Davis.

Once more the Chief Constable thumped the desk so that the ink jars rattled.

"We've got," said the Chief Constable, "to do something."

"Yes, sir," said Davis.

"What the hell," said the Chief Constable, "are we doing?"

For the first time Davis's face showed sign of embarrassment. He shuffled his feet. He cleared his throat.

"Of course, sir," said Davis, "we're making careful enquiries. . . . "

The Chief Constable exploded. "For God's sake is it necessary to work that stuff off on me?"

Inspector Davis smiled, a faint, embarrassed smile. "There's nothing else, sir," he said, "to say. . . . If only we could find someone that could have any possible *reason* for wanting this boy out of the way. . . . "

"I know," said the Chief Constable wearily, "I know. Well, there's nothing more I can say, Davis. Carry on as best you can. Only for God's sake get a pair of handcuffs on to somebody before we have the whole countryside about our ears."

"Yes, sir," said Davis.

The telephone bell by the Chief Constable's table rang shrill.

"Who's that? . . . " said the Chief Constable, "Yes. . . . Martindale speaking. Oh, yes, Jefferson . . . . *What?* . . . Yes. . . . Go on, yes. . . . Where? What time? . . . Good God! All right, I'll send . . . . Eh? What's that you say? . . . Just read that over again, will you. Slowly, while I write it down." He picked up a pencil; scribbled to the telephone's dictation upon his blotting pad; looked at what he had written; spoke again into the receiver: "All right, I've got that." His voice was no longer astonished but weary, and with something of fear beneath its weariness. He spoke again : " Yes. . . . Yes. . . . . I should think they would. Well, we'll do what we can as quick as we can. Ring off now, will you. Stay where you are and I'll let you have a word within half-an-hour." He hung up the receiver and, with an abstracted air, lifted the telephone and placed it at the edge of his desk. He looked at Davis for so long and in such pregnant silence that at last Davis was forced to break it. He said :

" What was that, sir ? "

" That," said the Chief Constable, " was Jeffson. You know Jeffson, I think, Davis. Jeffson, from Holmdale ? "

" Yes, sir," said Davis, half rising from his chair ; then throwing himself firmly into it again.

" Jeffson," said the Chief Constable, very slowly, " was telephoning to tell me that at 9.15 this morning, three-quarters of an hour ago, Davis, a man called Walters, who's a milk-roundsman in Holmdale, saw a small car—a Baby Austin—standing at the end of one of the roads. He would have taken no interest in this car, except that as he passed and happened to glance down into it from his float, he saw what at first sight looked to him like a bundle of old clothes. He thought no more about it—for the moment." The Chief Constable's words were coming now slower and slower : it was not so much that he was seeking dramatic effect as that he was, it seemed, trying to order his own thoughts. " But, Davis, he went back the way he had come, and as he got abreast of the Baby Austin, he looked down into it again. . . . And he saw that what he had thought was a bundle of old clothes, was a bundle of new clothes . . . . with something inside 'em. What was inside them, Davis, was a girl—a girl called Pamela Richards. . . . " The Chief Constable paused. The Chief Constable looked hard, over his hands which played now with a pen-holder, at Davis.

" Yes, sir," said Davis.

" Pamela Richards," said the Chief Constable, " was dead. Pamela Richards had been slit up the stomach in just the way that two days ago Lionel Colby was slit up the stomach. . . ."

Davis's lips, beneath his tight and tidy waxed moustache, pursed themselves. There came from them the ghost of a long drawn-out whistle of amazement.

The Chief Constable nodded. " Exactly, Davis. Only more so." The Chief Constable leant forward, pointing the end of the pen-holder at the Inspector. " *And*, Davis," he said, " almost at the moment when this milkman, Walters, was finding the body, three letters—letters like this "—here the Chief Constable tapped upon the centre of those three yellow sheets which lay upon his blotter—" letters like this were being read by Flushing, Jeffson and the Editor of *The Holmdale Clarion*—letters, Davis, which were unstamped, and which must have been delivered by hand during the night."

" Was that letter, sir," said Davis, eagerly leaning forward in his chair, " what you were scribbling down on your blotter ? "

" It was," said the Chief Constable. " I will read it to you. It was set out just like these here. It said:

My Reference Two. R.I.P. Pamela Richards died Sunday, 25th November. And it was signed . . ."

" The Butcher," said Davis.

2

" What's this ? What's this ? " said Percy Godly. " What's this ? What's this ? "

The boy with the red brassard of *The Holmdale Clarion* pushed forward the bundle of sheets which he held. "Special," said the boy. "Special extra. All about the Butcher." And that was in the official wire. "Blime, sir," said the boy, "ain't it torful!" And that was in the boy's own voice.

"Isn't what," said Percy Godly, "torful?"

He pushed sixpence into the boy's hand and waved away the change and snatched one of the broadsheets. He leaned against the corner of one of The Market windows and looked down at his purchase. He saw, in staring headlines two inches deep :—

"WHO IS THE BUTCHER?
HOLMDALE PANIC STRICKEN.
IS OUR CITY TO BE ANOTHER DUSSELDORF?
THE BUTCHER'S SECOND LETTER.

"PROMINENT LEADER OF HOLMDALE'S YOUNGER SET DONE TO DEATH.

"WHAT IS BEHIND THESE MURDERS?

"*Editorial Office, Claypits Road.*

"This morning, at 9.15 a.m. Richard Henry Arthur Walters, a milkman in the employ of The Holmdale Market Limited, driving in the course of his rounds down New Approach, off Marrowbone Lane, saw a motor car— a small motor car of the 'Baby' type—standing, apparently deserted, in the semi-circular sweep at the head of the Approach. As he passed, what Walters thought a peculiar bundle in the front seat of the car attracted his attention and later, as he returned, passing the car once more, this bundle again attracted his attention. So much so, that he halted his horse, got off the milk float, and investigated.

Horribly Mangled Body.

"To Walter's surprise and horror, he found that what he had thought was a 'bundle' was, in reality, the body of that well-known and charming young member of Holmdale's 'Upper Ten'—Miss Pamela Richards—the daughter of Mr. and Mrs. Arthur Richards, Sunview, Tall Elms Road. Walters discovered immediately that Miss Richards was not only dead, but that she had been dead for a considerable time. The injuries which had led to her death were almost identical with those which led to the death of that poor lad Lionel Colby, whose mother, the *Clarion* learns with regret, is likely to become dangerously ill with brain fever, brought about by her grief.

" *Police Activity.*

" Official enquiries into the circumstances of Miss Richard's death have elicited the following facts :—

(1) That in the opinion of the Police Surgeon, Dr. Billington, Miss Richards had been dead, when Walters found her, for at least eight hours.

(2) That Miss Richards, on the preceding evening, had left the house of Mrs. Rudolph Sharp in Tall Elms Road, after a bridge party, at 12 midnight.

(3) That Miss Richards, at Mrs. Rudolph Sharp's request, had spent some time in transferring to their various homes those of Mrs. Rudolph Sharp's guests who either had no motor cars, or who had not brought their motor cars.

(4) That the last known person to see Miss Richards alive was the last of Mrs. Sharp's guests that she carried home—Mr. Henry Warburton of 5 Oak Tree Grove.

(5) That Miss Richards had upon the day before broken off an engagement of marriage.

(6) That Miss Richards both throughout the evening and at 12.10 when she bade good-night to Mr. Warburton and his family, had seemed in the best of spirits and far from anticipating evil fortune.

(7) That Miss Richards had, so far as her parents and immediate friends and acquaintances can vouchsafe, no enemy whatever in the world.

"*Ex-fiancé.*

"It is rumoured that Miss Richard's ex-fiancé is a well-known figure in Holmdale, but that the engagement was broken off by mutual rather than individual arrangement.

"*Police Theories of the Crime.*

"In a long interview which our special representative had this morning with Inspector Davis of the County Constabulary, who is in charge of this and the Colby case, we learn that three letters signed, 'The Butcher,' were received this morning referring to the death of Miss Richards. These letters, except that the reference was two and the name—that of Miss Richards—was different, were identical in other respects with the letters received after Lionel Colby's death. Inspector Davis was very frank with our representative. He pointed out that in this case of murder without apparent motive, investigation must necessarily be slower at the start than in the case where a motive or motives are immediately visible. His considered theory of how the crime actually took place is as follows :—

"Miss Richards—after taking Mr. Warburton home—was proceeding towards her own domicile in Tall Elms Road, via High Collings, Marrowbone Lane and, as a short cut, New Approach. At the corner of New Approach (at the spot where the car was found this morning) it is the police theory that she was hailed and stopped the car, when the murderer—leaning into the car upon some pretext such as asking the time or the way—must have struck at her, killing her instantaneously and fearfully mutilating her in the same way that Lionel Colby was mutilated, namely, by terribly slitting her stomach. There can be no doubt, fortunately, that death was instantaneous, and therefore practically painless.

"Police enquiries have ascertained, Inspector Davis told us, that at that time all the households of the occupied houses in New Approach were abed. A small car of the type owned by Miss Richards does not make much noise and none of the occupants of New Approach heard a sound. There are no street lights in New Approach, and after the dastardly murder had been committed, there was nothing to prevent the malefactor from calmly and cold-bloodedly going quietly upon his way.

"Bereaved Family.

"*The Clarion* learns with deep regret that Mrs. Richards, Miss Pamela Richard's mother, is critically ill owing to the terrible shock imposed by her daughter's untimely' end. Mr. Richards also was prostrate with shock. It is truly terrible to think how these tragedies affect, not only their victims, but also those whose loved and adored ones have been so suddenly, and as it were, by some all powerful demon, snatched from them in such a diabolic and undetectable way."

Mr. Percy Godly, a little whiter than usual about his jowls which were so like gills, crunched the single sheet *Clarion* special into a hard ball; threw it viciously into the gutter; raised himself from his leaning posture and walked, a thought unsteadily, away. He passed in his walk the whole long green-painted front of The Market, Holmdale's one shop, and, at this time every morning, Holmdale's social centre.

A man stepped into Mr. Godly's path; a man who said: "Hullo, Godly. I say, Godly old man, I *am* damn sorry. Dreadful business!"

Mr. Godly apparently did not hear this man. He side-stepped and walked on, his eyes fixed in a wide and clear stare. Mr. Godly faced, at the far end of The Market, a group of young matrons who stood with neat and busily wagging heads, and talked together at the top of their voices, the subject for once being, in every case, the same. From this group the youngest matron detached herself and rushed towards Mr. Godly with hand outstretched as if to clutch him by the arm. But, still staring with that glazed look before him, he twitched the arm away before the hand could descend upon it, and walked steadily on.

The young matron stared after him. " *Well !* " she said, and went back to her group. The heads of the group had turned to follow Mr. Godly's progress until at the corner by Holmdale's Inn, The Wooden Shack, he disappeared from sight.

" Poor Percy ! " said the youngest matron. " I don't care what you say ! I think that when Pam. broke off the engagement it hit him very hard."

" Poor Percy ! " said the second youngest matron indignantly. " Poor *Percy*, indeed ! Poor Pamela, *I* say ! Poor darling Pam ! "

" I say ! " said another, with something in her voice which brought all heads round to her and stilled the chattering mouths. " I say ! Have any of you thought about this ? I've only just realised that I haven't. First that boy—that was awful—and then Pamela. They're dead ! Do you understand ? They've been *killed !* They've . . . . they've . . . . There's some inhuman thing going about that . . . . that . . . . " She stopped. She caught her breath. Her eyes were wide. White teeth caught at her lower lip. She suddenly burst into a peal of sound bearing some resemblance to laughter, but having in it no mirth.

The youngest matron put her fingers to her ears. " Oh, don't ! " she said.

The red brassarded boy came running up to the

group. Twenty yards from them he began to chant.
"Special! Special! Extra! *Clarion* Special! All
about the Butcher!"

"How dreadful!" The eldest matron fumbled in
her purse. "Here, boy. Give me one. How much."

"Tuppence," said the boy.

He had, it appeared, six copies left. The youngest
matron was left without one. The previous record
circulation of the *Clarion* for one week, had to-day with
this special and unprecedented daily edition, not only
doubled, but trebled itself. Holmdale was excited and
more excited. But Holmdale was beginning to wonder
whether excitement was so desirable as forty-eight hours
ago it had seemed.

3

The Holmdale Theatre is in the Broad Walk. Facing
it across the white, wide roadway and the railed off stretch
of turf and rose trees, is the red brick building which
houses the offices of The Holmdale Company Limited.

At nine o'clock upon Monday, the 26th November—
the evening of the day upon which Pamela Richard's
body was discovered—there was held, in the Board Room
in these offices, a special meeting of Directors and
others convened by Sir Montague Flushing himself.

Round the long table in the Board Room sat nineteen
persons : Sir Montague, the six Directors of the main
Holmdale Company, and the eight Directors of the
associated and subordinate companies. There were also
present Major Robert Wemyss John, who was honorary
yet active Captain of Holmdale's surprisingly efficient
fire brigade ; the Hon. Ronald Heatherstone, who was
Private Secretary to Lord Bayford, upon whose property
half of Holmdale was built ; Colonel Grayling, head of the
Holmdale Branch of the County Special Voluntary
Constabulary ; Miss Finch to represent the Press, and

Arthur Steele, Sir Montague's Private Secretary, to take notes of the proceedings.

The meeting had begun at seven-thirty. Now, an hour and a half later, it was drawing to its close. Sir Montague was speaking, and speaking, for once, without that pomposity which until to-day all those gathered about the table had thought part of the real man. He was saying :

" . . . . I take it then, gentlemen, that we are fully in agreement that as from to-morrow, unless by to-morrow night the Police have laid their hands upon this . . . this fiend, we'll take the steps we've been discussing . . . If you have got them down, Steele ? . . . . Thank you . . . . I think I'll read over these points, just to make sure there's no misunderstanding. First, Colonel Grayling, if he gets permission from the authorities, will have every road patrolled by one or more special constables, in addition to the regular constables who will be so employed. Second, Captain John will provide additional patrolling help out of his volunteers. Third, you, Mr. Heatherstone, will obtain, if possible, Lord Bayford's permission to use some of his outdoor staff, such as gamekeepers, for patrolling the entrances to and exits from the city, so that all incomers and outgoers after dark may be interrogated. Fourth, Miss Finch will issue another special edition of the *Holmdale Clarion* to-morrow, in which it will be clearly stated that the Holmdale Company are prepared to pay a reward of £500 for information leading to the capture of the . . . the . . . murderer. Are we all agreed upon that, gentlemen ? "

Sir Montague seemed somehow less portly than usual and certainly less sure of himself and his own greatness as he looked round the table. There was something not without pathos in the anxiously out-thrust face ; something almost pitiful in the man's pallor and uncertainty ;

something certainly admirable in his earnestness.
There were murmurs of assent.

"You needn't worry about my end," said young
Heatherstone heartily. "Bayford'll lend you all his
men. If he doesn't, I'll send 'em along without asking
him."

"I'll get a rush edition out before noon, if I can,
Sir Montague," said Miss Finch, and rose and fumbled
beneath her chair for the perpetual umbrella.

"I'll get permission for the Specials all right *and*
enroll a devil of a lot more." This in a growl from
Grayling.

"Thank you. Thank you," said Flushing. "Well,
gentlemen, I'm sorry to have kept you so long." He
glanced at his watch. "I see it's already well past a
normal dinner time. . . . "

There was a general shuffling as chairs scraped back
over the thick carpet and a sudden muddled hum of many
small conversations as men struggled into their coats.

Steele threw open the double doors leading from the
Board Room to the hallway. Thirty-eight feet
clattered along the hall and so to the main doors
and the flight of steps leading down to the pavement.
The porter, expectant of tips, flung open the doors.
The first rank shivered a little as the cold air struck
their faces. The night was dark, but stars blazed in a
black and moonless sky. The frost had held and there
was a chill wind from somewhere in the north-east.
Light, broken into a hundred little shafts by the bodies
of the small crowd, flooded out from the hall and
stabbed fingers at the darkness. Twenty-five yards
away, straight opposite, the red and yellow signs
across the face of the theatre winked cheerfully and a
yellow rectangle of light poured through the glass
doors of the portico.

Young Heatherstone tightened his muffler and turned

up the collar of his ulster. He said to Grayling beside him :

"Looks pretty cheerful, what? Hardly as if there was a . . . *Jumping Gabriel*, what's up !" The sudden change in his tone from one of idle pleasantness to one of urgent and vehement wonder brought a dozen eyes to peer in the direction of his pointing arm. From out of the theatre's portico there had rushed suddenly a man in the theatre's green and gold and scarlet uniform; a man hatless and to judge by his manner distraught; a man who, arrived upon the pavement, looked with quick turnings of his whole body to his right and to his left, and then, standing half crouched, put to his lips a whistle whose shriek throbbed across the cold, dark air.

"What the devil !" said Heatherstone, and was gone, crossing the roadway in four strides. He took the railings to the grass in a leap and arrived by the side of the man who whistled before any of his companions had moved a foot. The first few of them to cross the road and the grass saw him, after urgent and gesticulating talk with the commissionaire, disappear at a run into the portico. The commissionaire, turning suddenly, made off to his right at a long, loping run.

Grayling was the first to reach the theatre. He pushed open the heavy swing door which still vibrated with Heatherstone's entry. In the vestibule he found the beginnings of a white-faced and gaping crowd. From this he singled out a face—a face whiter even than those which surrounded it, but a face beneath the cap of green lace worn as part of their uniform by the women who serve in the theatre. A man of sixty-five, but a man, Grayling, who knew both what he wanted and how to get it. He cut the girl out from the swelling crowd—they were pouring now in gusty lumps from the exits—as a skilled sheep dog a desired ewe.

"Where ?" barked Grayling. "What is it ?"

The girl gasped something, pointing. He dropped her arm. He jumped for the arch upon his right which framed the stairs leading up to the Royal Circle and Balcony. Despite his years and weight, he went up the stairs three steps at a time and came, after thirty of them, to the first floor vestibule where was the Tea Lounge and the chocolate counter and main door to the Royal Circle. That door was closed and before it there stood white-faced but determined, the short and ungainly bulk of Rippon, the theatre's manager. The tall, broad, heavy-coated figure of Heatherstone was leaning, his hands flat upon the front of the chocolate counter, peering over it. At the sound of Grayling's footsteps he looked up, twisting over his right shoulder a face whose tight clenched mouth, out-thrust jaw and fierce paller brought the newcomer to his side quicker than would have any words.

" Look ! " said Heatherstone.

Grayling stood beside him, and now himself peered over the counter and down.

In the uncarpeted semi-circle of floor between the blank back of the counter and the shelves, gaudy with sweatmeat boxes, there lay, like a crumpled life-size doll, the body of a young woman. Her face was pressed to the floor. Her arms were doubled beneath her. Her legs were ungainly asprawl in a position impossible, it seemed, for a living person. . . .

And upon her back, between slight shoulders and waist, there lay like a square yellow lake, a piece of paper.

And out from the paper, staring up at Grayling's eyes, printed in black ink, were four words :

WITH THE BUTCHER'S COMPLIMENTS.

CHAPTER FOUR

I

SUPERINTENDENT ARNOLD PIKE of the Criminal Investigation Department was talking with his immediate chief. Pike was saying :

" Very well, sir, but you realise that I shall have to drop the Brandon business ? "

Lucas shrugged. " Of course you will. But Broxburn can take that on. Anybody could do that, Pike, but this Holmdale job *isn't* anybody's meat."

" If you asked my opinion, sir," Pike said, with a wry smile, " I'd tell you that the Holmdale job isn't really *do*able ! "

" Oh, rubbish ! " said Lucas. " Take two men and get off there by car as quick as you like. Get down there by lunch time. Who do you want with you ? "

Pike considered a moment. He looked among the pages of a small notebook pulled from his waistcoat pocket. " Blaine," he said, " and Curtis. They're not on anything special at the moment, sir."

Lucas nodded. " Right ! Take them and for God's sake catch this lunatic or whatever it is before we get any more questions in the House. If only these County Police would ask us in at once instead of waiting until they've made a mess of everything, life might be easier."

Pike nodded. " By jing, sir," he said, " I echo that wish ! " He turned towards the door.

Lucas recalled him. " Oh, Pike. You'd better stay down there, I think. And the men."

Pike nodded. " It's the only way, sir, to get at the

They dealt, now with the Chief Constable as main spokesman, and both Inspectors as chorus, with the murder of Amy Adams, the waitress at the Holmdale Theatre chocolate counter. And here Pike found more to say.after the others had finished.

"This girl Adams . . ." said Pike. "There's one or two points about her case. You're sure to have noticed, gentlemen, that this case is different from the other two at almost every point. First, while the others are killed by a wound in the stomach, which is ripped up— all untidy as you might say—Amy Adams is killed by a single thrust through the stomach which isn't anything but tidy. Second, third and fourth, while Lionel Colby and Pamela Richards are killed at night and in the dark and in the open, this Adams girl is killed in the evening, and in a well-lighted public place and under a roof. Fifth, that while the first two had no . . . . well, trade-mark of the murderer's on 'em when they were found, Amy Adams did. Seventh, that while Lionel Colby and Pamela Richards had parents at least in comfortable enough circumstances, the Adamses are really poor folk living in a small cottage with the father actually out of work and on the dole."

Pike sat back in his chair and looked, with his brown, bright eyes, at the Chief Constable.

The Chief Constable pondered, stabbing at the blotting-pad before him with a tortured pen nib. He raised his eyes at last to look at his two henchmen. "Thought of that ? " he said.

Davis nodded. "Of course, sir," he said, "we've seen all that." His voice was, as usual, a flat monotone, but there was in it also a rasping of bitter and elephantine irony. "We couldn't help ourselves but see all that. It was us, you see, who did all the work and found out these facts."

"What I asked," said the Chief Constable mildly,

" was whether you'd *thought* about it ? " He looked now at Farrow.

Farrow could not, as had the more controlled Davis, keep his eyes off Pike as he answered.

" Thought about it ! " Farrow exploded. " Thought about it ! "—And then, with sudden realisation of his company—" Beg your pardon, sir, I'm sure. But if we haven't been thinking, and thinking hard, about the whole bl——about the whole business for these past seventy-two hours and more, I'd like to know what we *have* been doing."

" Yes. Yes." The Chief Constable was soothing. " Yes. Quite ; quite ! " He turned to Pike and said : " And what was *your* thought, Superintendent, when you put this ' difference ' point to us ? "

Pike shook his head. A faint smile twisted his wide mouth. He said :

" Nothing . . . . I'll have to explain myself a bit, sir. It's always been my way not to think at the beginning of a job. I've found it pays me very well. I just turn myself—or try to turn myself—into a machine for recording facts without theorising. I don't worry about whys and hows and whats and ifs. I just try to collect facts whether they appear to have any bearing on the case or not. Then, suddenly, when I've been digging round long enough and hard enough, I maybe dig up something which seems to click in my mind and become a good starting-off place for a think . . . . I hope you follow what I mean, sir."

" *Chacun*," said the Chief Constable with a most un-Gallic accent, " *à son gout*." Kindly he translated : " Each man his own way . . . . I gather then, Superintendent, that you had no particular reason for drawing our attention to the differences which exist between the circumstances of Colby's and Pamela Richards's murders and Amy Adams's murder ? "

Pike smiled at the Chief Constable. " That's right,
sir. No particular reason except that, as the cleverest
man I know is always saying, in this sort of job, if
one collects oddities one sometimes—very often, in fact
—gets somewhere."

Inspector Davis coughed, breaking the little silence
which had followed Pike's speech.

" It seems to me, sir," said Davis, " that we might
get down, as it were, to brass tacks ; might get down,
that is, to deciding what steps we're going to take to
prevent any *more* of these murders. . . ."

Farrow grunted assent. " Ah, that's right ! That's
right, sir ! And I'd like to add, what steps 're we going
to take to ensure that we watch this blasted lunatic."
He turned to his colleague. " There's only one way,
Davis, to make *sure* of stopping these murders and that's
to catch the man that's doing 'em."

" What," put in Pike mildly, " are the arrangements
so far ? "

The faces of Davis and Farrow, which had been
turned each towards the other, turned now, outwards,
towards the interloper. The interloper remained unmoved. He was not smiling any longer, but his lantern
face was placid like a child's. The Chief Constable—
a man, perhaps, of more sensibility than sense—felt
strain in the air. He hurried in with his stubby oar.
He said quickly :

" What are we doing ? I'll tell you, Superintendent."
He fumbled among the papers stacked to one side of
the blotting-pad before him and produced at last some
pinned together foolscap sheets. " Here's a copy of
the present arrangements. I'll just go through them in
brief for you and then let you have the papers."

" Thank you, sir." Pike's tone was diplomatically
grateful.

The Chief Constable cleared his throat. " First,"

he said, " as from four o'clock this afternoon, every main thoroughfare and every secondary thoroughfare in this place will be patrolled by regular police drafted in from other areas of the county. The patrols will be in pairs and will be on throughout the night, coming off duty an hour after dawn. These patrols will be supplemented in regard to the secondary thoroughfares by volunteer patrols, composed of special constables, under the control of Colonel Grayling, who acts under my directions, and other volunteers under the control of the Holmdale Company, who also hold themselves at my directions. Further volunteers will be posted to cover the various cul-de-sacs, squares, keeps and other non-thoroughfare ways. Further, as from five o'clock this afternoon, specially authorised guards (they will all be enrolled to-morrow as special constables to give them further powers) will be posted at all the entrances and exits of Holmdale. These men are being supplied, Superintendent, by the courtesy of Lord Bayford. An elaborate code of signals, in the case of any discoveries being made or any assistance being required, has been evolved. You will find full details of the whole scheme in the papers. Further, a reward of five hundred pounds has been offered by the Holmdale Company for information leading to the arrest of the murderer . . . . What's that, Superintendent ? "

Pike shook his head. " Nothing, sir, nothing. I was only thinking what trouble you're going to have. I'm not sure that I believe in these advertised rewards."

" We couldn't," said the Chief Constable, " stop the Holmdale Company from offering the reward or the *Holmdale Clarion* from publishing the offer. And also, Superintendent, I'm not sure that the course isn't justified.

Pike shrugged. " Very likely you're right, sir ! "

" It seems to me," said the Chief Constable, folding

up the foolscap sheets and handing them across the
table to Pike, "that this lunatic who calls himself
The Butcher will be hard put to it to try another of
his games without getting caught. Eh? What?
Don't you agree?"

Once more Pike's wide mouth twisted into a little
smile; a smile doubting, but by no means offensive.
"Couldn't say, sir," said Pike. "I'm afraid I must
stick to my own way. And that, as I've told you, is
not to let myself form opinions in the early stages.
I'm sure I hope you're right though. The arrangements
seem fairly complete. The danger is, of course, that
they'll frighten this Butcher into stopping his games.
And then what'll happen?"

The Chief Constable stared. "Well? . . . . I'm
afraid I don't quite follow you."

"What'll happen," said Pike, "is that nothing will
happen and then, when after a month or six months, or
a year or six years, when all supervision is removed—
when all your arrangements that is, are, so to speak,
cancelled—well, then, this butcher gentleman will just
start his games all over again."

The Chief Constable frowned. "Something in that,
I suppose." He looked hard at Pike. "Meaning,
Superintendent, that that's what you think *is* going to
happen."

Pike shook his head. "I'm not thinking, as I told
you, sir. . . . There's no doubt that it's what *may*
happen. All we can hope is that it won't."

Inspector Davis muttered beneath his breath.

The Chief Constable turned upon him irritably.
"What is it, Davis? What is it? Speak up,
man!"

Davis flushed. "I was going to say, sir, that in my
opinion, we didn't ought to be talking about *hoping*.
We ought to be talking about *doing*."

The Chief Constable glared. He opened his mouth to speak, but Pike was before him.

Superintendent Pike smiled at Inspector Davis. "I'm not at all sure," said Pike, "that Inspector Davis isn't right." He turned his head to look once more at the Chief Constable. "These arrangements of yours, sir," he said, "they seem to me to be very good and there's nothing more that I'd like to suggest —at the moment. . . . After all, you gentlemen know this place and what can be done with it. I've only just got here and want to look round before I say anything . . . About the question of quarters for me, sir? . . ."

The meeting broke up in a spirit almost of amity.

CHAPTER FIVE

I

PARALLEL with the long platforms of Holmdale station, upon The Other Side of the railway line, runs, for two hundred yards, the thousand-windowed, green-and-white-painted back of the Breakfast Barlies Factory. At the southern end of the building there shoot into the sky, sudden and massive, the four great grain-elevators. These terrific towers are considered, by many of Holmdale's citizens, to be the one blot upon Holmdale's beauty. Actually they are the strongest claim to beauty which Holmdale has—their grouping; their smooth, sleek, immutable strength; their unbroken and unvarying shape; their almost brutal utilitarianism: all these—and something else; some indefinable and inner meaning not to be understood even by their makers—make them worthy to succeed the great trees which once stood where now the towers stand, but which, if still they grew, would seem shrubs clustered untidily about the tower's feet.

They stood now, these towers, a black mass against the bloodshot sky of a winter sunset. The thousand-and-one windows of the factory sprang from blackness into golden life. Behind them the work went on. Good honest grain, ton upon ton of it, was being beaten and thrashed, roasted and split, drenched and be-surgared until, behind the gleaming windows at the northern end of the building, its final and tasteless distortions were packed, by white-clad females, into blue-and-white cardboard boxes, bearing all, in letters of red and gold, the words Breakfast Barlies. Under the splendid insignia was a picture of the factory, the grain-towers omitted. Under the picture were the words : ' Breakfast Barlies beat the band, with cream and sugar they are grand ; Dad likes them, so does little Pete, no meal without them is complete.'

There were seven hundred and seventeen lay-workers in the factory. They were all well paid, well tended and worked under conditions almost painfully hygienic. They started work—girl-packers, men-machinists, roasters, clerks, porters, managers ; everyone—at eight a.m., and they finished work—again all of them— at five p.m. Save upon most unusual occasions, and then only when armed with an official permit, signed and countersigned and franked again, was a worker seen to leave the factory before the proper time. But it was only ten minutes past four when Albert Calvin Rogers, second electrician in the belt-room, came up the stairs from the belt-room whistling, with hands in his overall-pockets and cap over one ear.

Albert Rogers was a competent working electrician hating electricity. Albert Rogers was a brilliant player of Association Football, loving the game with a devouring love. And in a pocket of the trousers beneath his overalls there lay a letter signed " Yours faithfully, F. T. Lovelace." This letter had come by the previous morning's post and had been in the pocket or his hand ever since. Thirty-six hours and more he had had it ; but it had taken every minute of those hours and all the assurances of the many to whom the letter had been shown, to convince him that the letter was fact and no imagining.

But now he did believe it. Hence the small scene, most dramatic, which had taken place in the belt-room ten minutes before. He had, as most workers, often mentally dramatised the visionary occasion upon which he would tell his immediate superior what he thought of him but never—not at least, until just now—had it occurred to him that such an occasion would ever befall him in reality.

Yet it had. And down there was Masters, the foreman, with a flea in his ear and the other ear beginning already to thicken. And here was he, an hour before knocking-off time, coming up, by the forbidden stairs, a free and melodious man.

Sergeant Stelch, the Commissionaire, came out of his cubby-hole in resplendent wrath. In all the five-year history of Breakfast Barlies, Stelch had never before seen any one of the belt-room staff come up the Directors' stairs nor heard an electrician whistle. The sight of the one added, in the same person, to the sound of the other, had at first amazed Sergeant Stelch and then infuriated him.

" Oy ! " bellowed Sergeant Stelch.

Albert Rogers halted. He turned and his wide smile added fuel to the other's wrath. " If you speak a little louder," said Albert Rogers, " a fellow might be able to 'ear you."

Sergeant Stelch advanced. The fine tips of his waved moustache seemed to reach forward, bristling.

Albert Rogers stood his ground.

" It's you, is it ? " said Sergeant Stelch, his mouth not more than six inches from Albert Rogers's nose.

" Right," said Albert Rogers, " the very first time, my dear 'Olmes. Your methods are astonishing."

" None," said Sergeant Stelch, " of that ! You know very well that no one of you blokes ain't allowed up these stairs nor in this 'all. You know the rules and regulations of this firm just as well as I do."

The smile of Albert Rogers grew, incredibly, wider. His sparkling blue eye rested longingly upon the jutting corner of the Sergeant's jaw. " You know what it is," said Albert Rogers, " if you don't take that face away, I

might push it. Leave it there by all means if you like,
but I'm not guaranteein' what may 'appen if you do."

The scarlet face became blackly purple. The points
of the moustaches seemed to double their length.
Beneath them the thick lips moved in an effort to get
out words which would not come.

"If you're going to say," said Albert Rogers, "that
you're goin' to see that I'll get the sack, you're mistaken.
I shall *not* get the sack. You see, Stelchy, it's Breakfast
Barlies who've got the sack. I've just given it to 'em."

Albert Rogers took Sergeant Stelch by the arm and
spoke kindly to him. "You don't," said Albert, "look
very well. What you want, my little man, is to 'ave a
nice quiet sit down."

Still whistling, still with his hands in his pockets,
Albert Rogers walked out of the main doors of the great
building and down the sweep of the white steps. He
had never been that way before; had never, in fact,
wanted to. It was a much longer way than the way
he and his associates generally used. But to-night he
used it, savouring every step. He turned left at the
end of the steps and walked along the neatly gravelled,
white-bordered driveway to the great gates across the
top of which showed in letters of blue and white light:
" THE BIRTHPLACE OF BREAKFAST BARLIES." Presently,
as he came out under this arch and spat reflectively
behind him, his mind became really busy not with the
past but with the future. To-day was Friday and the
letter had said next Monday morning at nine o'clock.
And this meant that as from nine o'clock upon this
unbelievable Monday Albert Calvin Rogers would be a
fully fledged and comparatively highly remunerated
member of the Woolwich United Association Football
Club.

Half-way over the new iron bridge spanning the
railway line he halted. His fingers groped for the letter

and found reassurance in its comforting but by this time greasy crackle. There it was in black and white . . .

Albert Rogers went on a little faster. By now it would be nearing five and at five he could suitably crown this day by turning into the public bar of The Wooden Shack. So down the slope of the bridge he went and turned sharp to his right and went behind the lounge and dining-room of The Shack and so round to the back where are the billiard saloons and public bar. The doors were open and the lights ablaze. Already, although this was only a moment past five, there were three customers and of these three, one—Frank Howard—was a friend.

" Love us ! " said Mr. Howard. " Look who's 'ere. Wattle, Bert ? "

" With you," said Albert Rogers, " nothing. You'll drink with me and so will everybody else. This is my lucky day." He turned to the barman. " Stick 'em up, Ted."

The hand of Mr. Howard descended upon his friend's shoulder. " You don't bloody well mean to say," said Mr. Howard in tones of great astonishment, " that that bloody tale Wally was telling me about you bloody well being a bloody footballer is bloody well true ? "

" Frank," said Albert Rogers, " it bloody is ! "

" Kor ! " said Mr. Howard.

" On Monday next," said Albert Rogers, " . . . but 'ere, read for yerself." He pulled out from his pocket the letter, unfolded it and drew from its envelope the precious, be-thumbed sheet.

Mr. Howard read. " Well, well, well ! " said Mr. Howard. " 'Eere, 'ave another."

Albert Rogers had another ; and then, when more friends came in, yet several more. Albert Rogers, who had a good head but not great capacity for bulk, switched from bitter to whisky. By half-past six he was in a condition which he himself, even at the time,

described as three parts lit. He was, however, much in
love with Mary Fillimore and had an appointment with
Mary Fillimore for six thirty-five at a spot distant by
fifteen minutes' walk.

" 'Eu," said Albert Rogers, " I'm off."

" Not," said a voice behind him—a new voice for this
evening—" till you've had one on me, Bert."

Albert Rogers turned. " Blimey ! " he said, " if it
isn't old Todd." He swayed a little on his feet and held
out a ready hand.

Mr. Edward Bultivle, chief compositor at the Lakeside
Press, gripped the proffered hand, shook it warmly and
within two minutes placed firmly within it a glass containing yet more whisky. Mr. Bultivle then raised his
own glass. " Here," said Mr. Bultivle, " is to the most
promising Outside Right in League Football ! "

" 'Ear, 'ear ! " said Mr. Howard.

And " 'Ear, 'ear ! " came hearty chorus.

" How the hic," said Albert Rogers, " did you know
anyhic about it, Todd ? "

" Off the next edition of the *Clarion* of course," said
Mr. Bultivle. " 'Aven't I spent the whole flamin' day
settin' the darn thing up ? And didn't Tom Pearce
where you lodge drop word into the *Clarion* office this
mornin' ? Of course he did and of course Miss Finch
put somethink in, and a nice bit it is, I can tell you,
Bert ! 'Ave another ? "

" I will," said Albert Rogers firmly, " do nothink of
the such. I . . . I'm goinc. I . . . I've got a point-
ment. What's time ? "

Mr. Bultivle consulted a large watch. " The time,"
said Mr. Bultivle largely, " is twenty-three and three-
quarters of a minute to seven. You're late already, boy.
Stay and 'ave another."

But Albert Rogers had gone.

Albert Rogers was willing his unruly but magnificent

legs to carry his thirteen stone of well proportioned bone
and muscle fast, and as straight as might possibly be,
up the length of Market Road ; thus to Forest Rise and
so, eventually, to the hedged-in blackness of Links Lane.
Half-way up Forest Rise he broke into a staggering run,
He knew what Mary was when she was kept waiting. It
wasn't that she was cross with him or gave him the rough
edge of her tongue or anything like that. It was just
that she was hurt and it wasn't as though she made a
fuss about it like some sorts would. It was just that she
was disappointed-like at the waste of time and couldn't
help showing it however much she tried.

Albert Rogers, running uphill upon legs which although
steadier were still unruly, once more cursed himself for
a fool. At the top of Forest Rise and the steep downward
slope which joins this house-flanked thoroughfare with
the rurality of Links Lane, he slowed down to a walk.
No good charging, on these legs, down a steep and dark
and stony road.

He tried, as he began the descent, to calculate the
time. It must have taken him eight minutes at least
since leaving The Shack. What had Todd said ? Twenty-
three minutes to seven. That would make it, now, about
a quarter to . . . That would be all of twenty minutes
she would have been waiting before he got up the hill
the other side to the seat . . .

He found himself blowing hard, a thing he hadn't
done after a little run like that for perhaps four years. . . .
He despised himself. . . . He stopped to draw breath.
. . . Cold air went down into his inflamed lungs like a
sharp, hot sword. He got his breath. He went on again ;
walking. He got to the foot of the hill just by the little
white stile into Crosbies Wood. . . . He passed the
stile. . . . He was walking on the right-hand side of the
road and so he went by not more than a few feet from
the stile. He thought that he saw, dimly through the

dark, a figure leaning against the rail to one side of
the stile, but he was not certain until, from just behind
him, there came a voice. It said :

" I wonder whether you could help me."

Albert Rogers turned, swaying a little with the
movement.

Albert Rogers started to say—he was always a civil
boy—" I beg your pardon . . ." But he got no further
than the " beg."

Something very cold hurt him. . . . No, it wasn't
cold, it was fire.

A little stifled cry, like the squeak of a small injured
animal, came from his mouth. He doubled, his hands
clasped vainly to his stomach. His knees crumpled
beneath him. He felt light, light . . .

2

They had lodged Pike in Fourtrees Road, in Number
Twelve. This was, for Holmdale and Fourtrees Road,
a large house, having five bedrooms, a sun-parlour and
something over quarter of an acre of garden. The owner,
a spinster of fifty healthy years, was Miss Honoria
Marable. Miss Marable was a prosperously retired
seaside boarding-house proprietress who, after thirty
years of lodgers, was still weirdly unable to live happily
without being constantly surrounded by these animals.
Number Twelve was Miss Marable's ambition brought
about by Miss Marable's self. Number Twelve was,
necessarily upon a small scale, everything that boarding-
houses should be, but so very seldom are. It is doubtful
whether Miss Marable did anything but lose money over
it, but it is certain that Miss Marable's lodgers were
well fed and well housed and happy and, to be all
these, paid less than any other lodgers in Holmdale.

Pike was given the large bedroom in the front of the house, a much-windowed, cheerful room. Upon the evening of his first day in Holmdale, just after the evening meal, he sat up in his room looking out, through the glass of the bay-window, at the dark, clear night. There was no moon but the sky was encrusted with stars and there was that strange translucency to the darkness which sometimes comes upon a winter's night.

It had been cold all day and now was colder. But there had been a fire—and a good one—in the room since early morning and Pike, seeing that the air was already misted with his tobacco smoke, threw open a pane of the bay window. Keen, sweet-smelling air rushed in. He knelt upon the window-seat, took his pipe from his mouth and leaned out, taking deep breaths.

He could see dimly the black shapes of smaller houses upon the other side of the road and, a hundred yards or so to his left, a yellow splash of light where the street-lamp stood, outside the small white cottage which was the house of Sergeant Jeffson of the County Constabulary and, therefore, also Holmdale's Police Headquarters.

He put the pipe back into his mouth again, leant his forearms comfortably on the sill and waited until the measured, regular footfalls which he had heard when first he opened the window should pass beneath him.

They drew near and nearer, two men walking together, with slow and unvarying pace, upon the pavement upon his side of the road. He leant out and peered downwards, straining his eyes. In a moment he levered himself back, satisfied. A patrol—and a patrol of regular constables. He had just been able to distinguish their helmets. The patrol went by at the same pace. The sound of their walking grew fainter and fainter and died away altogether as they breasted the small rise and went down the hill towards the end of Fourtrees Road and the semi-circular sweep of Fourtrees Avenue which was one end of their beat.

Pike tapped the ashes out of his pipe against the window-sill, sat back on his heels and reached out a hand to pull the window close.

But he did not close it. The sound of more footsteps came to his ears. These were not measured, regular footsteps. They were hurrying, stumbling footsteps ; one person's. Pike threw the window wide and leaned out listening. The footsteps were coming from the same way as had the patrol's when he had first heard them. They must just have turned the corner from Marrowbone Lane coming, however, from the east end of Marrowbone Lane and not the west as had the patrol. They were thus upon the far side of the road from Pike. They came tripping and stumbling along with a sort of shuffling ring borne to Pike's ears on the frosty air. It was no good hoping that he could see their owner from where he was. Half he decided to whip out of the room and down the stairs in the hope of waylaying the maker of the sounds ; but he changed his mind immediately, realising that by the time he had got down the stairs and down the path and through the gate, the runner might be twenty or thirty yards ahead of him. . . .

The footsteps, loud now, were exactly opposite him. Craning out of the window he could hear another sound besides that made by the feet. He could hear laboured, gasping breathing—a wild sound. Whether it was made by a man or woman he could not tell. It was the strangeness of this and also the tale which the breathing told of the runner's distress that made him jump across the room in two leaps, fling open the door, go downstairs in four bounds, wrench open the front door, run down the path and vault the gate. . . .

Pike could run. Pike knew that he was gaining over a yard with every stride. But his running stopped

c

within a hundred yards. The pursued halted under the street-lamp opposite Jeffson's cottage, fumbled with Jeffson's gate and charged, reeling a little in his stride, up to Jeffson's front door. Pike slowed down to a walk, reached the gate himself and stood by it, waiting, unobtrusive.

The street-lamp took within the radius of its yellow light the small, green door and the figure which now was knocking upon it with loud and irregular beatings. Pike saw that he had been running after a man of considerable age. It was a tall, lean and stooping figure which knocked. It supported itself with its free hand against the door-post. Its shoulders were bent and heaved to shuddering breaths. It had no hat and a mop of white hair tossed disorderly to its movements.

The door was opened by Jeffson himself. Pike heard his deep growl and then a high-pitched, wavering voice in answer whose words were marred to Pike's hearing by their owner's fight for normal breath.

Pike pushed open the gate and strolled quietly up the path. He arrived at the door just as Jeffson had waved his visitor inside.

" Just a moment," said Pike.

Jeffson opened the door again. " Oh, it's you, sir," he said. He heaved a sigh of relief. " Glad you've come, I must say." He jerked a thumb over his shoulder towards the dark recesses of the passage. " That there, that's . . ." Jeffson never finished his sentence. His visitor's voice came again from just behind him.

" Quick," it said, " quick ! We can't stand here wasting time. Quick ! quick ! "

Pike and Jeffson looked at each other. Pike nodded. They stepped across the threshold and Jeffson closed the door.

There was a room on the right of the passageway which was half parlour of the Jeffson family and

half rural police office. A flood of hard light from
a yellow-shaded electric lamp showed to Pike's eyes a
slippered and coatless Jeffson, burlier even than in
his uniform, and a cleric of extraordinary leanness
from whose lined and working and ravaged face blue
eyes blazed out with a strange light—a light which
might have been mirth, or madness or sheer, naked
terror.

"This," said Jeffson awkwardly, "is the Reverend
Rockwall." He turned to the cleric. "Mr. Rockwall,
this is . . ." he hesitated, looking at Pike and receiving a nod, went on: "This is Superintendent Pike of
Scotland Yard who's down here about——"

"Yes, yes!" Rockwall seemed now to have mastered
his voice. It was still high-pitched and strained, but the
note of hysteria had gone.

"Yes," he said again, "yes. But there's been another
of these . . . in Links Lane. . . . I was walking down
there. I was going home. I tripped over something in
the road. It . . . it . . ." He put up long, lean fingers
and for a moment covered his face.

Pike pushed forward a chair. "You'd best sit down,
sir," said Pike. His voice was calm and soothing and
matter-of-fact.

Rockwall sank into the chair. From a pocket of the
black, long-skirted coat he took a crumpled handkerchief
and with it mopped the bony brow which glistened
with great beads of sweat. "I'm sorry," he said. "I'm
sorry. . . . What I stumbled against was the body of
a man. I could . . . I could tell that he was dead.
He had . . . he had . . . there was a wound in his
stomach." He shuddered and looked at his right hand.

Pike's small, bright eyes looked at the hand without
seeming to look. They saw that on the ball of the thumb
was a dark, drying stain. Pike said, quietly:

"How long ago was this, sir? Don't worry to tell us

any more. Just answer my questions, if you would be
so good."

"It seems," said Rockwall, "hours! But it can't
be. I came here. . . . I ran . . . all the way. I don't
know how long it took me."

Jeffson looked at Pike's raised eyebrows then, cal-
culatingly, at his other visitor. "Call it a quarter of an
hour to twenty minutes," said Jeffson.

"Did you," Pike said to Rockwall, "see anybody
else on your way? After, I mean, you had found the
body and were coming here?"

The white head was shaken. "No. Not a soul. All
the way I was looking for some one. I felt that I should
never get here."

Pike's hands were deep in his pockets and his eyes
were fixed upon the shining toe-caps of his boots. He
rocked a little from heel to toe. He was silent for a long
moment. And then the hands came out of his pockets,
the rocking ceased and he turned to Jeffson. He said:

"Get in touch with the patrol stations. Tell 'em to
pull in everybody from now on. Get ready yourself.
I'm going to get the car. Bring a man with a bicycle.
I'll be back in four minutes. Mr. Rockwall, will you
please stay here and then accompany us."

3

Two bright streams of white light—one stream from
the headlights of the blue police Crossley, the other from
the headlights of the Holmdale Cottage Hospital
Ambulance—flooded the narrow hedge-lined summit of
Links Lane. Where the two floods intersected in an
oddly theatrical pool of whiteness, a group of men stood
looking down at something which lay upon the road.
The road was black under the white glare. The hedges

were black, thick tracery against blue-black night. Every little irregularity in the road's surface showed under the lights as a bump and a dip eight times their real size.

Pike came suddenly into the centre flood of light.

" That's that ! " he said curtly.

" Anything, sir ? " said Jeffson.

Pike shook his head. " Not a thing."

" No . . . trace ? " said Rockwall.

Again Pike shook his head. " Not a trace, sir." He bent his head to look down at the sprawled thing, now covered roughly with a blanket from one of the ambulance stretchers, which lay at their feet. " What could you expect ? The Butcher keeps his weapon and I don't suppose ever so much as touches his victim. There's a hard frost and even if there wasn't this surface wouldn't take any prints. . . . No, there's nothing. Nothing at all. . . . Jeffson, you'd better tell the ambulance men to take this away." He nodded at the bundle which, so short a time ago, had been Albert Rogers. " The only thing we've got to be thankful for at the moment is that somebody knows who he is."

For a moment Jeffson stood motionless looking down.

" Poor kid," said Jeffson. And then, lifting his head sharply, turned and strode off and became brusquely official with the ambulance men.

Pike moved nearer to the cleric and looked at the him. Pike said : " You're *sure*, sir, that the body hadn't been moved since you saw it ? "

Rockwall shrugged thin shoulders helplessly. " So far as I can tell, Superintendent, the poor fellow hadn't been moved. . . . But you must understand . . . you must understand that I . . . I . . . I was overwrought . . . when I——"

" Quite, sir, quite. I just wanted to make sure . . . Jeffson ! "

"Yes." Jeffson came trotting up, moving his bulk lightly.

"Did you say something about this boy having had a girl?"

Jeffson nodded. "Yes. That's right. Mary Fillimore it is. In service. Parlourmaid at Mrs. Sharp's in Tall Elms."

The ambulance men came shuffling with a stretcher. They set the stretcher down. They stooped and lifted the shell of Albert Rogers and soon bore it away.

Pike went on as if there had been no interruption. "Happen to know where they used to meet? Here?"

Jeffson shook his head. "Couldn't say. We could wake the girl. Shall we? Or get her in the morning?"

Pike considered this. "In the morning," he said at last.

Jeffson, tilting his helmet forward over his eyes, scratched the back of his head. "What's to do now, then?"

"Get back." Pike was curt. "Get back and see if they have pulled any one in. What's the time?"

Rockwall answered this. He pulled out a watch, bent to see its story by the lights of the Crossley and said.: "Fifteen minutes to eleven." He seemed calm now and in the thin face the blue eyes too were calm. The hand that held the watch did not tremble and the voice, though high-pitched still, was steady.

"Thanks," said Pike. "Now we'll get back. Jeffson, send that bicycle man of yours the round of the patrols."

"I wonder," said Rockwall, "whether you would let me ride in your motor car as far at least as the beginning of Marrowbone Lane. This . . . this . . ."

"Of course, sir." Pike was quietly genial, in great contrast to his official curtness. "Come along."

There came a sudden roar as the engine of the ambulance started and then a swinging of its light beams.

It backed, turned, and then, with a soft purring in place of its roar, was gone. Against the hedge Jeffson spoke with a dim shape standing by a glittering bicycle.

Pike, his hand courteously ready to assist, led Rockwall to the car, settled him in the front seat and wedged himself into the driver's seat beside him. Jeffson came running and climbed into the back. More swinging of lights. More backing and turning. Another, deeper purr as the Crossley went. . . .

Links Lane was once more its black and empty and silent self.

4

The hands of the clock upon Jeffson's mantelpiece stood at five minutes to midnight. The little room seemed crowded. Behind the plain deal table, which seemed to be the end of parlour and the beginning of office, sat Pike in a chair with arms and Jeffson upon a chair without arms. Before the table, at an angle to them, sat huddled in one of the parlour armchairs the thin length of the white-haired clergyman. By the door, upright, uncomfortable and yet most pleasurably excited, sat, nursing an awkward helmet upon more awkward knees, Police Constable 4123 George Birch.

Pike was speaking to the Reverend Lucius Charles Arbuthnot Rockwall.

" . . . I think that's all. No, there's one other thing. If you wouldn't mind telling me, sir, purely, of course, as a matter of form, what the business was which had taken you, in these strange times, to such a place that you had to walk back through Links Lane ? "

" Certainly. Certainly." Rockwall sat upright in his chair with a sudden spring almost inhuman to view. " I had been to visit a sick parishioner of mine, who lived in the farm cottages at the top of Links Lane just within my cure——"

"Who's that, sir?" Jeffson put in. "Joe Starr?"

The white head was shaken. "No. Sarah Queen. You know her, Sergeant? Of course you do! Poor old dame! I'm afraid she won't last another week."

"What time, sir," said Pike, "did you get to this woman's cottage?"

The heavy lids were lifted from the strange blue eyes. "I really couldn't say, Superintendent."

Pike was looking down at the pencil with which his hands were toying. He spoke without raising his eyes. He said: "Surely, sir, you could give us some idea."

From Rockwall's mouth there came a queer sound, presumably a laugh. Its end was as sudden as the death of the sound of a loud speaker peremptorily disconnected.

"I daresay," said Rockwall, "that I could . . . Let me think . . . I left my house immediately after my small evening meal. . . . I should say, Superintendent, that that was at somewhere between seven and half-past. I remember that I did not want to go out but I had promised old Sarah that I would. I walked straight——"

"Just one moment, sir!" Pike's interruption was suave but interruption nevertheless. "Did you walk to the cottage by the same way that you came back? Through Links Lane, that is?"

Rockwall shook his head. "I did not, Superintendent. I took the short-cut over the golf course half-way up Tall Elms Road."

"But you came back," said Pike mildly, "by the longer road?"

Rockwall nodded. For a moment the very poll of the white head was presented to Pike's eyes. "I came back," said Rockwall, "by the longer road . . . as you say. . . . The reason, Superintendent, was that it was so dark to-night that I had a great deal of trouble walking over the golf course. . . ." His thin lips curved into a self-deprecatory smile. " As a matter of fact I twice measured my length upon the grass, tripping first over a wire fence which I altogether failed to see and secondly stumbling down over the edge of one of the greens. I really thought it safer, after leaving old Sarah, to walk back by the road. . . . Thank God that I did. Otherwise . . ."

" Otherwise what, sir ? " said Pike. His tone was gently curious and he still did not raise his eyes.

Rockwall stared. There was an instant's silence. " Otherwise . . ." he said, " otherwise . . . Why, Superintendent ? I am afraid I do not follow you. If I had not chosen to go back by Links Lane, I should not have . . . I should not have . . . made my terrible discovery, and if I had not . . . the . . . the . . . it might have been lying there still, uncared for and untended."

" Yes," said Pike. " Yes. I see, sir. . . . And we know from what you've already told us that it was somewhere about twenty minutes past nine when you found . . . when you made the discovery."

A film of vagueness seemed to have come over Rockwall's lean, lined face and his eyes, too, were now dull. He waved a white, thin, long-fingered hand. " As you say, Superintendent. As you say."

" Now the walk across the golf course, I should say, would take you . . ." Pike looked at Jeffson.

Jeffson twitched burly shoulders. " Say half an hour." He looked at Rockwall. " Do you agree, sir ? "

Once more the hand was waved while the other hand rested upon the arm of the chair supporting the white head. " Yes. Yes. I should think you are right. I have never timed the walk. Yes. Yes. I should say half an hour. Quite half an hour. A full half-hour."

Pike ceased to play with his pencil. "So that you would have arrived at the cottage of this Sarah Queen at about eight o'clock and, as I see it, the walk from the cottage to where this man Rogers was killed would take somewhere between five and ten minutes. You got to the cottage at eight and you left at a quarter-past nine. A longish visit, wasn't it, sir?"

Rockwall closed his eyes. "Why, yes. But that poor old dame, she's like all the rest of them . . . she was afraid." He raised his head from his hands and the lids from his eyes. He stared hard at Pike. "She was afraid, Superintendent, of death. . . . I gave her what comfort I could. One cannot tear oneself away on those occasions."

"Quite, sir. Quite." Pike looked at Jefferson again. "I don't think we need keep Mr. Rockwall any longer unless, Jefferson, there's anything you'd like to——"

Jefferson shook his head. "No, sir. No."

Pike rose and came out from behind the table. Rockwall rose to meet him. For a moment they looked at each other.

"I will be going on my way then," Rockwall said. "If there is anything further I can do—any small assistance which may lie within my power—I hope you will——"

Pike nodded. "Thank you, sir. We'll certainly call upon you. We are, of course, much indebted to you for acting so promptly and properly."

Jefferson opened the door. Police Constable George Birch sprang to his feet and stood, lumberingly, out of the way. There was a moment's silence. Tall and bent and almost unbelievably thin, Rockwall stood in the centre of the little room. His eyes were darting glances here and there about the furniture.

"Lookin' for something, sir?" Jefferson said.

"Eh?" said Rockwall, suddenly raising his eyes.

" Oh, thank you, Sergeant. Thank you. It was . . . I was looking for my hat."

" Hat, sir ? " said Jeffson and began, too, to look.

Pike interposed. " When you came, sir, you had no hat with you," he said quietly.

" Eh ? " Rockwall stared. " Oh, yes . . . yes . . . yes. It must have been lost in my run. Thank you. Thank you. Good-night ! "

He went through the door and into the passage in which there was now a light. At a nod from his Sergeant, Constable Birch followed along the passage and opened the front door.

Inside the room Pike and Jeffson, looking at each other in silence, heard the click of the door shutting and then slow, weary-seeming footsteps ringing down the frozen path.

CHAPTER SIX

I

PIKE looked at his watch. The hands stood at half an hour after midnight. He looked at Jeffson. He said:
"About time we were hearing whether the patrols have got any one, isn't it?"

Jeffson nodded and crossed the room with heavy tread to the corner where, upon a small and rickety table, the official telephone stood. He picked up the receiver and asked for a number. Pike walked over to the window, edged his way behind a parlour table and stood looking out into the dark, cold night. He drummed with his finger tips upon the glass. Behind him in the warm, brightly lighted little room Constable Birch was striving to master a November cough and Jeffson was holding a muttered conversation with his telephone. Pike went on staring into the darkness. He did not turn until, with the click of a replaced receiver, Jeffson spoke once more in his normal voice.

"They've got three," said Jeffson.

Pike wheeled, nearly knocking over the little table. "Where are they?"

"One," said Jeffson, "down at the police hut by the station and two on the way here now. What shall I do, sir? Tell 'em to get the one from the station up here as well?"

Pike nodded. Once more silence fell. Constable Birch mastered his cough. Jeffson sat upon the edge of the official table and swung massive legs. Pike turned again to the window.

It seemed nearly as many hours; but it was actually ten

74

minutes, before there came the sound of footsteps
upon the road outside. Jeffson nodded at Constable
Birch, who, putting on his helmet, left the room. They
heard his heavy tread in the passage and then, simul-
taneously with the sound of the front door opening,
the click of the gate latch and a tramping upon the
path.

Pike and Jeffson waited. There entered to them three
Special Constables and two others. The senior of the
Special Constables reported. He was a small and stout
and excited man. Jeffson handled him well and got rid
of him and his two henchmen with admirable speed.
The two prisoners were left standing in the middle of
the room. Again Jeffson and Pike sat behind the official
table, and again Constable Birch sat by the door nursing
his helmet.

The prisoners were a tall and dishevelled young man,
not quite steady on his feet—Percy Godly—and a small,
untidy, nervous and yet truculent person in a black
felt hat, enormous horn-rimmed spectacles and a very
short-coated and hairy suit.

Godly, swaying gently, rather as a young sapling
sways in a light breeze, seemed content to sway. The
other, if one could tell by his sudden and instantly
repressed movements and his tight-clenched mouth from
which the lips seemed completely to have disappeared,
was only restraining speech, and hot speech, with the
greatest difficulty.

"Sergeant Jeffson!" Pike was smoothly official.
"Do you know these men?"

Jeffson nodded. He indicated first the swayer.
"That's young Mr. Godly," said Jeffson, "the other
gentleman—I'm afraid I don't know his name—is
something to do with the film business."

"My name," said the small man in horn-rimmed
spectacles, using a voice surprisingly deep and

phenomenally fierce, " is Spring, Wilfred Spring, and I'd like to know what the hell——"

" Half a minute, sir, half a minute ! " said Jeffson. Pike smiled a pleasant smile.

" Sit down, Mr. Spring," he said. " Constable, give Mr. Spring a chair."

Spring exploded. Beneath the shadowing spectacles his dark, clever, somewhat weasley face seemed to grow thinner and darker with his anger.

" I don't want your damn chairs," he said. " All I want to know is what the hell——"

" Excuse me, sir ! " Pike was smooth. " You've said that before. If you wait a moment I'll tell you. Are you resident in Holmdale ? "

Spring seemed on the verge of another outburst, then controlled himself with a visible effort.

" Yes," he said, " 14 Collingwood Road."

" And this other gentleman ? " Pike looked at Jeffson.

" Mr. Godly," Jeffson said, " lives with his father, Mr. Emanuel Godly, just outside the city at Links Corner."

" Qui' ri' ! " said Mr. Godly affably. " Absolooly ri' ! " He smiled largely upon the room. The effort seemed to unbalance him, and the sway turned into a stagger.

" Sorry ! " said Mr. Godly.

Constable Birch, displaying initiative, rose and took a chair from a corner and thrust it neatly against Mr. Godly's legs from behind and so had him neatly seated.

" Good ! " said Mr. Godly.

" Look here ! " burst out Spring. " I mean to say, damn it all ! "

" One moment, sir." Pike's tone was noticeably curter. " At 9.30 this evening the body of another murdered person was discovered within the bounds of this town. Acting upon my instructions, delivered at about half-past eleven, the police detained every one found within the town out-of-doors. I am naturally sorry to cause inconvenience, but I am sure you will agree with me that some such step as I took was absolutely essential in the interests of the public."

Spring glared. The horn-rimmed spectacles slipped a little on his nose. He thrust them back into position with an impatient hand.

"But, good God!" he said, "you don't suspect me of——"

"Don't go so fast, sir. Naturally I don't suspect anybody. And yet to do my duty I suspect everybody. It is possible, you know, to do both."

Pike looked hard at his indignant prisoner. The gaze of his brown eyes met and held the gaze of the other brown eyes behind the spectacles.

"I am sure," said Pike, "that you will agree with me, Mr. Spring, that personal inconvenience must be borne in these strange circumstances. . . . May I suggest that you sit down ? "

"But blast it, tell me . . . Oh, all right!" Mr. Spring sat down so hard upon the chair which Constable Birch pushed forward that he almost rebounded from it.

"Carefoo!" said Mr. Godly, raising an admonishing finger.

"Jeffson," said Pike, "where did that Special report that Mr. Spring was taken in? "

"Junction," Jeffson said, "of Market Road and Collingwood Road. According to the report Mr. Spring was coming up Market Road from Chaser's Bridge—that's the bridge over the Railway, sir—and he just got to the corner of Collingwood Road when the patrol stopped him. Just after twelve it was."

"The blighters," said Spring, "grabbed hold of me as if I was a criminal." He glared at Pike. "God alive, man! Can't you hurry, I want to go home. I've just done a hard day's work—a harder day's work, I expect, than you've ever done in your life. I've been on the go ever since half-past four this morning, and I'm tired, damn tired! So would you damn well be! I've been on my feet the whole day. I'm directing a film in which we're using half the blasted Air Force and as their own officers don't seem to be able to tell the men what to do, I had to do it for them! Always the same story!"

"Quite!" said Pike. "I'll try and see that you get back to your house as quickly as I can, Mr. Spring. I'm afraid, however, that I shall first have to worry you with some questions. I can assure you, sir, that the more readily and more concisely you answer these questions, so to speak, the quicker you'll be off home. . . . Now then, Jeffson, please take notes of the questions and Mr. Spring's answers."

"Right, sir," Jeffson said. "Ready when you are."

"Now, Mr. Spring, would you please tell me what you were doing when found by the patrol."

"Walking home."

"Where from?"

"Garage."

"What garage is that, Mr. Spring?"

"Damn it, don't let's waste time! There's only one garage in the place." Spring twitched about in his chair as if he would like to jump off it and wave frantic arms and legs. His spectacles kept slipping and the thrusts with which he jammed them back into place grew more and more savage.

Jeffson chipped in. He said to Pike:

"That's quite right, sir. There's only one public garage in Holmdale. It's down by Chaser's Bridge."

"Thanks," Pike nodded. "Now, Mr. Spring, what were you doing at the garage?"

"What the bloody hell d'you think I was doing at

the garage? Having coffee and cake? ... I was putting my car away, of course. I keep my car there. It's too big to go into the garage at the house. Besides, our other car is always in the house garage."

"I see. And am I to understand that you had come straight into Holmdale from outside and gone straight to the garage to put your car away and were walking directly home?"

"You are."

"Where had you been outside Holmdale, Mr. Spring?"

"You must forgive me for saying so—I'm afraid I don't know who you are—but it does seem to take you a very long time to get an idea into your hea▬▬ .. I'd been working. I told you that. All day. An▬ I've got to work all day to-morrow and I should be very, very much obliged if I could go home. If you're looking for this lunatic who calls himself The Butcher, it's not me, although I'm not at all sure I'm not beginning to sympathise with him."

Pike smiled at that. "All right, sir. But we can't help being slow, you know. We've got to be careful. I'm afraid I'm still not clear on this point. Where exactly do you work?"

The tight and somehow fish-like mouth of Mr. Spring opened in amazement. He shut it again with a decisive click so loud as to betray the origin of his splendid teeth.

"Good God!" he said, and then: "Sorry! I'm a film producer. I'm at present working outside Holmdale at the Empire Studios in Enswood. You may have heard of the picture. It's called 'Death in the Air.' I've got half the Air Force out on the job——"

"Yes. Yes. And you finished work at Enswood Studios, Mr. Spring, at what time?"

"I don't clock off but I should say that when I finally

got away it must have been about . . . let me see. . . .
I came home at a steady eighty and it's about seventeen
miles from Enswood. . . . You can say I left Enswood
at between twenty and ten to twelve, getting to the
garage at about twelve and getting hauled in by your
busybodies at just after midnight. I was going home,
and, I might tell you, looking forward to a whisky and
soda and some food."

Pike nodded. " I see. Was there any one in the garage,
Mr. Spring, when you put the car away ? Any night
porter or anything ? "

Spring was silent for a moment. Behind the horn-
rimmed spectacles his hot brown eyes were veiled under
heavy lids. He said :

" Can't remember. . . . Let me see. . . . No, don't
think I saw any one. I've got a special private lock-up
there. All I did was just to ram the bus inside, lock the
door and start off for home."

" I see. Did you happen to notice whether you passed
any one, Mr. Spring, between your entrance to Holmdale
from the main road and your arrival at the garage ? "

" Couldn't say." Spring shrugged. The black felt
hat which had been balanced on the back of his chair
fell to the ground with a soft plop. " I wasn't looking,
of course."

" I shay," said Mr. Godly, " I shay ! "

" Did any one, Mr. Spring," said Pike, " happen to
see you leave the Studios at Enswood. I suppose there's
a gatekeeper there or some one ? "

" I shay," said Mr. Godly indignantly, " the chap's
dropped hish hat. Hatsh on the floor. Shome one might
have the deshenshy pick it up."

" Yes, there's a gate-keeper," Spring said. He paused
a moment. " Half a minute though, he wasn't there
to-night, I remember noticing, and the gates were open.
I say, though——"

" Well, that doesn't matter, sir. There's sure to have been some one on your staff about when you left the studio building."

Spring laughed—an awkward little sound. " Funny thing, but I'm pretty certain there wasn't now I come to think of it. I sent them all home about half an hour before I left myself. I was going with the others and I suddenly remembered some notes I had to make for the morning. I went back to my room and jotted them down. . . . Now I come to think of it, I don't suppose there was a soul saw me from the time my assistant went till I was pulled in by your men."

" I shay, ol' chap," said Mr. Godly, " I shay, d'you know your hatsh on the floor."

Again Spring laughed. He was staring hard at Pike. " Makes it a bit awkward, doesn't it ? I mean the whole thing's perfectly absurd. . . ." His tone was noticeably milder.

Pike leaned near to Jeffson and said something to him in a voice so low that it did not carry to any other ears in the room.

Jeffson nodded. " Yes, they did, sir. Nothing."

Pike sat back in his chair again and once more looked at Spring.

" If shome one," said Mr. Godly suddenly, " doeshn't pick that hat up, I'm going to. Can't shtant hatsh on the floor. Get dushty."

" I think," said Pike, " that if you'd like to get along home now, Mr. Spring, we could arrange it. No doubt we can get hold of you at any time if we want any further information."

Behind their shields of glass and tortoise-shell Spring's eyes for a moment looked astonished. But he said, after a moment's pause : " Thanks. . . . Thanks. . . . Very good of you." He stood up—a short, cheeky little figure

rather offensively sure of itself. He stooped and picked
the black felt hat from the floor.

"Thank God," said Mr. Godly. "Can't shtand sheeing
hatsh on floor."

Constable Birch opened the door. With a jerky,
bouncing walk, Spring went to it. He paused on the
threshold, half turned and flung a "Good-night" over
his shoulder.

There was a murmur in answer and he was gone.

"You're sure," Pike said to Jeffson, "that they went
right over him?"

"The Special assured me of that, sir. It's written
down in these notes here. They went through all his
pockets. There's nowhere he could be carrying a
weapon." Jeffson's jaw suddenly dropped. "Unless..."

"The car, you mean?" Pike said. "Tell you what ·
Send this man down to the garage now. He'd better
knock up the watchman or whoever's there and go over
the car. He'll have to do it without a warrant, but he
should be able to if he's sensible."

"The best man I've got," Jeffson said.

The round, childlike face of Constable Birch warmed
to a rich red flood of colour.

"And now," said Pike, "what about *this*?" He was
looking at Mr. Godly.

Mr. Godly, still upon his chair, was, by this time, fast
asleep. His head lolled so that his left cheek lay cosily
upon his left shoulder. His mouth was wide open. He
looked like a stupid but happy child.

Jeffson got up, took two heavy strides and stood over
the sleeper. Jeffson's finger and thumb, each as big as
a sausage roll, clamped themselves upon Mr. Godly's
right ear and twisted.

"Wow!" said Mr. Godly, awake. "I shay, dam' shilly
thing to do."

Jeffson went back to his chair.

" Mr. Godly," said Pike. His tone was very different from that which he had used to Wilfred Spring. It was the tone of a just but stern parent. " Mr. Godly," he said, " I must ask you to pull yourself together. I want you to answer as best you can the questions I am going to ask you. Just a few simple questions. Do you understand ? "

" Not," said Mr. Godly, " one little bit."

" I am going to ask you," said Pike, pausing long between each word, " to answer a few questions."

" 'S not," said Mr. Godly, " a bit of ewsh. Can't ansher 'em." He smiled beautifully, first at Pike, then at Jefffson and lastly over his shoulder at Police Constable Birch.

Jefffson coughed. He said to Pike :

" If you'll excuse me, sir, the boy's right himself. He's been three parts canned all his time and now he's right under, if you follow me."

Pike's mouth twitched to a half smile. " Right," he said. " Best thing we can do is to keep it here till the morning. Got anywhere to put it ? "

" It'll do anywhere," Jefferson said.

" Isn't it about time," Pike said, frowning, " that that other catch was up here ? "

Jefffson looked at his watch. He pursed his lips and a little whistle came from them. " I should just say it was, sir." His glance travelled to the telephone and then, as if actuated by that glance, the telephone bell rang shrilly. He crossed to it in two strides and plucked off the receiver.

" Hallo ! " he said. " Yes, Jeffson speaking. . . . I was just going to ring you. . . . Where is 'e ? . . . What d'you say ? Well, it doesn't matter a damn who 'e is, 'e ought to have been up here by this time, even if 'e was the Archangel Gabriel. . . . Eh ! what's that ? I can't hear you. . . . And who the hell told you to do that ? Oh ! . . . *All right !* "

Jeffson slammed back the receiver on to its hook with
a jar that might have broken it. He turned a frowning
face to Pike.

"Look here, sir," he said, "that third man was a
doctor. Dr. Reade. Practises 'ere. They're just bringin'
him up 'ere when they get stopped by Colonel
Grayling——"

"Who the flop," said Pike, "is Colonel Grayling?"

"Head of our branch of Specials. Colonel Grayling
knows Dr. Reade very well, as we all do in fact. Well,
Colonel Grayling tells the patrol—who, very unfor-
tunatelike, were Specials and not our men—it's sheer
foolishness to arrest Dr. Reade and that you won't want
to see 'im. And then they go and loose him at once!"

Pike's brow's met together in a harsh, deep-cut frown.
"Where's this Reade live?" he said.

"Marrowbone Lane, sir. 172. Big house on the left
at the Market Road end. Maybe you've seen it."

"Come on!" Pike said. He nodded at Police Constable George Birch. "And you," he said, "look after
that." He nodded again, this time towards Mr. Godly,
once more asleep.

2

It was ten minutes past one when the blue police
Crossley pulled up outside Number 172 Marrowbone
Lane. Pike switched off lights and engine.

"This the place?" he said.

"That's right, sir. Empty or all asleep by the looks
of it."

They stood at the gate looking through the darkness
at the dim bulk of a low-built, verandahed house.

Pike leaned his elbows on the gate. "This Reade
married?"

"Yes." Jeffson dropped his voice. "But Mrs. Reade's

away. Been away for some months now. Besides Dr.
Reade, there's a housekeeper and a maidservant. Oh!
and of course, there's the dispenser; but I don't think
she sleeps in. She's a Holmdale girl—Marjorie Williams."

Pike put his hand to the latch of the gate, passed
through and went up the path. His boot-soles rang out
a brisk tattoo upon the frozen path. He made no effort
to dull their sound. Jeffson followed. They came to the
end of the path and three steps which brought them up
to the verandah. They crossed the verandah and were
at the door. There were two bells on it, one with "Night"
written above it in bold letters of brass. There was also
a heavy iron knocker wrought like a snake. Pike set his
thumb on the bell marked "Night." From somewhere
within the house came to their ears a steady peal. He
took his thumb away. They waited. After two minutes
waiting, he once more pressed the bell. This time he
held his thumb upon it. The pealing went on within,
steady and insistent, but they could hear no other
sound. Pike lowered his hand.

" Knock ! " he said.

Jeffson knocked.

" Knock harder ! " Pike said.

Jeffson knocked harder.

Pike pressed both bells. . . . And then a light shone
out above their heads and there came the sound of a
window violently flung open and a voice which said:

" What the devil's all this row ? "

Pike nudged Jeffson. Jeffson went back off the
verandah and stood in the path looking upwards.

" I'm Sergeant Jeffson," he said. " I'm afraid we
must trouble you to come downstairs and let us
in."

There was a muttering from the window, its words
indistinguishable. Jeffson came back up the steps on to
the verandah and stood beside Pike at the doorway.

They heard movement within the house and then footsteps descending the stairs and coming along the hallway towards them. Bolts were drawn and there was the clanging of a safety chain. The door opened and the lantern above the door sprang into light.

" Dr. Reade ? " said Pike. He was looking at a thickly-built, broad-shouldered, man in the middle thirties, with a white heavy-jowled face under wiry and crisply curling jet-black hair. The black brows were a straight bar across his face and from under them bright almost black eyes darted flickering glances.

" That's me," said the man in the door. " What do you want ? "

Pike put a foot across the threshold. For a moment it seemed that Reade was going to bar his entrance but almost at once he drew back.

" Come in ! " he said.

Behind Pike came Jeffson. Reade moved away from them. They could hear him near them fumbling at the wall. There was the click of a switch and three wall lamps shed a soft gold glow over the hall. Pike looked about him. He said :

" Can we talk here, sir ? "

Reade's eyes darted glances this way and that ; everywhere except at the faces of his two visitors.

" No," he said. " Better come into my surgery." He led the way to a door in the right-hand wall, opened it and stood while they passed through before him.

Jeffson, burly and blue-clad but helmetless, stood with his back to a fireplace in which there flickered an electric fire. Pike, in answer to unspoken invitation, sat in one of the red-leather armchairs. There was a small, square, oaken table in the centre of the room and upon the edge of this its owner sat himself. He looked from one of his visitors to the other, quickly and almost furtively.

" We understand, sir," said Pike, " that you were

taken up by one of the patrols this evening at some time after midnight. Mistakenly and against my orders——"

" I'm not clear," said Reade, " exactly who you are." The dark head was bent until only the top of it was presented to Pike's gaze. The deep voice was querulously angry.

" I am from Scotland Yard, sir," Pike said. " At the present moment, I am, as you might say, in charge of the police activities." His tone was bland and there was a smile upon his mouth but his eyes did not smile. He paused a moment. At last, as if he could bear the silence no longer, Reade lifted his head. For the first time Pike saw his eyes ; then spoke again : " I must inform you, sir, that at about nine-thirty this evening we were informed that another of these murders had taken place. Immediately I had verified this, I gave word to all the patrols that any persons found in the streets of this town should be held, pending investigation of their movements. Mistakenly and against my instructions, the patrol let you go. In these circumstances, Sergeant Jeffson and I came round to have a word with you and to ask you to explain to us where you had been this evening. This is a matter of form, of course, but, I am afraid, one which must, in the interest of the whole community, be carried out. . . . I am sure that after a moment's thought, Dr. Reade, you'll see the necessity of carrying out investigation like this, utterly irrespective of persons."

" Yes . . . Yes," Reade said. " Of course. . . . Yes, I see." He raised his head, flinging it back with a movement almost theatrically defiant. " I suppose you want to ask me a lot of questions. Isn't that the way you do it ? "

Pike shrugged. " Well, sir, that's as you like. You can either make a statement on which we may want to ask you questions afterwards or you can answer my questions as I put them to you without making any original statement at all."

"When I was stopped by the patrol," Reade began in a voice which seemed deliberately emotionless, "it was a few minutes after midnight. I was walking down Broad Walk coming in this direction. I've been over-worked lately and suffering from insomnia. To-night I went to bed just after dinner. I thought I *could* sleep to-night. I soon knew sleep was impossible unless I took drastic measures. So I went out for a walk. I daresay it was foolish of me and may seem incredible to you but my own state of mind had made me forget all about this . . . this Butcher business. I just went out as I would've done at any normal time in the same circumstances. I walked straight up Marrowbone Lane, round the Poultry Farm and back down Runborough Lane, across the Playing Fields and into the top of Broad Walk like that. I was half-way down Broad Walk when I was stopped. . . . That's all!" He sat staring at Pike. The eyes, Pike thought, were covered with a hard, protective glaze through which a man could see nothing of feeling.

Pike pondered. "Tell me, sir," he said after a moment, his voice urbanity itself, "while you were on this walk how many people did you see before you met the patrol?"

Reade shook his head. "None." His mouth shut, after the word, in a hard, lipless line.

"No one at all?" Pike was insistent.

"No one."

"And how long would you say the walk occupied, Dr. Reade?"

The broad shoulders were lifted, somehow despairingly. "I can't give you any accurate estimation. All I can swear to is that I was not out for less than an hour and not out for more than two."

There ensued a long silence. Jeffson, shifting from one foot to the other, looked first at the doctor's pallid defiance and then at the inscrutability of Pike. Jeffson knew what he would do, yet had a sinking suspicion that this would be wrong. A good man, Jeffson, and one knowing his own limitations. He waited, almost unbreathing, for what should happen. When it came it was so unexpected an anti-climax that he let out his breath in a long hissing whistle instantly repressed.

For Pike got to his feet and said :

" Well, thank you very much, Dr. Reade. I'm sorry to have had to disturb you." He looked round for his hat which lay upon a chair to the left of the door. He made for it. " We'll be getting along, Jeffson," he said.

Reade sprang to his feet. " Look here ! " he said violently. " What I . . ." And then once more closed his mouth into a tight line.

Pike stooped to pick up his hat ; turned with it in his hand. " Yes, sir ? " He was suave.

" Nothing," said Reade. " Nothing ! "

Pike set his fingers to the door handle but dropped them as if struck by a sudden thought. " I'm sorry," he said. " Just one more question. Is there any one besides yourself, Dr. Reade, sleeping in the house ? "

There was a little movement of Reade's bulk ; a movement almost like the recoil from a light, sharp blow. " Housekeeper," he said. His lips hardly opened to emit the word.

Pike raised his eyebrows. " No one else ? "

" No." Reade shook his head.

Pike took his soft hat in both hands and began to knead the brim. He seemed, now, a personification of diffidence. " I wonder," he said, " whether we might have a few words with your housekeeper ? "

Reade seemed to have grown bigger. As he stood, he

looked taller, burlier, more self-assured. "What the
devil for ? " he said.

"Verification," said Pike. The hat brim twisted in
his fingers. "I'm sure you'll see, sir, that it may save
you some unpleasantness, as you might say, and us,
perhaps, some work, if we just saw whether we could
get some nearer hint as to the time you left the house..."

"Good God!" said Reade. His tone was one of un-
leashed anger. "D'you want to wake the poor old woman
up? She was in bed and asleep before I went to bed."

"Mrs. Reade, sir," said Pike inconsequently, "is
away, I understand?"

"Thank God," Reade said, "she is!" He came round
the corner of the table and stood to face Pike, his hands,
which were clenched into fists, thrust into his pockets.

Pike laid his hat upon the chair from which he had
taken it. "I think, sir," he said, "it would be best if
we saw the housekeeper. And by the way..." He
turned for an instant and his eyes met Jeffson's.

It was much to Jeffson's credit that he understood
the unspoken message. He came forward from the
fireplace. He said, heavily, looking at Reade:

"Isn't there a maid too?"

Reade glared. He made a little movement as if his
arms, the hands still fists, were coming out of their
pockets. But what he did was to turn and take a pace
and once more sit down upon the table. He said,
answering Jeffson's question but looking at Pike:

"There *was* a maid. I discharged her last week. She
was impertinent and unsatisfactory. My housekeeper's
been looking for another girl, but so far hasn't got one.
Therefore the only person in the house besides myself
to-night is Mrs. Flewin."

"I see, sir." Beneath the diffidence of Pike's tone
had come a subtle hardness. "Now, what I think's best
is if you take Sergeant Jeffson here and go and wake this

Mrs. Flewin and tell her you would be much obliged if she would come down and answer some questions which Sergeant Jeffson will put to her. If you would then, sir, come back here, we could have a further little chat ourselves while Sergeant Jeffson is talking to Mrs. Flewin. . . . Once more I must apologise for being so pestering, as you might say. But it can't be helped."

Reade stood motionless for a long moment. Four eyes watched him. "Oh! *All* right!" he said at last. He swung himself off the table, passed Pike and went to the door. He set his hand to the door-knob and turned. "This way, *Sergeant,*" he said. The accent upon the last word was heavily ironic as was the little bow which accompanied the words. Jeffson, unmoved, crossed like a silent and agile elephant to the door.

Pike, straining his ears to listen, heard the footsteps— Reade's quick and light like a cat's; Jeffson's solid and ponderous yet quiet—go down the hall, turn left and begin the ascent of carpeted stairs.

When the sound of the footsteps had died away and been replaced, after a small bridge of silence, by a rat-tatting of knuckles against a door, Pike ceased to listen. He crossed the surgery and sat himself upon the table in the spot where Reade had been sitting. He pulled from a pocket of his blue suit an oilskin pouch and a new but pleasantly maturing pipe. He began to fill the pipe from the pouch. The filling was complete and the pouch rolled up and once more put away when he heard, following a broken murmur of voices, feet coming down the stairs—three pairs of feet this time : two leather-clad and softly ringing, the others soft and slip-shod. He slipped off the table and crossed with light steps to the door. He waited, leaning against the door-jamb so that without obtruding himself into the passage he could yet see the foot of the stairs.

He saw the little procession. Reade first, and then an

elderly and many-angled female wrapped in a dressing-
gown of blue flannel, with curling pins clustered thick
about a head whose raven blackness seemed too black.
And lastly, Jeffson, blue-clad and silver-buttoned,
heavy and apparently unmoved by humour or any other
emotion. At the foot of the stairs the cortege halted.
Opposite where it stood was a door, Reade reached out
a hand and flung this open. The woman passed in first
and then Jeffson already fumbling in left-hand breast
pocket for pencil and notebook.

Pike drew back a little. Down the hall towards him
Reade came with slow steps. By the time he got to his
surgery, Pike was once more seated upon the table. He
had the filled but unlighted pipe in his mouth and a box
of matches in his hand.

" Mind if I smoke in here, sir ? " he said.

Reade shook his head. " No ! " he said savagely.
" You can do anything in here. . . . After all, you're a
big noise, aren't you ? "

" I try," Pike said with urbanity, " not to make
one."

Reade flung himself into a chair. He, too, pulled out
pipe and tobacco. While he fumbled for matches, he said :

" Well, Inspector or whatever you are, where's these
other questions of yours ? "

Pike smiled, friendly enough. " I don't think," he said,
" that I'll be worrying you. Not yet anyhow."

Reade laughed ; a short, barking sound. " Thought
so," he said. " All you're waiting for is for that hulking
bobby to see what he can get out of old Flewin and keep
me here in the meantime. What ? "

Pike did not answer. There was no other sound in
the room until, heralded by his footsteps, Jeffson came.
He stood in the doorway, seeming to fill it. He looked
at Pike and, in answer to Pike's raised eyebrows, shook
his head.

Once more Reade let out a harsh, barking laugh.

Pike got to his feet. " I think, sir," he said, " that that'll be all . . . for to-night." He turned towards the door.

Reade sat where he was. " You'll forgive me," he said, " if I leave you to let yourselves out." There was a sneer in voice as well as words, but there was something else behind the sneer. As Jeffson said to Pike when the car started, its headlights cutting a white swathe down the blackness' af Marrowbone Lane :

" Seemed some'ow to me, sir, as if 'e was more scared than he liked to let on ! "

CHAPTER SEVEN

THE car had not gone a hundred yards before Pike halted it. He felt in the darkness of the saloon the little start of surprise which Jeffson gave.

"What is it?" said Jeffson.

"Had an idea," said Pike. "Get taken like that sometimes. Where's the post-office? Never mind. Don't tell me, I know. What I mean is this: Know the postmaster?"

"Yes, sir. Name of Myers."

Pike grunted. "Hmm! Where's he live?"

"'Bout two hundred yards," Jeffson said, his tone shewing his endeavour to conceal curiosity, "of where we are now."

Pike started the car. "Stop me," he said, "opposite his house. When we get there, get out, knock him up, shove him into some clothes and bring him along. Can you do that?"

In the darkness Jeffson nodded. "I can, sir. Know 'im well."

The car went on at a smooth fifteen miles an hour.

"Whoa, sir!" said Jeffson.

The car came to a halt. There was the click of one of its doors opening and a scraping shuffle as Jeffson got out. Pike switched off the car's lights and waited in the darkness. He remembered his own theory of "not thinking." He smiled wryly to himself as he realised that, now, even at this stage in this case, his mind was working as hard as never before. With a small percentage, as it were, of his senses, he was aware of Jeffson's approach to the dim bulk of a little house; aware of the sound of a knocker; a silence; voices

and then, after another and smaller silence, the opening
and shutting of a door.

In what seemed an amazingly short time, there came
the sound again of the door, this time followed by
footsteps crunching upon the half-frozen gravel. Pike
came to himself with a start. He shivered a little as he
realised the cold. He leaned over as the footsteps
drew nearer and opened the door.

" 'Ere's Mr. Myers!" came Jeffson's voice. "In
you get, Myers."

Behind Pike there came a scrambling and puffing and
then the sound of a body settling itself upon the back
cushions. Jeffson climbed in beside Pike. Once more
the headlights cut a swathe through the night. The
car moved off.

"Which," said the driver, " is the nearest way to the
post-office ?

"First left, second right, first left," came a high,
eager voice from the back.

The car, seeming to gather speed all the way and take
its bends without pause, did the half-mile in creditable
time. There was a squeaking of brakes and a flurry of
gravel, and the car came to a stand.

"Out you get!" said Pike, and within a moment was
peering at a thin and bespectacled person introduced
by Jeffson as Mr. Myers, our postmaster.

"I don't know yet, Mr. Myers, what the Superintendent wants. . . ."

"Easy!" Pike said. "Can we get in? Got a key,
Mr. Myers ? "

Mr. Myers had got a key and, leading them round to
the back of the small brick-tiled, rough-cast plaster
house which was the post-office, used it.

The side door of the post-office clicked behind them.
They stood in darkness until at a touch of the postmaster's fingers the lights sprang up all about them.

D.

"This," said Mr. Myers, "is the Sorting Office." He peered at Pike with an avid curiosity. "Now, sir?"

Pike looked about him and saw two desks, walls bare save for almanacks and a clock, and three long trestle tables. The windows of the room—long, narrow windows—were barred and netted. "Sorting Office, eh?" said Pike. "Now then, Mr. Myers, that nine o'clock collection. The nine o'clock is the last collection, isn't it?"

"Except," said Mr. Myers, "in the very outlyin' boxes like Arrowcourt, Forest Road, Two Tiddlers Corner over The Other Side and such, the last collection is nine, Superintendent. With a final collection here at nine-thirty."

"Right!" said Pike. "Right! When are letters cleared at this last collection sorted?"

"The succeeding day, Superintendent, at 5 a.m. We have to have a five o'clock sort so's to catch the 6.10 up-mail and the 6.30 down-mail. Letters wanted to be delivered in London first post have to be posted by the eight o'clock, but we have a nine o'clock collection to get London letters up by the second post and some others like Cambridge."

"What I want," said Pike, "is to have a look at the mail. Can we do it?"

"Cer-tainly, cer-tainly!" Mr. Myers bounded like a consumptive, but eager antelope. In three strides he was at a small door facing the one by which they had entered. It swung upwards and closed again, only to re-open a moment later to admit the back of Mr. Myers bent into the shape of a C. Mr. Myers was dragging with both hands and all his inconsiderable weight at a bulky mail sack. With Jeffson's help the sack was hoisted to one of the tables, tilted and emptied of a cascade of envelopes and cards and little parcels. Pike, with eager fingers and a look of concentration

which somehow lent a sharp, knife-like appearance
to his lean face, was busy among the great scattered
pile of paper. There was a crack like a distant pistol
shot : Jeffson had slapped his thigh.

" Kor ! " said Jeffson. " Got it ! " The creased
frown of worry which had been on his face since their
arrival at the cottage of Mr. Myers disappeared and was
replaced by a grin of triumph at his own perspicacity
and of admiration for the Superintendent. Jeffson,
too, became busy. Mr. Myers, his head on one side, his
eyes twinkling like a small bird's behind their metal-
rimmed spectacles, watched them. . . .

" Right ! " said Pike suddenly and straightened
himself.

" God strike me dead ! " said Jeffson. He was
staring round-eyed at what Pike was holding in his right
hand. It was a square, yellowish envelope bearing a
superscription written in a backward-sloping handwriting, and with curious jet-black, shining ink.

Pike, the envelope between his fingers, advanced upon
Mr. Myers. " Any way of telling," said Pike curtly,
" which box any of these letters came out of ? "

Mr. Myers shook his head decisively. " 'Fraid not,
Superintendent. They're all pitched in here together
to wait the five o'clock sort." Suddenly his eyes fell
upon the envelope and widened slowly, while the bright
spot of colour upon each cheek-bone faded to leave a
ghastly green patch. " The Butcher ! " said Mr. Myers.

Pike nodded. He turned and spoke over his shoulder,
and Jeffson produced a knife.

Jeffson, watching, saw that Superintendent Pike
had only held this letter by its edges, and that now
that he wished to open it he laid it down carefully upon
a sheet of paper and, still taking great care not to touch
more of its surface with his fingers than was necessary,
carefully slit the top of the envelope.

There was a rustling. Delicately Pike drew out the envelope's contents. Three sheets of paper this time. He opened the first. He read. Over his shoulders the other men read too. They saw:

" My Reference THREE
R.I.P.
Amy Adams,
died Monday, 26th November, 193 . . .
THE BUTCHER."

Pike opened out the second sheet. It read:

" My Reference FOUR
R.I.P.
Albert Rogers,
died Friday, 30th November, 193 . . .
THE BUTCHER."

Pike opened out the third sheet. It read:

" DEAR POLICE,—Enclosed please find my memos regarding those unfortunates, Amy Adams (what a terrible name) and Albert Rogers (what a far worse one !)

I really am so very sorry that I am late with my memo, in regard to Amy Adams, but pressure of business (after all, you know, I have had a lot of staff work to do) has made it impossible for me to let you have this earlier.

I must now pass quickly on to the main point of this letter, and that is to tell you to keep your spirits up. I quite realise how disheartening, to say the least, it must be for you never to know when and how and where and who I am going to strike next. I hate causing unnecessary pain to others and am, therefore, undertaking to give you warning wherever possible of any future little jobs which I may be contemplating. This will, don't you think? add quite another spice of excitement to our game?

Believe me, Police,

Yours tolerantly,

THE BUTCHER."

CHAPTER EIGHT

I

*(EXTRACTS from report to Assistant Commissioner C.I.D. by Detective Superintendent Arnold Pike. Dated Saturday, December 1st, 193 . . .

Received Scotland Yard by special messenger 11.30 p.m. same day).

Arrived Holmdale with Sergeants Blaine and Curtis at 2.30 p.m. on Wednesday the 28th ult. Was met by Chief Constable of County and Inspectors Davis and Farrow. Sent Blaine and Curtis to pick up what they could from local Constabulary, under Sergeant Jeffson, and proceeded myself immediately to meeting with Chief Constable and two Inspectors above mentioned. Relations between myself and Inspectors at first strained. Usual resentment, though under control, fairly evident. Smoothed matters down and am now on good terms. Both Inspectors capable men. C. C. content to leave real control to me. At meeting learnt of steps already taken to safeguard population against further outrage. Scheme (for an unavoidably hurried and patchwork measure) very good, but naturally merely protective. (I attach copy of the scheme with pencil notes in its margin shewing the alterations and additions I have proposed and which have been carried out).

* * * * * * *

*It should be noted that although this chapter is an extract there are no germane points whatsoever omitted. The only omissions are of purely routine and, in this context, unnecessary detail. For instance, plans of patrol placing and details of patrol scheme quoted by Pike as being attached to the document are among the omissions.

Thursday, 29th ult.

Put in long day, with two conferences not worth reporting, and many hours reading mass of documentary evidence (all of it worthless) collected by police in regard to first three murders. During day was 'phoned for by local sergeant to go to station as a man had just given himself up, stating that he was "The Butcher." Sergeant in a state of excitement. Proceeded immediately to station. Found elderly man, in state of nervous collapse, who stated himself to be Edward William Marsh, a Holmdale resident. Failed to get any coherent statement from him, merely reiteration of "I did it. I did it. I am 'The Butcher'" At once sent Curtis to Marsh's house where, after enquiry of his sister who keeps house for him, it was found, beyond doubt, that upon all the occasions when the murders were being done, Marsh was in the house. He is a mild epileptic and, according to Dr. Reade, his medical adviser, a neurotic subject. Called Doctor who recommended removal to a Nursing Home. Since this "confession" there have been three more. Two from elderly women and one from a garage mechanic known to be "simple." Have also had trouble with would-be detectives, vindictive gossips and over-imaginative persons. These troubles so acute and apparently so upsetting to the normal work of the local police that have put Curtis in sole charge of this side. Every one properly investigated but must note that have very little faith in catching our man this way. Curtis doing invaluable work. Blaine on patrol organisation. His report for last three days copied below.

. . . . . .

Progress

Naturally no actual progress except in regard to safety measures. I have, however, satisfied myself

upon one or two points which should go some way
towards eventual solution. In order to make these
points more clear, I give table of murders. Would like
to have this studied carefully before my conclusions
are read.

.   .   .   .   .   .

Conclusions drawn from comparison of murders.

(1) The expert opinion (see attached docs.) tends
to prove that all wounds were caused by the same
implement. All wounds are the same except in the
case of Amy Adams, the girl killed in the theatre,
where there was only the piercing and not the post-
piercing rip. (This latter accounted for by need for
extra caution on murderer's part owing to locus of
murder.)

(2) Every case a " Butcher " letter.

(3) Implication must be that murderer is not only a
resident in Holmdale, but one who has some intimate
connection with Holmdale in all its class-spheres. As
proof of this we have—

(a) Murderer's knowledge of whom his victim is
(in the case of Pamela Richards it is true that
there were cards in a pocket which the murderer could have seen, but there were only
initials on Lionel Colby's clothes. There were
no identifying marks or papers upon Amy
Adams, nor did the murderer have time to look
at them if there had been. And on Albert
Rogers the only means of identification was
a crumpled and torn envelope which had not
been disturbed from his pocket and from
which his name had been almost obliterated).

(b) Silent delivery by hand, during the night, of
the letters in the case of Pamela Richards
(showing too murderer's knowledge of Holmdale geography).

TABLE A.

Name.	Age.	Cause of Death.	Type of Place.	Time and Date.	Social Standing.	
Lionel Colby	11	Stomach pierced then ripped	Populated road	Approx. 9.30 p.m., 23rd Nov., 193—	Clerical class	Only child. Brilliant at studies. Very athletic. Capt. school football team. Promising little boxer. Both parents devoted. Butcher letter received per post by Police, Holmdale Company Chairman and Editor Holmdale *Clarion*. Postmarked Holmdale, 10 a.m., Nov. 24th.
Pamela Richards	19	As above	In motor car on semi-populated road	Between midnight 25th Nov. and 5 a.m. 26th Nov	Leisured class	Very popular. Beautiful. Parents devoted. Troublesome engagement broken off at girl's own wish. Happier engagement foreshadowed. Butcher letters received next morning, having been delivered by hand.
Amy Adams	17	Stomach pierced but not ripped	Theatre lounge	Between 8 and 8.30 p.m. 26th Nov.	Labouring class	Winner of County Beauty Contest, and therefore possible source of increased income to family. Butcher notice (see attached docs.) found on body. Butcher letter delivered with Albert Rogers below.
Albert Rogers	21	Same as Colby and Richards above	Unpopulated road	Between 6.30 and 9 p.m. 30th Nov.	Skilled workman class	Ambition realised by recent engagement as professional footballer. No parents, but "walking out" with girl. Football engagement would have made marriage quickly possible. Butcher letter found in post early a.m. 1st December, 193—

NOTE.—For steps taken by local police immediately following discovery of murders 1, 2 and 3, see documentary extracts attached. These need not be carefully considered as they are non-productive, though this is no fault of the police work, which seems to have been as efficient as can be expected. In regard to 4, Albert Rogers, this murder was done last night and the steps I have taken to deal with it are outlined below, but after my statement of conclusions to be drawn from above table.

(c) The very short time in which these letters must have been prepared (such a short time that it looks almost, in some cases, as though the murderer must have known beforehand who he was going to murder).

(d) (See separate conclusion No. 4 below, which applies separately, but is also proof of this conclusion).

(4) That the "Butcher" chooses for his victims young persons of either sex

(a) whose deaths come at a time when they are having a run of good fortune, and

(b) who leave behind them persons, *resident in Holmdale*, to whom the deaths are more than usually painful.

Summarising these points (at the risk of repetition) I submit as a final conclusion, the following:

That these are a pervert's "lust murders" with a triple satisfaction in them for the murderer (*i.e.* the killing itself; the youth and happiness of the victim, and finally the observation of the distress caused by the killings), and that the murderer is a resident of Holmdale, who has business, or perhaps official opportunities of mixing with all classes of the community, *and therefore is certain to be found, not among the labouring classes or skilled workman class, but must belong to the clerical or governing class, probably the latter of these.*

.   .   .   .   .   .

Further reference yesterday's case of Albert Rogers. This is the first of the cases which has happened whilst I have been in charge. I accordingly submit precis of steps taken. Using fifty men in charge of Curtis and Blaine, had carried out, between 7.30 a.m. and 3.30 p.m. a house-to-house canvas. Each householder, or householder's representative, had submitted to him the following form of questionnaire.

(1) Give particulars of all people staying in this house as from evening of November 25th, to December 1st.

(2) Were all these persons in the house last night ?

(3) If not, who was absent, during what times, and why?

(4) If unable to state why, give present whereabouts of absent person.

These reports are now being checked, so far with no result. The questionnaire was easily filled in as regards individual houses, but as regards block of flats, and one guest-house or hotel, results cannot be hoped to be so satisfactory. I do not anticipate a definite result from this questionnaire, but felt the step ought to be taken, particularly as if it brings no suspicious movements to light at all other than those we know about already (see below) we shall have a basis for supposing that the "Butcher" is (i) *a householder, living alone*, or (ii) a householder who has the co-operation of his household (most unlikely) or (iii) *a resident in the flats or hotel.*

Suspicious Persons held by Authorities.

After my inspection of body at 11 p.m. three men were held by the authorities—W. Spring, P. Godly and Dr. Reade. All are residents. For details of questioning, etc., please see Sergeant Jeffson's notes attached.

The murder was reported by the Rev. Rockwall. His movements were questioned and a report of the questions and answers is also attached.

I have not detained any of these four men, though none of their stories can be called satisfactory. I have let them go, but am having them watched. I can do no good at the present stage by wholesale and indiscriminate arrests.

Further reports as to progress in the Rogers case will be submitted from time to time.

    .   .   .   .

Proposals.

Subject to not receiving contrary instructions from you, I propose to put the two following schemes into operation at such time as I think fit.

(1) To expend a certain sum, probably not in excess of £30 in having a concealed light fitted over the wall letter box at the main post-office here. The letters posted into this box go straight down the shoot into the first sorting room. The proposed light will be controlled from the bottom of the shoot. As from the installation of the light, a man will be constantly on duty at the foot of the shoot, and as soon as he sees one of the yellow " Butcher " envelopes, he will press the switch. The light will then flash momentarily from the top of the box. There will be outside the post-office, inconspicuously, three plain clothes men who, on seeing the light will, by the aid of whistling signals, close the single road which leads between the post-office and The Market. Any one who has been observed to post a letter during the time immediately preceding the flashing of the light will then be held and questioned as to what letter he had posted. I have chosen the main letter box for the obvious reasons that such a scheme could not be carried out at outlying pillar boxes, and also because I think it highly probable that the " Butcher " letters are all posted at the main box, this being more frequently used and therefore less liable to provide opportunity for observation. This scheme may not have many good points, but we must try everything in the circumstances. I submit that any constructive scheme is better than none. I should be glad of authority for the expenditure.

(2) To obtain similar paper and ink to those with which the " Butcher " writes his letters, have his disguised handwriting carefully imitated and start a " fake " correspondence of my own, addressing the

letters to the same three people (the Editor of the
Holmdale Clarion, the Chairman of the Holmdale
Company, and the Sergeant of the Police) in the hope
that I may thus force the " Butcher " into some slip.
I do not propose taking this course at present, but sub-
mit it herewith for consideration and comment.

(NOTE.—The obvious objection to any schemes of the
sort outlined above is that to be a hundred per cent.
efficient, such scheme should be carried out with the
co-operation only of persons who are demonstrably not
capable of being the " Butcher." In the case of the
" fake " letters, this could be done, but I am afraid in
the case of the letter-box suggestion, one or two Holmdale persons will *have* to be " in the know," I would
however, pick those with due regard to the improbability
of their being in any way connected with the outrages.)

ARNOLD PIKE,
Superintendent.

2

(Additional report enclosed in same envelope as full
report above. Dated 1st December, and time 5.30 p.m.,
marked " Confidential and Urgent.")

Further to my long report enclosed herewith of to-day,
and in confirmation of telephone message just now—
I have to report that at 4.45 p.m. this afternoon, Mrs.
W. Reade, wife of Dr. Reade (one of the persons
mentioned in the long report as being taken by the
authorities last night) called at the Police Station and
informed the Sergeant in charge that returning un-
expectedly from a long holiday she had found that Dr.
Reade's dispenser, a Miss Marjorie Williams, had left
the house on the afternoon of yesterday (Friday, the

30th), and had not since returned. The Housekeeper, Mrs. Flewin (see also statements attached to long report) had heard Miss Williams in an agitated voice answering the telephone at about half-past two in the afternoon and had then seen her rush out of the house, pulling on her coat as she ran, and holding a hat in her hand. She (Mrs. Flewin) had been in her room upstairs at the time. She had told Mrs. Reade that she had assumed at the time that Miss Williams had thought her away from the house, as it was her afternoon off. Dr. Reade had been out at the time. He had returned just before dinner at about 7 o'clock and then acted as set out in attached report.

On interviewing Mrs. Reade myself, I soon discovered that she is jealous of her husband and Miss Williams. It seems to have been some rumour that there was a liason between these two which had brought her back on this unexpected visit to her home. I asked her why she thought it necessary to come to the Police because Miss Williams has gone out and failed to return. She replied that Miss Williams, though a Holmdale resident, lived alone, was an orphan, and had no one to look after her, and that this curious behaviour seemed to her (Mrs. Reade) especially in view of the recent outrages, a matter in which the Police should be informed. I tried to gather from the lady what Dr. Reade's attitude would be towards her action in coming to the Police. She stated that she had not yet seen her husband, but thought that he would be annoyed. This did not, however, deter her from endeavouring to do her duty. I am trying to get in touch with the plain clothes man watching Dr. Reade, and if there is anything in his report which shows Dr. Reade's movements to have been at all suspicious, I shall use one of my special warrants and hold him for the time being.

ARNOLD PIKE.

P.S.—Dr. Reade has returned and the plain clothes man D/O Harboard is now with me. He reports as follows :

" Reade left house 11 a.m. this morning and proceeded on (apparently) usual round of medical visits, returning own house 12.45 p.m. After lunch (2.0 p.m.) Reade again left house and got into car. I followed. For three hours he drove round and about Holmdale (on outskirts) frequently stopping car and descending to enter copses and thickets. Owing to necessity of being unobserved could not get very close while he was thus away from car ; from what I could see, however, he seemed to be watching for something in every instance. Behaviour very strange. Demeanour nervous, apprehensive, excited. Returned home 5.3 p.m."

Under these circumstances I am taking immediate steps to execute warrant so that Reade may be held pending further investigation.

There is, of course, nothing yet to connect Reade's strange behaviour with the outrages, but his unaccountable " walk " last night and unsatisfactory statements, added to his behaviour this afternoon, have made me decide that he must be held for the time being at least. I shall charge him according to the formula you devised for emergency arrests during this case.

CHAPTER NINE

I

ACCORDING to many, the chief among Holmdale's much advertised amenities is the fact that the bars of the Wooden Shack open every morning at ten. At one minute and thirty seconds past ten, Mr. Percy Godly leant over the wooden counter of the saloon bar.

"George !" said Mr. Godly. "George !" He rapped upon the counter with a florin. "George ! For God's sake, George, I'm waiting !"

George came at last. "Mornin' sir," said George. "Usual ?"

Mr. Godly nodded, "Only twice as strong as usual."

George busied himself with a large wine glass and many bottles. Mr. Godly, anxious to while away the time until the filled glass should be his, picked up a copy of the *Holmdale Clarion* which lay upon the bar counter. With unsteady fingers he flicked it open and began to read. . . .

"Jumping Gabriel !" said Mr. Godly. "What's all this."

George set the glass, now nine-tenths full, gently upon the counter before his customer. "What's all what, sir ?" said George.

"All this," said Mr. Godly, and read aloud :

"PROMINENT HOLMDALE GIRL MISSING.
MYSTERY OF DOCTOR'S DISPENSER.
WHERE IS MARJORIE WILLIAMS ?

"The *Clarion* learns with alarm and consternation

that Miss Marjorie Williams, a popular figure in Holmdale circles, has mysteriously disappeared. As all her
friends are aware, Miss Williams was the able assistant
and dispenser of Dr. Reade, one of Holmdale's leading
physicians.

" On the afternoon of Friday last, the 30th November,
Miss Williams was seen to leave Dr. Reade's house—
Dr. Reade being absent upon his afternoon rounds—
in what appeared to be an extremely agitated condition.
Before leaving the house, Miss Williams had been heard
to answer a telephone call and appeared to be much
agitated thereby. On leaving the house, Miss Williams
was seen, as she ran down the path into Marrowbone
Lane, to be struggling into her coat. She carried her
hat in her hand. She was seen thus leaving the house
and was seen again at the junction of Marrowbone Lane
and Holmer Road. After that she seems to have
vanished into thin air !

" Nothing has been heard of Miss Williams since. The
Clarion are empowered to offer a substantial reward to
any one able to inform the police, either through the
Clarion or direct, of any further movements of Miss
Williams, either upon Friday the 30th November, or
subsequently—either upon the Saturday or Sunday."

Mr. Godly finished his reading with an air of triumphant, if somewhat weary, melodrama. " What d' you
think of that, George ! " said Mr. Godly, and reaching
for his glass, emptied it at a gulp.

George closed one eye, very knowingly.

" Same again," said Mr. Godly, pushing his glass
forward.

George once more busied himself with bottles.

" Marjorie Williams ? " Mr. Godly was saying to
himself. " Marjorie Williams ? Damn funny thing,
George, I thought I knew all the girls in Holmdale."

Again George set down the glass, this time filled only to seven-eighths of its capacity. " R ! " said George, darkly. " Tell you what you ain't done, sir. You ain't looked at the Stop Press. 'Ave a dekko at that ! "

Mr. Godly, having half emptied the second glass, turned for the paper with fingers which already were a little steadier. Again Mr. Godly read, this time silently. He saw :

" LATEST

" *Prominent Medico detained by Police.*

" The *Clarion* are authoritatively informed that following Police enquiries regarding the disappearance of Miss Marjorie Williams, Dr. Reade has been detained by the Police upon a certain charge.

" LATER

" Upon being interviewed, Mrs. Reade, the wife of Dr. Reade, stated emphatically that she was convinced of her husband's innocence of anything to do with Miss Williams' disappearance. ' My husband,' said Mrs. Reade, ' is not that sort of man. I am sure that this dark mystery will shortly be cleared up and that those responsible for my husband's detention will be brought rapidly to book.' "

Mr. Godly pursed his loose-seeming lips and breathed out a small, thin whistle.

" What," said Mr. Godly, " d'you know about that, George ? "

George shrugged his shoulders ; a shrug which spoke volumes but which implied that what George did not know about anything which George might be asked was not worth knowing.

2

They were talking about it everywhere. In The Market; in the Wood Cutter—the Wooden Shack's only rival; in the factories; at the Golf Club; at the corners of the streets; in back gardens; in drawing-rooms and lounges and parlours.

" I tell 'ee," George Farmer was saying in the public bar of the Wood Cutter. " My girl Francie, she bin an' seen 'um. She war goin' home, along about six last evenin,' when a girt stubby sort of a feller joomped out of 'edge like. Girt face 'e 'ad on 'im, Francie said, like 'e war some sort on a goberlin."

" But this 'ere," said Ted Lorry, tapping the *Clarion*, " did say summat about a Dr. Reade."

George Farmer shook his head. George Farmer spat ruminatively into a far corner of the bar. " Carn't 'elp what paper says. This 'ere what joomped out of 'edge like on my Francie was a girt, stubby sort on a goberlin sort-of-a-chap."

Mr. Colby was on holiday. That is to say, he was at home and not at his office. Following his terrible loss, Mr. Colby had been granted by his office a month's leave of absence. He had wanted to take Mrs. Colby away from Holmdale for this month. But women, as Mr. Colby, in those happy days which seemed so far behind him, had often said, ' were kittle cattle,' and Mrs. Colby strangely preferred to stay in Holmdale and in their little house. Mr. Colby acceded to her wish, but had a private wish of his own that soon she would ask him ' take me away.' Personally he found that every corner of every street in Holmdale; that every square

inch of every room in his house ; that every sound and
sight and smell in this neighbourhood reminded him of
Lionel, and his one wish nowadays seemed to be to
attain a state where thinking of Lionel was, if not
impossible, at least infrequent. For to think of Lionel
was, to Mr. Colby, most acutely painful. The thought
of Lionel seemed to grip him with a cold bony hand
which clamped its fingers about his insides.

Mr. Colby sat apathetic in his parlour. Beside him,
upon the arm of his comfortable chair—the chair upon
whose arm Lionel had so frequently been reprimanded
for bouncing—there lay one of the now almost daily
'Special' editions of the *Holmdale Clarion*. Mr.
Colby, sucking at an empty pipe, kept looking at this
paper. He supposed that he wanted to read it, but
although once or twice his mind had bidden his hands to
take hold of this paper and bring it properly within his
field of vision, so far his hands had refused to obey. . . .

Odd ! thought Mr. Colby. He'd found this sort of
thing happening more than once during the last week.
And it seemed to be getting worse. This, he thought,
would never do. . . . He made a great effort. A
frown, deeper even than the perpetual frown which
had come since Lionel's death, creased his brow. . . .
The hands obeyed. They moved and took up the
paper and opened it and held the centre page so that
his eyes could properly read it. . . .

Mr. Colby read. For a few moments what his
eyes were reading was not communicated to his brain.
He went on staring at the same few lines of large-
lettered print. As, however, his eyes did not move
from these few lines, gradually their meaning sank into
his mind.

Mr. Colby shot to his feet as if impelled by a giant
spring. Clutching the paper in a hand which shook as
if agued, he blundered towards the door. There

must have been something the matter with his sight, for, although he had often boasted that he knew the way blindfold not only about his own house but about the whole of Holmdale, he now got to the door through a series of collisions.

But he did get to the door, and he did open it, and he did run out into the passage crying:

"Mother! *Mother!*"

Mrs. Colby's uncertain cry came faintly to him down the narrow stairs. Up them Mr. Colby blundered, twice falling and twice picking himself up without knowing that he had fallen.

"*Mother!*" said Mr. Colby again. He blundered into the bedroom. Mrs. Colby was sitting huddled—staring rather vacantly at the wash-stand—upon the edge of the bed. Her hands were squeezed between her knees. During these past few days her plump comeliness seemed to have sagged, so that now she was, as it were, withered behind her shell. Her shoulders drooped. Her hair was lank and wispy. Her cheeks sagged into two pendulous little jowls. Beneath her eyes were two black half moons and the eyes themselves had over their erstwhile beauty a hard, glittering, permanent-seeming glaze.

"Mother!" said Mr. Colby, blundering to the bed and somehow seating himself upon the edge beside his wife. He held out the paper and the shaking hand.

Mrs. Colby turned dull eyes, first upon her husband and then upon the paper to which her husband seemed to be drawing her notice. . . . She stared. She shut her eyes; then opened them wide. . . .

"I don't believe it!" said Mrs. Colby.

Mr. Colby's fingers opened and the paper fluttered down from their grasp to the floor where it lay like an untidy mound of pantomime snow against the dark red carpet.

"My *God!*" said Mr. Colby. "My God: Don't

believe it! Don't believe it! What d'you mean:
Don't believe it!" He pointed the shaking hand
downwards at the paper, making little stabbing movements with a stubby fore-finger.

"Doesn't it say so in the paper?" said Mr. Colby.

Mrs. Colby's head dropped until her face was veiled
from her husband's gaze.

"I don't care," she said dully. "I don't care. I
don't believe it."

Mr. Colby sprang up from the bed, a strange quaint
little figure with, just for this instant, a wild power and
dignity about it.

"If I had that man here!" said Mr. Colby.

Mrs. Colby shook her head wearily. "I don't care,"
she said. "I don't believe it."

Mr. Colby suddenly raged. "*Don't believe it!*" he
mimicked savagely. "What d'you mean with your
'don't believe it!' Don't believe it! . . . Seen it
there, in that paper? Seen he's been arrested? Don't
they know he's the Butcher? . . . My God!" said
Mr. Colby. "If there was any justice in this Heaven-
forsaken world, they'd have him burnt to death."
Suddenly he broke. The force which had been in him
went away from him. He was like a lighted candle,
suddenly snuffed by ruthless finger and thumb. He fell
upon his knees by the bed. His head lolled awkwardly
upon Mrs. Colby's knees. Strange convulsions shook
him. Mrs. Colby put an absent-minded hand to his
head and passed its fingers through his hair.

Over his head her lips still shaped the words: "I
don't believe it!" And suddenly she said aloud, in a
new, strange voice:

"It wasn't him. He's . . . human. Lionel . . .
Lionel . . . What killed Lionel wasn't human. . . ."

Upon her knees Mr. Colby's round untidy head rolled
and lolled like an insane child's.

4

" My dear," said Mrs. Lightfoot, " you can't *imagine* what I felt like, to think that that man was here only last Tuesday, putting a swab down Ted's throat, and all the time he might have been murdering us all, without any one to stop him ! "

" I know, Lucy," Mrs. Stirling nodded her head so hard that she bumped her chin upon the top railing of the fence dividing the two gardens. " I always did think there was something queerish about him."

Mrs. Lightfoot pegged a pair of her husband's long woollen drawers on to the line with decisive and almost vicious thrusts. " That white face he's got, and that black hair. . . . "

" I know ! And my dear, those sort of odd-like eyes. And to think of him—the doctor that we all looked up to, to put our kids right when they were ill, all the time being this horrible Butcher !" Mrs. Lightfoot shuddered, covering her face with well-shaped but washing-wrinkled hands.

5

" Stans to reason !" Bilby thumped the work bench until all the tools rattled. " Stans to reason, you don't get a feller like that, a feller as'll stay up all night same as 'e did with my Jack, lookin' after a sick kid—you don't get a feller like that, goin' round stickin' daggers into innercent people's stummicks. Stans to reason ! "

" Stans to reason," said Bilby's mate. " My left bloody ankle. Here's this dispenserer of 'is, vanished like. There 'e is, wandering about, so they say, the same night as young Bert Rogers is done in, and there 'e is, wot's more, in stir. . . . Course 'e's the Butcher.

All I wisht is they'd let the guy out and let a few o' the boys get at 'im. It'd do more good, that would, than this respectable ' angin ' ! "

The voice of the foreman chipped in on the conversation. In the foreman's hand was a copy of the same edition of the *Clarion* as that which lay upon the bench between Bilby and his argumentative mate.

" You," said the foreman's voice, " can say what you qualified-well like. This 'ere doctor may 'ave done away with this 'ere suspencer, but what I *can* tell you is this ; this 'ere doctor is *not* the 'Olmdale Butcher. And I'll tell you for why ; this 'ere doctor ain't the 'Olmdale Butcher, 'cos 'e don't look no more like the 'Olmdale Butcher than your foot, Bilby, looks like the Queen's ! " The foreman came near to Bilby. He bent until his face was opposite Bilby's, and prodded Bilby in the chest with a bony forefinger which felt like the end of a spanner. The foreman sank his voice until it became a sinister and rasping whisper.

" The O'lmdale Butcher, Bilby," said the foreman, " *'as bin seen.*"

" Koo ! " said Bilby.

" Yes," said the foreman. " Seen by a reliable witness —my brother-in-law. I dunno whether you knows my brother-in-law, but 'e works at Breakfast Barlies' : 'is name's Leslie Todd—'e married my sister out o' pity and now 'e's the one to be pitied. Well, Leslie, 'e was comin' 'ome the day before yesterday, acrosst the fields between Breakfast Barlies' and Attwater Road. 'E's just goin' 'ome whistlin' merry like to keep 'is spirits up, just on account of all the talk on account o' this 'ere Butcher, when 'e sees somethink *and* 'ears somethink which, I might tell you, sends 'is spirits down with a bump. Somethink seems to pop out from the ground 'afore 'im, somethink which 'e sees as 'e approaches is an old man, a very, very tall old man with a very, very

long beard, and this old man, 'e 'as waving white 'air,
Bilby, and in 'is right hand, Bilby, 'e's got a gleamin'
knife—and this old man 'e lets out a 'owl and it makes
one spring toward Les——"

"*Koo!*" said Mr. Bilby again.

"Well," said the foreman, still in his dreadful whisper,
"may you say so! Leslie, 'e gives one shriek-like and
then 'e's orf, an' 'e don't stop, I might tell you, till 'e
gets 'ome. 'E 'asn't got over it yet. 'E wakes up in the
night a-shiverin' and a-sweatin' and a-cryin' out that
the Butcher's arter 'im. 'E says 'e'll 'ear them poundin'
feet comin' arter 'im in 'is sleep for the rest of 'is
natural. . . . Well, and what's the matter with *you*,
me lad?" This last sentence, in his natural and ireful
voice, the foreman addressed to Bilby's mate.

"I only said," the mate said with forced humility,
"why the 'ell don't your ruddy brother-in-lor go and
report 'is blood-curdlin' narrative to the p'lice?"

"My brother-in-law," said the foreman with slow
wrath, "is no B.F. 'E did report the 'ole 'orrible incident
*eggz*akly as it occurred . . ."

"Koo!" said Mr. Bilby.

6

The house of Mrs. Rudolph Sharp lies a little back
from Tall Elms Road. It is the fourth house in that most
exclusive of Holmdale's thoroughfares, and it has,
rather like its owner, a good deal more in front of than
behind it.

There were guests at Mrs. Rudolph Sharp's, for she
was giving one of her periodic luncheon parties. All
her progeny were there, the three girls Pamela, Priscilla
and Prunella; the two boys Francis and Ronald and
also—though he was indeed of small moment—Mr.
Rudolph Sharp. The guests were Martin Prideaux and

his wife, Moll. Prideaux was the Swiss-American pro-
duction expert recently imported by the Empire Educa-
cational Film Company who had, at great price, reft
him from Hollywood where he had been, so he frequently
would tell the world, the right hand man of Donald
Blacklawn.

Mrs. Rudolph Sharp had met the Prideaux only a
week before. She was taken with the Prideaux. She
felt that the Prideaux were *worth-while*. She sat, now,
at the head of her pleasant dining-table and behind a
mask of supreme but sufficiently pleasant boredom was
titillated to the very marrow of her being by the casual
references to great public figures—references usually
made by Christian names but in such manner as to
leave the surnames beyond doubt—which passed so
nonchalantly between Martin Prideaux and Moll
Prideaux. *Greta* for instance—who could this be but
Garbo? *Big Bill*, who could this be but Tilden? Wait
a minute! Might it not be Fox? Harley Wood, what
could this be but the home of Douglas and Mary, Rod
and Vilma, Charles and Chaplin? . . .

But the family of Mrs. Sharp was not impressed to so
great an extent. The family of Mrs. Sharp began to talk
among themselves. Said Francis to Ronnie:

" I say ! Seen the *Clarion* to-day ? "

" No." Ronnie shook his head. " What's on ? More
Butcher ? "

" You haven't seen it ! " Francis was incredulous.
His voice, full of the triumph of the bringer of news,
was raised even above the strident nasalities of Moll
Prideaux. " Then you don't know ! " He leaned forward and said with great empressement :

" There won't be any more Butcher murders ! They've
got the Butcher ! "

There was a stir round the table. Many voices simul-
taneously said :

" What ? What's that ? Say that again ! "

Francis sat back in his chair. He was a small and greasy-looking but moderately intelligent youth of twenty-four. He suffered from the suspicion that the world's valuation of Francis Sharp was not quite upon a par with Francis Sharp's own. When there came, therefore, isolated moments like this into his life, when a company fixed their attention upon himself even momentarily, he was in the habit of making such moments last for so long as they might. He placed his hands together, finger-tip to finger-tip, upon the edge of the table. He said, after a deliberate pause :

" It's all in the *Clarion*. They've arrested the Butcher. Of course they don't say that they know he's the Butcher, but it's obvious. . . . I must admit it was a surprise to me, knowing the fellah and all that. But then, the longer I live, the more I realise how surprising life can be. . . . To think that a decent fellah like that that we all know——"

" For the Lord's sake," said Ronald, " hurry up ! Who is it ? "

" You don't mean to say," said Mrs. Sharp, " that you *know*, Francis ? " She turned with pride upon Moll Prideaux. " Francis is an extraordinary boy. He always gets to hear of everything. He's always first."

" Who," said Ronald, thumping the table, " is it ? Say at once or I'll——"

He was never to tell what he would do, for at the moment of his thumping the table there descended upon the back of his neck an avalanche of spinach.

" What the hell ! " said Ronald, for the spinach was very hot and very wet.

He sprang up, scraping with clawing fingers at the back of his neck.

The noise of talk and movement was cut off as suddenly as if a dumbness had smitten the world. Every one at the table was gazing, petrified, at the spectacle of a black-frocked, white-aproned, be-capped parlourmaid, two dishes slipping from her nerveless hands, her healthy pretty face blanched to a deathly pallor, giving slowly at the knees and slipping in a huddled, crumpled heap to the floor. For this was Mary Phillimore, and Mary Phillimore had been betrothed of Albert Rogers, the Butcher's last victim.

Poor Mary. She had held out against ghoulish enquiry and a sympathy which seemed to her more than half based upon curiosity. She had carried on with her work. She had done her weeping decently and orderly by herself. She had made a mask to put on against the world, but now, with the news of the finding of the beast who had turned a pleasant life into a very fiery Hell, she had lost herself.

7

"My dear fellow!" said Mr. Runciman. "My *dear* fellow! You don't mean to tell me seriously that dear old Reade has been jolly well arrested!"

"My dear Runciman," retorted Mr. Calvin, "I think you heard me. If you didn't hear me I can only suggest the application of slightly more soap and water last thing every night and first thing every morning."

"Well," said Mr. Runciman, "I'm damned!"

Mr. Calvin smiled. "Very possibly, Runciman; in fact I should say, inevitably. But there it is. It appears that Reade has been taken up under suspicion of being the Butcher."

Mr. Piggott-Smith put in his word. "Can't understand," he said, "haow on earth a decent chep lake Reade kems under suspicion lake this."

Mr. Piggott-Smith subsided under the combined glares of Runciman and Calvin. Piggott-Smith was a retired

Something-Or-Other while Runciman was manager of the Holmdale United Laundries Limited, and Calvin the manager of the Holmdale Electricity Supply Company Limited. Runciman and Calvin detested each other, but were as one in determination to blot out Piggott-Smith and all his kind. They were on their way to the Club House. Runciman fell into step beside Calvin. In the rear Piggott-Smith trailed along disconsolate, dragging behind him a bag of clubs which were too heavy for him to lift.

"The whole thing is nonsense," said Runciman. "Blasted rot, my dear fellow! What I mean : a chap, a decent chap like Reade, the sort of a chap who's always good for a hand of Bridge and that sort of thing ; the sort of chap one has to dinner and all that ; well—you know what I mean, Calvin—that sort of a chap—he can't possibly be this Butcher."

"I see no valid reason," said Calvin, "why any one shouldn't be the Butcher. For all you know, Runciman, I might be. For all I know, you might be : in fact, looking at you, I'm not at all sure that you're not."

Runciman laughed, both an annoyed and an annoying sound. "As a matter of fact, my dear Calvin," he said. "You are, as I am afraid is pretty usual, quite utterly wrong. What I want to know is this : why don't the police *do* something! For all I can see, they might just as well not be here at all. . . . Now if they'd only get some one with a *business* head to help them get some *method* . . . For instance, I had a theory ; still have, if it comes to that. But would they listen to me when I took it to them ? Of course they wouldn't. . . . Time, however, will show."

8

All that happened upon the morning of Tuesday,
December 4th. At half-past three in the afternoon of
that day, a busy time at The Market and also at the main
post office which faced the most southerly door of The
Market, four men—four unobtrusively loitering men—
became, on a sudden, no longer loiterers and no longer
unobtrusive. Their eyes, as they had loitered, had been
fixed upon a spot just above the wall-slit letter box of
the post-office, and they had seen for one little flash
of time, so infinitesimal as to be unseen by any eyes
except their own, a red glow of light from the spot which
they had watched. The one nearest to the letter box,
though upon the far side of the road, ran forward, and
as he ran, he put a whistle to his lips and blew three
short sharp blasts. His three companions converged
upon him. There was one behind him at the western
end of the short road (it joins Market Road and Norfolk-
gate) closing that exit, and there were two before him,
half-way between the post-office outside which he now
stood and the junction of this road with Market Road.

To watch these four men was like watching a sheep
dog trial. Out of a scattered little throng of some
hundred and twenty persons, each picked a number.
The first man two ; the man behind him three, the other
two, respectively, four and one. This made a total of
ten, and these ten persons presently were gathered,
like bewildered sheep, in the postmaster's room which
opens out of a door to the left of the main entrance to
the post office.

The man who had blown his whistle, seeing that the
necessary work had been completed without aid, came
out to the steps of the post-office and once more whistled,
this time using only two blasts. At either end of the

short road, the four uniformed constables who had
appeared in answer to the first summons of the whistle
melted away like leaves before the wind. The man with
the whistle turned on his heel and went back into the
post-office and the postmaster's room. The selected
ten were huddled into a sheepish group. The room was
bare save for a desk, a chair, and three long trestle
tables. They stood in the centre of the barrenness.
They shuffled their feet and whispered indignantly one
to the other. There were three women, two boys of
apparently under sixteen years of age, and five men.
The three women were, as to two of them, well advanced
in middle age and of the respectable small-retired-trader
class, and as to one of them, of the would-be-smart
artificial-silk-stockinged live-on-your-credit class. The
two boys were—two boys. The five men were, at first
sight, so alike as to seem brothers. It was only when one
had been close to them for some time that one saw
that really the differences between them were so great
as to make their brotherhood most unlikely. It was their
uniformity of clothes (the cheap ready-made "sports"
suits of the holiday-making clerk) and the uniform
pallor of their faces which gave the initial impression
of similarity.

The man who had whistled went to the telephone
and spoke into it in a voice so low that not even the
ear-straining sheep could hear. He put the receiver
back upon its hook and turned to the sheep. He said :
"I am afraid you ladies and gentlemen will have to
wait until the Superintendent comes."

More muttering amongst the sheep, but not one voice
raised in hurried wrath. Sheep they looked like and sheep
they were ; sheep, moreover, lacking a bell-wether.

The Superintendent was not long in coming. He must,
it seemed even to the sheep, have been very closely at
hand. He came in upon them in a suave and friendly-

seeming rush which made them immediately feel, if
not less like sheep, at least less like sheep waiting outside
the abattoir.

Pike surveyed his catch and spoke to it. He said:

"Shan't keep you long, ladies and gentlemen. Just
one moment, if you please, then we'll start our business."

He went out through the door by which he had come
to return immediately followed by Myers the postmaster.

The postmaster, ignoring the flock, went out by
another door.

Pike, after a word with the whistle-blower, followed.

The whistle-blower went up to the flock, and from it
detached one of the elderly women.

"If," said the whistle-blower, "you would follow
me, madam . . ."

The woman followed. Separated from her enforced
companions she seemed, perhaps paradoxically, to gain
not only in individuality but in strength. There was
about her, as she passed through the door which the
whistle-blower held open and so into the presence of
Pike sitting behind the postmaster's table, an air of
shrewd, mind-your-own-business efficiency.

Pike, seeming courtesy personified, leapt to his feet
and placed a chair. "Take a seat, madam," he said.

She sat upon the chair with an air of protest. She
perched herself so much upon its edge that a fall seemed
imminent. Pike remained standing. He said:

"Madam, I am informed that just now you posted a
letter in the box outside this building. Is that so?"

The woman's head was bonnetted. There were dangling
bugles upon the bonnet and these shook with the
vehemence of her nod. In her craggy face the lips had
disappeared, but momentarily they showed again as
she spoke. "I did," she said, "and what of it?"

Pike at some length, and with a grave courtesy wholly
admirable, explained his position.

" . . . and so, I am sure, Madam," he concluded, " you will realise that it is only for the good of yourself and the community that I am forced to take these rather drastic steps and ask you the questions which I shall have to ask you."

Once more the bugles danced, though whether this time to a nod or a shaking of the head it was hard to determine.

" How many letters, Madam," said Pike, going back to his chair and resting his elbows upon the table, " did you post ? "

" One," was the answer.

" To whom ? " said Pike.

The woman bridled. Her hands which had been folded in her lap came up until in the palm of each there rested an elbow. The thin-lipped mouth emitted one word : " Imperence ! "

Once more Pike went over his explanations, this second time fully as courteous as he had been the first. His bright, small eyes were veiled with a smiling veil of deprecatory innocence and yet there was beneath his manner a quality of adamant which communicated itself.

The woman gave in. " If you must know," she said, " it was to my boy Alf. It was a white envelope. It had one penny and one ha'penny stamp, and it was addressed to 28706, Lance-Corporal A. Hitchin, 3/4th Duke of Gloucester's Own Light Infantry, Tidworth."

Pike glanced down at a slip of paper tucked into the corner of the postmaster's blotting pad.

" Thank you," he said. " Now—Mrs. Hitchin is it ?— you are not bound to do this, but I must say it would make our labours much easier, and possibly save you a good deal of annoyance, if you could just give me a rough outline of what this letter contained. I have explained to you that we have, in connection with our investigation, to check the letters posted just now, and if you care to just give me the outline I have asked for, well . . ." His shrug intimated how delightful such information would make the future relations of Mrs. Hitchin with the police.

Mrs. Hitchin's thin-lipped mouth writhed into a soundless and doubtless genteel epithet, but Mrs. Hitchen gave her information. Mrs. Hitchen had written to her Alf the usual letter. Was he well? Had the last lot of socks fitted him? She had not yet received the 5s. 0d. he had promised three weeks ago. She did hope that he would not have to go to India to fight them blackamoors. Cissie and Fred and Alice's children were all well. Hoping this found him as it left his loving mother at present. . . . And that was that.

Through yet another door Pike bowed Mrs. Hitchin, having first, however, written down her full name and her address. He went back to his seat and touched a bell. There was ushered in to him the second sheep, this time one of the five men, a person bearing the startling name of Loosebutton.

Mr. Loosebutton, it appeared, had posted two letters, one to a "lady friend," Miss Gwladys Frenchem, at an office in Holborn Viaduct asking her whether she would like to come to the pictures with him upon the next Thursday evening, and one to his father, a commercial traveller working in the north, asking for the loan of 10s. 0d. presumably to enable him to carry out the appointment made in the first letter. Addresses and details duly taken, Pike got rid of Mr. Loosebutton and once more pressed his bell.

The next was another woman, this time the young and automatically charming apex of the feminine triangle. After Pike's preliminary she smiled. She was ready enough with her information.

"Eunice Doulton," she said. "My father's very well

known here. He's assistant Secretary of the Company."
She looked at Pike and found him "interesting." She
made good use of her eyes.

Pike asked his next question. "I don't mind," said
Miss Doulton, "telling you at all. . . . Of course I
don't! What I mean is, Superintendent, I think *everybody* ought to do *everything* they can to help the police
to find this . . . this . . . terrible creature. At least
I hope I'm right in supposing that's what you're
after."

Pike's shrug and nod were triumphant masterpieces of
the non-committal, but he reiterated his question.

"Of course I don't mind!" Miss Doulton was most
obliging. "I only posted a letter to a boy I know. One
letter. Rather a difficult letter. As a matter of fact,
Superintendent, as a matter of fact he wrote to me last
Thursday asking me . . . asking me . . ." She paused
in some confusion, assumed or not.

Pike was gallant. "And this letter was your answer,
Miss Doulton?"

"As a matter of fact I'm afraid he'll be fearfully cut
up. D'you know, Superintendent, I don't know exactly
how to put it. As a matter of fact I hardly got any sleep
last night . . ."

"I quite understand." Pike, of necessity all things
to all men, was at once courteous, gallant and business-
like. He took his notes of Miss Doulton's address and all
particulars, and he bowed Miss Doulton out.

He came back to his table and once more pressed the
bell : but this time there entered to him not the next
of the ten letter-posters but his own aide, Blaine.

Pike looked up sharply. "What's up?" he said.
He knew his man.

Blaine raised his right hand to a level with the table.
In it was a square piece of yellow paper covered with
writing in a deep black ink.

"This," said Blaine. He set it down upon the post-master's blotter.

"Good man!" said Pike. "I was going to send Walters down for you in a minute. I ought really to've seen this first but I couldn't keep these people hanging about. . . . What's he got to say this time?" He bent over the letter. He read; and read again. What he read was this:

"DEAR POLICE,—You will remember that in my last letter I promised to let you know of any future jobs I intended to carry out. Now please don't get excited. This is not, exactly, the first of my 'warning' letters, as I shall call them, but it is a line to let you know of a job of mine which has been completed without your knowing anything about it, and over which, I gather from our local broadsheet, you have made a grave or comical error. You have arrested Dr. Reade, and although you have given no reason for his arrest, it is clear to me at least, that this has to do with the dis-appearance of his dispenser (dispenser of what?) Marjorie Williams.

"Marjorie Williams was an experiment of mine in a new technique. I must say that the whole job has given me the very greatest satisfaction. I am far from vindictive, however, and would not wish poor Dr. Reade to languish in prison much longer. I will therefore tell you where you may find the body of Marjorie Williams.

"If you will go out of Holmdale and along the by-pass road, travelling southwards, until you come—just before the Batley cross-roads—to four new bungalows which are built but not yet inhabited and will go to the third of these, you will find that the door of the cupboard under the stairs is not quite shut. I am afraid one of her feet *would* get in the way.

" Good-bye, Police, for the present, and please let
poor Dr. Reade out of jail.

"Yours in sportsmanship,

" THE BUTCHER."

Pike looked up at Blaine in silence.

" Yes, I know," Blaine said.

Pike grunted. " Do you ? Wish I did." He tapped
the letter before him. " How many of these this time ? "

" One, sir."

" Addressed ? "

" County Police. At the Station."

" Envelope ? " said Pike.

Blaine smiled reproachfully. " I've done all that, sir.
As usual, nothing. I've kept it, of course. . . . Excuse
me, sir, had any luck with these people ? "

Pike shook his head. " No," he said bitterly. There
was a pause. The silence was broken by the squeaking
of a chair as he rose to his feet. He said :

" I'm going to leave these people. Walters can keep
'em. I was being considerate, but I think for once consideration won't pay. They can blinking well wait and
blinking well cool their heels. Blast 'em ! "

Blaine almost staggered. He had known Pike and
worked under him for four years, but never before
had he heard from that thin-lipped but pleasant mouth
in the lean, brown, lantern-shaped face any oath,
however mild. He thought : Getting him down, this
is ! He said :

" What's to do now then, sir ? "

" Get a car," said Pike, " and two men and yourself.
We're going down to this bungalow."

Blaine for one half-second looked at his Superintendent
curiously. Never before had he seen quite that look upon
his Superintendent's face—not even during the Ponsonby
case.

" Hurry," said Pike.

The tone sent Blaine out at a run.

Pike pressed the bell, keeping his finger upon it. The plain clothes man, Walters, came at once. He was told, curtly : " Keep the rest here till I come back. It doesn't matter how long I am."

" Very good, sir," said Walters, and was gone.

CHAPTER TEN

I

THE Blue Crossley swung out of Pearmount Road into Dale Road at speed. Police Constable George Birch, on duty in Dale Road, opened his eyes first and then his mouth. He had been standing upon the left-hand pavement at the junction of the two roads and the wind of the passing car had seemed almost strong enough to blow off his helmet. He was about to shout after the car when he saw what car it was. He shut his mouth but his eyes remained widely open, staring.

The Crossley gathered speed and shot down Dale Road towards its junction with the Main Road. Pike was driving and though he was not yet fully admitting this to himself, he was both angry and afraid ; not afraid, of course, for his own skin, but afraid of the intangible in this business as a child is afraid of the intangibilities which the dark may hold.

It is, from the junction of Dale Road and the Main Road, a matter of six miles to the bungalow of which the letter had spoken. The car covered the distance in under seven minutes. It screamed along the macadamed road with its white curbing and the flat grasslands upon its either side. Suddenly turning the bend just before the Batley cross-roads, the engine was switched off, its gears thrown into neutral and the brakes rammed on. It drew up with a shriek of protest opposite four little gaily painted boxes of red brick and white stucco.

Almost before it was motionless its doors opened and

four men scrambled out—Pike and Blaine and two plain clothes county policemen.

They ran. Of the four, two were under twenty-seven years of age, one thirty-four and the other forty-two. It was forty-two who reached the door of the third bungalow a good twenty yards in front of his fellows. The door, Pike found, was, though it appeared shut, merely pushed to. On the threshold he turned, waved imperiously and disappeared within.

Blaine was next and by the time that Blaine was within the small green front door, it was to find his Superintendent kneeling a few feet beyond the threshold before an open cupboard and looking at something which lay in this cupboard. . . .

They took what was left of Marjorie Williams out by the back way. The second of the county policemen was sent to the car and came back from it, running, with a blanket. With this blanket they covered what was left of Marjorie Williams and, between them, carried the shrouded thing to the Crossley and laid it somehow in the back seat.

Pike drove. Blaine sat beside him. Marjorie Williams filled the back. The two county policemen stood one upon each running board and thanked their Gods that now the Superintendent drove never at more than forty-five miles an hour.

2

It was five minutes to five o'clock when Pike once more mounted the steps of the post-office, pushed open the swing doors and found himself face to face with a group from whom anger had now chased all resemblance to sheep. He did not look at them. He turned sharp to his left and went once more into the postmaster's room. He sat down at the table. He was about to ring the bell when Walters came. Walters, previously calm, was now red of face and damp. At any other time in any other circumstance Pike would, at least privately, have laughed. But now he merely barked :

" Had any trouble ? "

Walters took a handkerchief from his pocket and mopped his large brow. " Had any trouble ! " said Walters. " Look here, sir, I——"

" All right ! " Pike snapped at him. " Next one in. Send in the most troublesome."

For a moment it seemed that Walters had more to say ; but only for a moment.

" Quick ! " said Pike. And Walters was quick.

There was ushered in to Pike a very angry man ; one of the five men who when they had first been gathered together had looked all exactly like each other, but who now, after an hour and a half's incarceration, were as dissimilar as well might be. This one went, as after some trouble, Pike was to find out, by the name of Crawley. And Mr. Crawley had much to say and very many words in which to say it.

" . . . kept here," said Mr. Crawley, " for three or four hours and not knowing what we're kept here for ! I want to know what the meaning of this is ! " Mr. Crawley, who had refused a chair, leaned over the table and thumped with the soft part of his fist upon the postmaster's blotting paper. " It's damn scandalous ! " he said. " Damn scandalous ! Can't think what's come over the place, when a decent orderly citizen can't go out in the afternoon without getting held up by a lot of plug-uglies ! Life's come to a pretty pass ! " Mr. Crawley was rapidly working himself up into an even greater rage than that in which he had entered the room. " By God ! " he said, " I don't know who you are, but they tell me you're something to do with Scotland Yard. If you're a specimen

of Scotland Yard and what Scotland Yard can do, all
I can say is God help England ! I've got a cousin in the
Home Office. He knows all about these things. As soon
as I get away from here I'm going to get straight on the
'phone to him. As I said before, I don't know who you
are, and I don't care, but I'll damn well see the place
is made too hot to hold you. Some of you chaps seem
to think that because you've been three or four years
in the police force it gives you the right to act like
Mussolini." Once more he banged upon the desk.
" I'll see that you're discharged and discharged damn
quickly," said Mr. Crawley, and went on mouthing.

Pike looked at his watch. Pike, in the interests of his
work had a certain amount of time to waste, but no
more. He decided that Mr. Crawley's annoyance must
now cease. He said, quietly, cutting into the froth of
Mr. Crawley's speech as a knife will cut into soft
cheese :

" One moment. I'm doing my work. I don't need to
be told how to do it, you know. It's no good glaring
and frothing at the mouth, as you might say. Listen while
I tell you that if you continue this behaviour I shall
consider that you're preventing me from carrying out
my work properly and in that case I shall have no other
alternative than to put you somewhere where you'll
cool down. You know what I mean. In Holmdale,
Mr. Crawley, these are extraordinary times, and extraordinary times need extraordinary measures. I don't
want to use them, but I'll have to if you go on
like this . . ." His small bright eyes were boring now
into Mr. Crawley's whose frothing speech was subsiding
bubble by bubble.

" In other words," said Pike, " if you go on behaving
like this, I'll have you taken up . . . so it's no good
shouting your half-baked legal knowledge at me. I've
told you that these are extraordinary times and I've

told you that I've got extraordinary powers at the moment. Now, shall I use 'em or shall I not ? "

Although he did not say so, Mr. Crawley apparently decided that he would not give occasion for the use of these sinister sounding powers. Mr. Crawley became tame, and Mr. Crawley, tame, was very shortly got rid of. He had posted three letters; one had been to his mother in answer to a request for financial aid ; a second had been to Messrs. Selfridge containing a cheque in payment of an account for 17s. 11d. ; the third had been to his sister who had just become engaged to be married and to whom Mr. Crawley wished to offer his congratulations. The full names and addresses of the persons to whom his letters were addressed were given and fully noted by Pike, as also was Mr. Crawley's own full name, address and description. Mr. Crawley, much chastened, was dismissed.

There followed him, in this order : Miss Elsie Frost, Mr. Philip Frognall, Mr. Edward Thatcher, Mr. Israel Gompertz, and Masters Percy Burr and George Evans.

Miss Elsie Frost, a frigid and ill-dressed virgin, had posted one letter only and this to her solicitors, altering her will in favour of her niece, Ariadne Frost. Miss Elsie Frost, from Pike's point of view, was satisfactory. She took up no more than two moments of his time. She was very acid during these two moments, but that was of no matter.

Mr. Philip Frognall was a watered-down edition of Mr. Crawley. He was very angry, but not so angry as Mr. Crawley. He was very violent, but not so violent as Mr. Crawley. He was subdued more easily than Mr. Crawley. Mr. Frognall had certainly posted three letters, but none of them were letters of his own. They all belonged to his wife. Fortunately he was able to explain, not only to whom these letters were addressed,

but also their contents. They were all as innocent as
Mr. Frognall's appearance.

Mr. Edward Thatcher was neither as mild as Mr.
Loosebutton nor as irate as Mr. Crawley. Mr. Thatcher
looked colourless and was colourless. He had posted
one letter, addressed to Messrs. Sole and Harding,
ordering a set of loose covers for the interior of his
Baby Austin Saloon.

Mr. Israel Gompertz was difficult. He was, very
obviously, a Jew. He was, even more obviously, anxious
to oblige. But he took a very long time in obliging.
Mr. Gompertz beat about the bush. It cost Pike ten
minutes and more of intensive questioning before he
found out so much as the first reason for Mr. Gompertz's
hesitancy.

" You thee," said Mr. Gompertz, " it ith tho awkward,
Thuperintendent. . . . If Mitheth Gompertz were to
hear about thith, the'd go thraight up in the air ! . . ."

" I see. I see," said Pike, somehow managing to
retain the air of sympathetic consideration which he had
judged the best method for Mr. Gompertz. " But if you
would just tell me, in confidence, sir, what was the purport of this letter to Miss Aarons—just the broad out-
lines, you know—I could just make my official note and
we could probably see that you got home at once."

Mr. Gompertz rose from his seat. He came round
the table and leant over the astonished Pike. Supporting himself with one hand upon the edge of the table, he
bent still further over until his lips were no more than
half an inch away from the left ear of Pike. Mr.
Gompertz made hissing noises like a kettle.

But something must have been clear. For Pike made
his hieroglyphic notes and, so soon as he had given
details of his address, Mr. Gompertz was allowed to
depart.

There were now left only the two boys—Masters

Percy Burr and George Evans. Of these, Percy Burr was first. Percy Burr was much afraid. It seemed to Percy Burr that he was in imminent danger of being strung up, and he said so, with, at the end, an outbreak of blubbering. If Mr. Crawley had been present to see Superintendent Pike's handling of Master Percy Burr, he would have been astonished. He would have found it difficult to believe that this was the same man who had browbeaten him into submission.

Percy Burr became calm at last, and explained that he had indeed posted letters, four letters to be exact. He did not know what letters they were because they had been given to him by his mother. At the same time as giving him the letters, Master Burr explained, his mother had given him threepence with which to buy sweets. This he had done before posting the letters.

Pike looked at Percy Burr. Behind his pleasantly smiling face the thoughts raced furiously. He said at last :

" Is there a telephone in your house ? "

Percy Burr nodded emphatically and was then left alone in the postmaster's room for a matter of four minutes. When the police gentleman came back, he seemed even more pleasant than he had been before, and Percy Burr, much to his relief, was allowed to depart ; allowed to depart not quite as he had come, for upon his departure he was suddenly enriched by the presentation of a very new and very shiny two-shilling piece. . . .

Pike had spoken with Mrs. Burr and Pike was satisfied as to the three letters which Percy had posted. They tallied, as did the others, with the letters posted immediately before and during the flashing of the light from above the post-box.

After Percy Burr's departure, Pike sat a moment in thought. So far all these persons had not only properly accounted for their posted letters but had, each of them, seemed as little like what might be the Holmdale Butcher as any man could imagine.

And yet the letter had been posted, and the poster of the letter must be within this group. Must be so, that is, if the four specially picked rounders-up had not let any one slip through their fingers. And Pike did not believe—could not believe !—that they had let any one so slip. Each man of them had been most especially picked, and the job, in itself, had not been difficult. And the men themselves, when he had questioned them, had been certain and emphatically certain.

And yet the letter had been posted and here was he, faced with the fact that there was only one more person to be interviewed, and this a boy, who would probably be—allowing for the normal differences in human animals—a replica of Master Percy Burr !

There was, of course, the possibility that the Butcher —or at least the poster of the Butcher's letter—had been one of the persons whom he had already seen and a person who, having posted another checkable letter about which to talk, had so disguised his bearing of the other all-important missive. This was, indeed, a new thought ; an intriguing thought. But yet not a satisfactory thought. Pike, who relied more upon his well-trained and imagination-aided judgment of character than perhaps he knew himself, could not believe that any of the persons whom he had interviewed and let go were at all likely to fill his bill. . . . With an effort, he banished the frown from his forehead and once more pressed the bell upon the post-master's desk. Within a very few moments, the boy George Evans was with him.

George Evans proved to be not only dissimilar in appearance but also in spirit from Percy Burr. George Evans was not in the least frightened. If anything he was most pleasurably thrilled. He felt that for once he was an important person. He was not used to being an important person and, as so often happens in higher spheres than George Evans's, the feeling had gone seriously to his head.

But he answered the questions put to him with commendable decision and rapidity. . . . It seemed that George Evans was a messenger boy employed by The Market. At 3.15 that afternoon George Evans had been told by his immediate superior to go to the cashier's office, and, as usual, collect the afternoon's post. . . . Here George Evans explained, in answer to a question, that the afternoon's post usually consisted of some fifty or sixty letters of varying shapes and sizes which he found laid out upon one of the assistant cashier's tables. His duty in this connection was simply to pick up the letters and carry them through The Market and outside and across the road to the letter box. When he had posted them, he went back. He had followed this programme to-day. In answer to more questions George Evans explained that this afternoon the post had been of about the usual size—that is the wad of letters had been " thickish but not too thick." He had been able to carry them all in one hand quite easily. Perhaps there had been fifteen letters ; perhaps there had been thirty ; he could not say. . . . No, he had noticed nothing unusual until he had been commanded by one of the detectives to wait. . . . George Evans dared to make so bold as to ask whether this hold-up by the police had anything to do with the Butcher and they-there letters which the Butcher was wont to write. . . . But Pike was not listening to George. He was staring over George's shoulder into vacancy and the rough partition wall which separated the post-master's room from the main office. And presently Pike slapped once upon the table with his palm ; a slap

so hard that it made the post-master's ink-wells rattle
in their sockets.

And Pike said, " Got it, by *jing !* "

George Evans was dismissed with a similar gift to
that which Percy Burr was still clasping hotly in his
hand. It was explained to George that, if there was any
trouble in The Market about his prolonged absence, it
should be put right without delay. . . .

He had gone away with plenty to talk about but then
so had the others. This was inevitable. And yet. . . .
And yet. . . . Pike cursed himself for a fool. He ought
to have known better. Now, however, he saw his way
clear to one scheme at least which could be carried out
with outside labour and therefore more efficaciously and
less dangerously.

He sat, completely immersed in thought, for perhaps
five minutes, and then rousing himself, he reached out
for the postmaster's bell and pressed it, this time with
a long steady pressure. Walters came again, a Walters
now briskness personified. Pike looked at him. " Get
Blaine," he said, and very presently Blaine was with
him.

Blaine did not speak. He stood at the other side of
the table looking down at his chief and he raised his
eyebrows.

Pike shook his head. " Nothing doing."

Blaine's eyes opened wider. " *Nothing !* " he said.

" Nothing. And yet, Blaine, I feel those three fellows
and Walters got the right people."

" But it doesn't sound sense, sir, to me," Blaine began.

" I know." Once more Pike shook his head. " But
it's right nevertheless." He leaned right forward over
the table, his arms propping him up. He said :

" Look here, Blaine. That letter was posted, but you
might say it wasn't posted by any of the people I've
just seen. . . ."

Blaine shifted uneasily. " It's no good, sir," he said as last. " I can't see it."

" Nor could I," said Pike, " until just now." A little half smile fluttered fleetingly across his lean brown face. " We've been had, Blaine ! Had well and had proper. . . . That letter, Blaine, was posted by a certain person, but that certain person didn't know what he was posting. He knew that he was posting letters, but what those letters were—there must have been about thirty which we can soon verify—he didn't know. Most specially he didn't know that among the letters was *this*." Here Pike tapped meaningly upon his inner pocket which contained a note-case holding the last of the Butcher's effusions. " This fellow, Blaine, is getting a bit too much for me. He's getting on my nerves. I *must* get him. *I will* get him ! . . . But he's fly ! Somehow or other I feel that he'd got wind of this light stunt. He somehow or other managed to slip his letter among The Market's letters so that the boy posted a bunch without knowing what was in the middle of 'em."

Blaine whistled between his teeth, a quick and yet long exhalation of breath.

" Right, sir," said Blaine. " What's to do now ? "

Pike got to his feet. His movement was so sudden that the chair upon which he had been sitting shot backwards from him with a wild protesting shriek across the stone floor.

" I'm darned," said Pike, " if I know. . . . At least I *do* know, but I haven't got it straight yet. . . . First, though, we'd better read the letters and check these people's statements about them. I've got notes here. Just slip down and get 'em, will you ? Not that we shall find anything . . ."

They didn't find anything.

CHAPTER ELEVEN

I

THE finding of Marjorie Williams had been, you will remember, upon Tuesday, December 4th. Somehow, after it, the nerves of Holmdale were tautened to so tense a pitch that the two blank days which followed were almost unbearable. It was a time of terror in Holmdale; yet, when the terror seemed temporarily to cease, these tightened nerves did not relax. Rather, they went on, as it were, screwing themselves up. They had reached by the Wednesday night a point where, paradoxically enough, any actual horror would have been relief; relief, at least, from this waiting. They had borne with this crazy evil in their midst, and borne with it for many days which seemed more than twice the number of years. They had, in other words, got used to the Butcher. They expected the Butcher; and expecting the Butcher, they had come very nearly to the point—an hysteric point no doubt, but none the less real for that—when the news of a fresh activity of the Butcher's was, to them, normality.

It is said that the human animal can adapt himself to any constant circumstance; those who doubt this might well have their doubts refuted by an argument pointing to Holmdale during this time of the Butcher's activities.

After the Tuesday night, and Wednesday morning's revelation of the Butcher's magnanimity in procuring the release of Dr. Reade, Holmdale was turned inside out. Holmdale was beaten about the head and laid prostrate. Men in Holmdale suspected their neighbours;

144

many—as even Pike's early report had shown—began, perhaps, to suspect themselves. Citizens of Holmdale would not venture out of their houses, even during dusk, unless they were in parties of five or six, and not even then unless such parties were eighty per cent. male and able-bodied male.

Suspicion led to much trouble in Holmdale. There was the case of William Richards who, upon being accosted at 4.45 on the evening of Wednesday, December 5th by a stranger who asked him for a light, suddenly became more violent than ever in his life and smote and kicked the stranger until a patrol arrived, after which it was proved—not without much trouble—that the. stranger was a genuine person and no stranger at all, but a man who, in normal circumstances, Mr. Richards would have known by sight as one of the cashiers from The Market.

And the futile spying went on, and the reports to the police by Mrs. This of sinister activities by Mrs. That, Mrs. That being discovered, in every case, to have been for many months an enemy of Mrs. This. And there were letters to the papers ; letters not only to the *Clarion*—which in any save the most exalted cases refused to publish them—but to the big London daily and evening papers such as the *Mercury*, the *Planet* and the *Looking Glass* ; letters signed " Ratepayer," " Indignant," " Victim " and, of course, " Pro Bono Publico."

And there were questions in the House, showers and showers of questions ; question upon question. The Home Secretary answered more questions during Wednesday and Thursday, December 5th and 6th, than ever before during his three-year term of office. He did not, as was only natural, answer them satisfactorily, but answer them he did. He said that the police " had the matter in hand." He said that " every step was being

the fast express must pass. He marvelled at Millicent's knowledge of railways and how railways function. He perhaps discounted the fact that of her three years of life, Millicent had spent something like a quarter in railway carriages.

" Millicent ! " said her mother. " Millicent ! You're being a nuisance."

The tunnel disintegrated and became, in a gymnastic flash, a man and not a tunnel ; a man in a quiet blue suit and very shiny boots ; a man whose lean brown face was darker than usual by reason of its sudden flush.

Millicent, too, rose to her feet, but much more slowly. She was still a train and the train was a disgruntled train as any train might be disgruntled at finding its tunnel suddenly taken away from around it.

" Not," said Millicent, " nuisance. Train." She turned to Pike. She added, with some indignation : " The *tunnoo* went ! "

Molly Brade smiled upon the untunnelled Pike and said :

" It *is* good of you ! "

Pike fidgeted. He put his hands into his pockets and immediately withdrew them again. He looked down at his boots and then up at the ceiling. He said :

" If you'll let me contradict you, Mrs. Brade, it isn't at all." He looked down at the still frowning Millicent. " It's a pleasure, as you might say. And I *mean* that." He looked everywhere but at Molly Brade's smiling blue eyes.

" All the same," Molly said, " it *is* good of you. Especially when you must be so busy ; so . . . so rather terribly busy."

There came from Pike's mouth a short, hard laugh. " Busy ! " he said, and laughed again. " Busy ! I

wish I was, Mrs. Brade. I almost wish I was so busy
I didn't have time to play with this very charming
young lady. Almost, but not quite ; because no one
could quite wish that . . . Busy ! If you ask me,
Mrs. Brade, I tell you that I ought to be busy, but that
I can't *be* busy." Now he was looking straight into
Molly Brade's eyes, and now the flush of embarrassment
had gone and the frown, which had been absent during
the game of Chuffers, had returned in full measure. He
said, after a long pause :

"I've always said—give me something to do and
I'll get on with it. . . . But I take that back now as
you might say. Right back ! . . . I've got enough
to do, haven't I ? I've got to catch this . . . this
. . . Well, anyway, I've got something to *do* ! I've
got to catch something. But can I do it ? I can't !
If you knew. . . ."

"But I do know." Molly Brade smiled ; a charming
smile at which a tired and harassed and self-doubting
man might warm himself.

Pike looked at his watch. "All the same, Mrs.
Brade," he said, "thanks very much for reminding me.
I must get along now. . . . The least I can do is to put
in an appearance." He stooped down and kissed
Millicent. He bowed stiffly—a curious, jerky little
bow from the middle of his back—to Millicent's mother.
He left the room with long, quick strides. The door
shut softly but decisively behind him, and presently
Molly Brade heard the opening and shutting of the front
door, and then, after this, the click-clicking of the
front gate.

She dropped upon her knees beside her daughter.
She said : "Have a good game, darling ? "

Millicent nodded gravely. "Nice man," said Millicent. "Very good train."

"What shall we do ? " said Millicent's mother.

"Market," said Millicent firmly. "Bockey money."

"But, darling," said Molly, "it isn't pocket money day until to-morrow. And anyway, I haven't got two pennies. We'll have to get change."

"Bockey money," said Millicent, with dispassionate firmness. She looked up at her mother with a gravely concentrated stare which made her blue eyes seem larger than they were by nature. She wore a tense pre-occupied look, so pregnant with the curious appeal of the infant, that her mother, with that feeling so common to parents, had for a moment some ado to keep from tears.

"Bockey money," said Millicent. "Market. Buy little tin chuffer."

3

As he drew abreast of the lamp-post, and the small green gate leading up to Jeffson's white cottage, Pike's heart sank, for outside the gate, drawn up to the curb, was a big green old-fashioned Daimler Saloon, which he knew belonged to the Chief Constable. The Chief Constable alone could be handled so that he was very little trouble, but with each aide that he brought with him, his awkwardness as a "proposition" was increased quite disproportionately. And Heaven knew how many the green Daimler would hold and this morning had held. Pike opened the gate, walked up the little path, pushed open the front door which was ajar and so went into the little room upon the right, which, with every succeeding day, grew less like parlour and more like police station. The Chief Constable was there and with him were Davis and Farrow. The Chief Constable sat behind Jeffson's official table. There was no decline in his plumpness, but there was in his colour. Where, when Pike had first seen him, he had been ruddy though worried looking, he was now pasty and with new lines etched upon his comfortable face. Davis was unchanged; the lean type of Sergeant-Major. Farrow, the burly, seemed to Pike's quick eye to be a little more stupid and a little less aggressive.

As Pike entered, he became aware that the hum of talk which he had heard as he walked up the path and through the door into the narrow passage, had died down to an expectant and yet somehow minatory silence.

There were greetings all round; curt greetings merely sufficiently suave. Pike, at the Chief Constable's invitation, sat himself upon a chair to face the Chief Constable. Davis and Farrow who, Pike was sure, had been sitting before his advent, now stood stiffly behind the Chief Constable, one at his left shoulder, the other at his right. The Chief Constable, the greetings over, looked at Pike.

" Well ? " said the Chief Constable.

Pike's face was a studious blank. " If you mean, sir," he said in a very official voice, " is there anything to report, I'm afraid the answer's in the negative. There's nothing to report. I'm not sure. . . . "

The Chief Constable cut him short. He slapped with his finger-tips upon the edge of Jeffson's table. He said :

" What I would like to know, Superintendent, is what we are *doing*."

Pike shrugged. He was finding it difficult this morning to keep his temper. He waited a moment, swallowing down certain hot speeches which had suggested themselves to his mind and which almost had begun to come out of his mouth. He said :

" You know, I think, sir, all that we are doing. I've taken no steps at all other than those you suggested.

Except, of course, the letter box—which didn't come off. . . . "

There came a stifled sound from Farrow and its echo from Davis.

Once more the Chief Constable hit the table. " D'you mean to tell me, Superintendent, that we've got to go on . . . go on . . . *letting* this—I hardly know what to call him . . . this . . . lunatic . . . have his own way with every one of us ? "

Pike swallowed. He said, after a longer pause than his first :

" I'm afraid that's what it means, sir . . . . At the moment anyhow."

The Chief Constable looked at Pike. The Chief Constable in the next instant proved himself a shrewder man than most would have expected. He said :

" I think you've got something up your sleeve, Superintendent. If you have, I think we ought to know about it. You must follow your own judgment in these matters, but I must say I don't like the idea that you're not taking us fully into your confidence."

Pike, momentarily, was taken aback. He said at last :

" I'm sorry, sir, I'm sure. If you feel that there's anything wrong about the way I'm handling this matter. . . . "

" It isn't that . . . " The Chief Constable at this direct riposte to his attack seemed to grow slightly discomfortable. " All that I meant was . . . well . . . fact is I've had one or two suggestions made to me, Superintendent, and I think I'd better give them to you right away."

Pike crossed one leg over the other. He sat looking hard at the Chief Constable. " Please do so by all means. We're not up against an ordinary job here, or we'd have had some results by now. We're up against something strange, as you might say: something almost . . . or *quite*, inhuman. . . . Therefore, sir, my idea is this: that if any one's got any notion whatsoever about dealing with this matter; if any one can give us any sort of workable suggestion whatever, about how to lay our hands on the man we want. . . . Well then, I'm all attention."

The Chief Constable coughed and gave a half glance, instantly repressed, over his right shoulder at Farrow. The Chief Constable said:

" Well, for one thing, Superintendent, it has been suggested to me, that whatever the cost, we *ought* to try and double the patrols."

" Getting the men, sir," Pike said, " from where? "

The Chief Constable swelled out his cheeks and exhaled with a puffing sound.

" My dear fellah! " said the Chief Constable. " My dear fellah! You surely must know of all the offers of volunteers we've had since this business began! And now I come to think of it, I know you know. The last time we met we were talking about it. . . . And now Jeffson tells me the number of offers he's had in the past forty-eight hours has almost doubled the total previous offers. . . . Well, what's the matter with that? " The Chief Constable's last words were heavy with repressed ire.

For Pike had shaken his head in some subtly clever way which was not rude, and yet was most emphatic. And Pike said:

" I'm beginning to think we not only ought not to increase patrols, but we ought not p'raps to have any patrols at all. . . . "

There came a snort from Inspector Farrow, and this time a quite audible snigger from Inspector Davis.

The Chief Constable wisely went on as if there had been no sound from behind him. He said:

" You'll forgive me, Superintendent, but that sounds damned nonsense to me ! Damned nonsense ! Doesn't seem to be any sense in it, damn it ! " He glared at Pike, waiting.

Pike took his time. He discovered within himself a desire to rise from his chair, to seize the large ink-pot which stood just before the Chief Constable and to empty it over the Chief Constable's bald head. Successfully he restrained himself. But he didn't look at the Chief Constable as he spoke. He said :

" If you'll allow me, sir, I'll explain. The reason why I didn't think we ought to add to our patrols— the reason why, sometimes, I even think we should have no patrols at all, is that *we do not know who the Butcher is*. . . . "

This was too much for Davis and Farrow. Once more Davis sniggered, and this time Farrow spoke. " You don't say so, Superintendent ! " he said. His tone was so heavily ironic as to be either insulting or ridiculous or both.

Pike ignored him. " I daresay, sir," he said, looking at the Chief Constable, " that you think I'm dithering. I'm not. I said 'we don't know who the Butcher is ' on purpose. I thought that if I put it like that you might get a new angle on this business and see it as I do. . . . And the way I see it is this : this Butcher is someone who knows Holmdale—*all Holmdale*—upside down and sideways and backwards and through and through. This Butcher is not only a resident in Holmdale and knows everybody and, therefore, *one that everybody knows*. . . . and if we start putting every Holmdale resident into Special's armlets, we're just asking ourselves to give shelter to the Butcher. . . . "

The Chief Constable opened his eyes wide. There came no sound from Davis and Farrow behind him.

" We're just asking ourselves," Pike repeated, " to

give shelter to the Butcher . . . *if* we're not doing that already." These last words of Pike's were said without raised voice or seemingly stressed emphasis but yet they fell upon the silence of the little room like lumps of pig-lead into a shallow pond ; their ripples set up vibrating circles which could almost be seen.

The Chief Constable twisted uneasily in his chair. He was being forced to realise that determination and courage and hard work were not necessarily of use in this matter. The Chief Constable said, with an uneasy attempt at humour :

" Yes, I see what you mean, Superintendent. . . . But aren't you going rather far ? I mean to say, damn it ! I don't live in Holmdale, but I know Holmdale; You might almost be saying that you don't know I'm all right."

" If you will forgive me, sir," Pike said with firmness, " that's exactly what I am saying."

" Eh ! " said the Chief Constable sharply, and Farrow made a movement as if to step forward round the table, only to be repressed by Davis's fingers on his arm.

" You must not, sir," said Pike, " misunderstand me. I don't think you do, really. What I'm saying is this : the only thing I do know about this Butcher is that he doesn't know me and he doesn't know the two men I've brought down with me. But, so far as we're concerned, there isn't a single person in and about this place who mightn't be him. Hope you follow me, sir. You've got to remember this man's that most dangerous sort of lunatic—the sort of a lunatic who doesn't *show* as a lunatic as you might say. . . . He's the sort of man that you meet and I meet every day—we probably *are* meeting him every day. He's the sort of man that when we find out who he is we shall all, maybe, get the shock of our lives ! "

There was no sound in Jeffson's small room save the ticking of the clock upon the mantel.

At last the Chief Constable, clearing his throat, spoke awkwardly. " Then I take it, Superintendent," he said, sounding somehow shy, " that you don't advocate the policy of taking any more recruits to the special branch ? "

Pike nodded decisively. " I don't, sir. In fact, while I remain of any importance down here, I shouldn't let that happen. I am referring, of course, to recruits from Holmdale and district. If you could get 'em—or better still, regular police or military, from other quarters, well and good. Very good. But not from this quarter."

The Chief Constable grew peevish. " You know very well, Superintendent, we've drafted in all the men we can from anywhere and it's costing Heaven knows what. . . ."

" I know all that, sir," said Pike, blatantly interrupting. " I've said all I've got to say."

" Ah ! " said the Chief Constable. He paused ; then went on, rather in the tone of a sixth-form boy doubtful as to the reception of a suggestion he is going to make to his House Master : " The only other suggestion we need put to you, Superintendent, is the one Inspector Davis here made. Inspector Davis suggested to me last night that it might do a good deal for public safety if we could manage somehow or other to establish a curfew. . . . What d'you think about that ? "

This time Pike did not pause before he answered. " I have thought about it, sir. The idea occurred to me—probably about the same time it occurred to Inspector Davis—and I've been thinking it over. I must say I'm against it."

" Against it ! " said the Chief Constable in astonishment. " Damn it, man ! I thought it was good.

Damn it! This Butcher can't wander into people's houses; at least, if he does, we'll soon catch him."

Pike nodded. "I know, sir. But it's like what I said to you the first time we met, if you remember. If we make everything so safe for everybody that the Butcher *cannot* operate, well, what he'll do is to lay low, *or* move on somewhere else. I don't think he'll do the latter, but I'm pretty certain he'll do the former. He's cute, this gentleman. And what should we do, and where would Holmdale be if he did lay low? Right, as you might say, in the soup! You can't keep up this expense we're incurring every day indefinitely. What would happen would be that after about a month with no Butcher stuff, all the extra police would be taken out and all protections would have to be removed. Then, after a nice fortnight's holiday at Blackpool or somewhere, the Butcher would start his tricks again, and we should have to start our tricks again. All over again! With no good done to any one by the work we're putting in now. . . . No, sir, it won't do. We've got to be like the scientists in this game. If necessary, sir, we've got to let one or two or three more people run the risk of meeting the Butcher—that's the way we're going to catch him. If we make them all safe from the Butcher *before* we know any more about him, then. . . . " He broke off. He shrugged. It was an eloquent shrug.

There was another small silence in the small room.

It was broken not by any one within the room, but by the sound of heavy footsteps upon the narrow flagged path of Jeffson's front garden. The Chief Constable—he did it with the air of a man welcoming any diversion, however small—turned in his chair and peered out of the window, craning his head to see between Mrs. Jeffson's lace curtains.

" Postman," he said, in some disgust.

Pike looked up sharply." Postman d'you say, sir,"
he said.   He was out of the room in a flash.

The men in the room heard the opening of the front
door and a few muttered words and then the door
shutting.

Pike came back to them slowly.   He had in his hand
a letter.   It says much for what the Butcher had done
to Holmdale and these men who were bent upon getting
him, that just one glimpse of the envelope in Pike's
fingers brought the Chief Constable out of his chair
and round the table in a rush, with Farrow and Davis
close behind him craning over his shoulders.

Pike did not at once show them the letter. Pike
said, heavily :

" When you said ' postman,' I knew that there was
something up." He was looking at the Chief Constable.   " I know the posts here by heart.   There isn't
one at this time . . . but the postmaster's had orders
to send any of *these* up at once. . . . "

The Chief Constable was glaring at the yellow
envelope.

" Open it, man ! " said the Chief Constable. " For
God's sake open it ! "

Pike opened it.   The sound of his pen-knife hissing
through the thick linen paper sounded as loud to the
ears of the listeners as a shell-burst.

Pike, using only the tips of his thumb and forefinger,
pulled from the envelope a single sheet of square,
yellow paper.   He read the note once to himself,
slowly and deliberately.   And then he read it aloud.
He read :

" DEAR POLICE,—In accordance with my promise, I
hereby inform you that I intend to do another of my
little jobs upon Friday, December 7th—and that,

Police, is *to-morrow*. Or it will be by the time that you read this letter.

"Yours pityingly,
"THE BUTCHER.

"P.S.—I don't know which one of you Police will read this letter, but if it isn't Superintendent Arnold Pike, of Scotland Yard, I hope that whoever it is will convey to Superintendent Arnold Pike of Scotland Yard, my respects and kindest and warmest regards. I should like to suggest to Inspector Arnold Pike of Scotland Yard that he take some early opportunity of altering his sphere in life. He is not cut out for a detective ! But then, who is ? "

CHAPTER TWELVE

I

THEY were still in Jeffson's room, which now was shrouded in a blue mist of tobacco smoke. It was an hour since the arrival of the postman with this last outrageous epistle of the Butcher's. The hour had been spent in discussion, never very amicable, of what steps should be taken to make utterly certain that the Butcher should not be allowed to carry out his threat.

Pike had taken very little part in the talk, but the Chief Constable—mercifully for Pike, who was thinking his own thoughts—had been disagreeing with his subordinates; more, the subordinates had been disagreeing among themselves. The Chief Constable was in favour of an immediate and Police-enforced order that all persons resident in Holmdale should be forced to remain in their houses from 7 o'clock, or earlier, upon the following night. Davis agreed with him, but went even further. Davis suggested, and kept on reiterating his suggestion, that the confinement to houses should start much earlier, say at 4 o'clock in the afternoon—so far as the residents actually in Holmdale at that time were concerned: in regard to those persons resident in Holmdale, but not having returned to Holmdale from their business or pleasure by that time, he suggested that these should be held up at their points of entrance to Holmdale—whether these were the railway or the roads—interrogated, and escorted in bunches to their homes.

Farrow, surprisingly, held a very different view. Farrow, Pike was astounded to note, seemed a sudden convert to Pike's way of thinking for, while he disagreed, he kept sending his eyes towards the yellow splash upon the table which was the Butcher's letter. Farrow, since the arrival of this last letter, had been a different person. He was now a man, perhaps not of vivid intelligence, but a man of sound if slow commonsense. Farrow, not looking at Pike, stoutly opposed this rigid curfew measure. He said, gazing at the Chief Constable :

" It won't do, sir. It won't do at all ! We've got Heaven knows who among the Specials and the Fire Brigade and even the Regulars. If we make a curfew and shut everybody else up we're just giving the chap —if he *should* turn out to be this here Butcher—an extra chance, and a double-plated chance ! "

Davis shook his head. So, a moment later, did Davis's admiring mentor, the Chief Constable.

" You're wrong, Farrow," said the Chief Constable, " quite wrong. If, as you suggest, and as I believe the Superintendent here suggested before you, this Butcher is one of the Specials or some one like that, and we *do* have the curfew, *then*, if there was—God forbid !— another crime, we should know, shouldn't we, where to look for the murderer ? And that should be something, eh, Davis ? " The Chief Constable turned round to look, with some pride in his own lucid reasoning, at Inspector Davis.

Davis nodded emphatically. The Chief Constable glared triumphantly at Superintendent Arnold Pike.

" Eh ? " said the Chief Constable. " Eh ? What about that ? Eh ? "

Pike who had been listening to all this with one half of his alert mind, nodded his head.

" I'm sorry, sir," said Pike, " I can't agree. I agree most strongly with Inspector Farrow. . . . "

" Eh ? " said the Chief Constable, " what's that ? What's that ? "

"I don't," said Pike, speaking now very clearly and allowing a pause between each word, "agree with you and Inspector Davis. I agree with Inspector Farrow. . . . You are quite wrong, sir, in supposing that, if we had your curfew to-morrow night, and there *was* a murder, we should necessarily know that we had to look among the patrols etcetera for our murderer. We should know nothing of the sort. . . . This Butcher, sir, is a clever devil. He has proved that not once, but twenty times, and if he's so clever, well—he might be someone nothing to do with the patrols etcetera and yet get out and do his job, and then laugh at you up his sleeve for watching among the patrols for the murderer."

One of the now frequent and very pregnant silences held the little room in its quiet grip.

Another silence broken at last by the Chief Constable. He said, uncomfortably:

"That's two for curfew and two against; me and Davis against you and Farrow." The Chief Constable's glance at Pike was compound of deference to the institution which Pike represented and personal hostility to the man himself while his glance at Inspector Farrow was just plainly irate.

Farrow coloured; coughed to hide his embarrassment; shifted his great weight uneasily from foot to foot.

Pike was unmoved. He merely nodded his head.

"Quite so," he said. "Mine and Inspector Farrow's opinion, against yours and Inspector Davis's." There was nothing in his words to startle the Chief Constable, and it would have taken a masterly analyst to show what there was in his tone to startle the Chief Constable and yet, somehow, the Chief Constable was startled. He stared a moment, grew rather redder in the face even than was his habit, and said at last:

" You seem to be very decided, Superintendent. . . . "

Pike interrupted, " I am, sir. . . . Completely."

Another pause. . . . But at silence, as in other things, Pike was more than a match for the Chief Constable. It was the Chief Constable who spoke first.

" Very well, Superintendent," he said in a voice thick with mingled emotions. " What do you suggest?"

Pike uncrossed his legs. He deliberated for a moment before replying, but said eventually :

" Just yet, sir, I don't know. What I *will* do is to agree with your suggestion made at the beginning of this talk, that the patrols should be given extra instructions and the existing arrangements generally tightened up. I *do* agree to that. Obviously it's necessary. But I do like to remind you, sir, that we've got a good few hours before us—that is if the Butcher's going to try and keep to his word—and you can bet he is because that's the one thing these madmen are proud of. If I've got any more suggestions I'll let you know them by telephone or any other way you like, this evening. This is not a thing one can decide upon after a few minutes talk. We've got to think not only of this present threat, but of the whole composite threat of the Butcher's actual existence. . . . If you see what I mean, sir—while we might be able to take steps to stop this lunatic's games just temporarily, it is that that wouldn't do much good. What we *have got* to do is to make sure that we get him. When we've got him, then the people, as a whole, are safe."

The Chief Constable shifted uneasily in his chair. The chair creaked loudly beneath his bulk. He had opened his mouth to speak when there came to their ears the sound of brisk tapping footsteps upon the path outside and then a brisker rat-tat-tat on Jeffson's knocker.

Jeffson himself went to the door, to return in a

moment to face the Chief Constable, spring to attention, and say :

"It's Miss Finch, sir. Lady editor of the *'Olmdale Clarion*. She wants a word with you, sir—or someone in 'thority, very, very special. She wouldn't take no for an answer, sir."

The Chief Constable, after automatically glaring for one moment, seemed to welcome this diversion. The briskness with which he welcomed it seemed to suggest that he was out of his depth in this business and that any floating log which came along within his reach was certainly to be snatched at. He said :

"Show her in ! Show her in !"

Jeffson went back to the door and opened it. He stood upon the inside of the room and made a beckoning movement with his head. There entered to the company, Miss Finch.

Miss Finch's appearance was, as usual, severe, but extremely well tailored. She wore a coat and skirt of some dark, subtly-patterned tweed which fitted her pleasant and slimly strong figure to perfection. Under her close-fitting hat of dark felt Miss Finch's face showed pleasant and composed at first sight ; at second sight, however, one saw that beneath the pleasantness and composure there was the tautness of a great strain. Miss Finch nodded to Jeffson as she passed into the room. She bowed, very slightly, to the Chief Constable. She gave to Superintendent Arnold Pike, whom she had met at one of the many meetings of the Holmdale Company which had taken place since his advent, a fleeting but wide and delightful smile. Miss Finch, knowing what was what, managed somehow to address her words ostensibly to the Chief Constable while conveying the impression that Pike's ears were the ones for which she really spoke.

She said : " I hope you'll forgive me, Sir Geoffrey, for

crashing in like this, but to tell you the truth, a letter has just come to me at the office which I felt I ought to bring up to the Police as soon as possible." The gravity and tenseness of Miss Finch's face relaxed for a moment into a smile which made her seem considerably younger. The Chief Constable rose to his feet. He was gallant. He had a penchant for women just of Miss Finch's type; pleasant-faced, well-cared for, sophisticated women who knew how to dress well without flummery; witty, self-reliant, perhaps rather 'managing' women who looked as if they might, quite easily, manage Sir Geoffrey. And Miss Finch, in particular, had very fine and very lustrous dark-brown eyes.

The Chief Constable came forward. He took a chair from the hands of Jeffson and set it for Miss Finch. He took from her hands her bag, and the umbrella from which she was never, so folk in Holmdale would tell you, separated. Having put his burdens down upon one of the parlour chairs, the Chief Constable returned to his visitor. He answered her as if her words had only just been spoken. He said:

"Of course I don't mind, Miss Finch, of course. . . . We're here to do what we can. You've frequently helped us in the past and we're here to help you as far as is in our power. . . . " He was very pompous.

Miss Finch, a busy woman, had not much time for this. She cut across the flow. She said briskly:

"Had to come and see you. Because just now a boy from the post-office slipped down to my place—my *office*, you know—and gave me this." Miss Finch produced from a side-pocket in her admirable tweed coat a yellow square envelope covered with backward-sloping and angular and very black writing. . . .

The Chief Constable's eyes seemed to be starting out from under his prawn-like eyebrows. For a moment he stared, dumbfounded, at the envelope in Miss

Finch's fingers. Collecting himself, he stretched out a hand to receive it, but he never did receive it. A hand came from somewhere and suavely took it before his fingers had closed upon it. This other hand was Pike's. And Pike said :

" Excuse me, sir . . . . I'd like to add this to my collection. If I may, sir, I'll open it."

It appeared that he took the Chief Constable's assent for granted, for before the Chief Constable could speak, he had borne the letter to the table and, treating it as gingerly as he always seemed to treat these epistles, had taken out his pocket-knife and gently slit its flap. . . .

Inside the envelope was a replica of that letter which still lay, now slightly askew, like a yellow blot upon Jeffson's table. . . .

" But how on earth," said the Chief Constable to Miss Finch a little later, " did you get it at this time in the morning. We had ours up here ; but then the Superintendent here had arranged for a special delivery. . . . "

Miss Finch interrupted the Chief Constable. She smiled, and the smile took the edge from any discourtesy which the words might have implied. She said :

" I'm sorry, Sir Geoffrey, but you're asking me to give away trade secrets. However, seeing that it's you who ask—and seeing the . . . the . . . rather awful gravity of the whole thing, I'll tell you. I'm afraid that I've been guilty—I am trusting you, Sir Geoffery, not to let this go any further—I'm afraid that I've been guilty of bribery and corruption. I know one of the post-office staff, and I gave one of the boys a rather handsome tip the other day in return for which he has undertaken to deliver to me, in advance of the usual delivery, any yellow envelope of that . . . of that

. . . . of that sort, which might come." Miss Finch here appeared slightly embarrassed, but instantly recovered herself. " I do assure you, Sir Geoffery," she said earnestly, " that the boy hasn't done anything wrong. I should have reported this in any case and, anyhow, I guessed that the Police would have a special service for . . . . for . . . . these *Butcher* letters."

" This letter, Miss Finch," said the Chief Constable, tapping upon the desk by the sheet which had just come out of Miss Finch's envelope, " is, if you want to know, an exact replica of one which we received here a full hour ago." He smiled brightly upon Miss Finch and added: "So that you see you are quite exonerated. I can only say that I thank you very much for your public-spirited action in leaving your work and coming up here personally to deliver this. You could not know that we had already received our version." The Chief Constable, duty for once holding its own against the opportunity for gallantry, made it clear by tone and attitude that, however grateful he was to Miss Finch, he now expected her to depart.

Miss Finch, however, seemed of a different mind. She said, blankly unreceptive both to attitude and tone :

" I was wondering, Sir Geoffery, whether I could have a little consultation with you about whether this letter . . . this terrible letter . . . could be used by my paper. . . . I quite see that in some circumstances it might be dangerous or against the public welfare, as we say, to see it, but if in any way it would help the Police investigation if I did give it prominent publicity —why, then, I should be only too glad to do so." Here Miss Finch paused a moment and laughed, a friendly little laugh, at the Chief Constable which made him momentarily forget that duty should go before beauty.

The Chief Constable was about to answer. What he

was about to answer he may himself have known, but nobody else will ever know for he was not allowed to answer. The courteous voice of Superintendent Pike cut across the tête-à-tête. It said:

"May I suggest, sir, that we are not yet sufficiently advanced in our plans to know whether it would help us to give publicity to this letter or not ? May I suggest that in the circumstances the best thing we can do, both from our own point of view and this lady's, is to promise to let her know within a couple of hours whether she is to use this or not ? "

The Chief Constable started, stared for a moment. He said, after that moment: "Yes—er—Yes. . . . Yes. . . . Yes. . . . Quite." He turned to his visitor. "I think, Miss Finch," he said, "that the Superintendent here is right. We're just having an er—er—a meeting. We've got to take some further steps. Until we've decided what they should be, we'd better leave your knowledge in abeyance if you don't mind."

Miss Finch rose to her feet. She was brisk and business-like, She took from the Chief Constable, as he brought them with gallantly ready hands, her bag and her little umbrella. Miss Finch said brightly, that she quite understood. . . . At the doorway, she turned round and added, that she hoped that they would not forget to ' give the *Clarion* a call.' They must not forget that while the Press, in a horrible business like this, would do anything within reason, or perhaps beyond reasonable bounds, to help the Police, the Press must nevertheless live, and that therefore the Press expected a tit-for-tat. In other words, if the Police could not eventually see their way to letting her publish this latest effusion of the Butcher's, would the Police give her something else. She was very keen to get a special edition out to-morrow. It was not so much that the special editions were desired by the *Clarion*, to whom they gave a vast deal of extra work, as that the public were so eager to have first-hand and locally-originated news. . . . .

The Chief Constable, escorting Miss Finch to the door, promised that when there was anything that the Police could ' give ' to Miss Finch and the *Clarion*, he would see that they did so. He went back, rather swollen by the fascinating smile which the *Clarion* had given him, to sterner work.

He found Inspector Davis sullenly gazing out of the window, while, their heads together, Pike and Farrow—this sudden, strange alliance—bent their heads over the two letters now side by side.

As the Chief Constable came up Pike raised his head, looking over his shoulder, he said :

" If you'll come here, sir, and just have a look at this you'll see that these two letters, though they look at first sight like duplicates, are not really anything of the sort. They've each been written by the same hand, on the same paper, with the same ink, but they aren't duplicates ; one's a copy of the other." As he finished speaking, he suddenly straightened himself. Without another word he went to a corner of the room and from one of Mrs. Jeffson's many occasional tables, picked his hat.

He said, " If you'll forgive me, sir, I'll be getting along."

" Eh ? " said the Chief Constable sharply.

" If you'll forgive me, sir," Pike repeated firmly, " I'll be getting along."

" Eh ? " said the Chief Constable again. " What's that ? Getting along. . . . What for ? Damn it, man, we haven't finished."

But Pike was adamant. " I'm afraid you'll have to excuse me, sir," he said. " I've got what you might call a small idea. I'm going to see whether it's workable before I tell you about it. Don't think it's anything big

because it isn't. But it might help. . . . Where will
you be this evening, sir ? "

" Here," said the Chief Constable fiercely. " Here."

" Very well, sir, I'll report here," said Pike and was
gone.

The Chief Constable glared at the closed door. " How
that fellah "—he spoke ostensibly beneath his breath
but actually with considerable volume—" ever got
where he is at the Yard, *I* can't think."

Inspector Davis from beneath his waxed moustache
emitted a coughing sound which was echo of his master's
voice.

Farrow, very glum, said nothing.

2

When Pike had, so summarily, left the meeting in
Jeffson's cottage-Police-Station, the time had been
two o'clock. He was not a man who needlessly cut out
meals. His experience had taught him, sometimes
painfully, that to go without food and drink, when
food and drink may properly be had, is to impair a
man's ability. And so the first thing that he did was
to call at the garage next to Miss Marable's where the
Police Crossley was housed, and take out the Police
Crossley. This took him about an eighth of the time
that he could have walked the distance to the Wooden
Shack, and at the Wooden Shack, not unduly hurrying,
but yet getting it over within twenty minutes, he had
a meal, and within five minutes after the bill for the
meal was paid, the Blue Crossley was nosing its way
over Chaser's Bridge.

The offices of the Holmdale Electricity Supply Company lie three hundred yards south of Chaser's Bridge
upon the left-hand side of the road. At ten minutes to

three, after a wait of seven or eight minutes, Pike was shewn into the Manager's room.

Mr. Calvin, though curt, as was his way, and a thought sardonic-seeming, was nevertheless brisk enough and obliging.

"Anything we can do," said Mr. Calvin, " of course we will do. I think we've told the Police that already."

"You have. And, needless to say, we are grateful." Pike was curt and business-like too, though of an equal politeness. He put to Mr. Calvin certain questions. Mr. Calvin having made calculations upon a scribbling pad and once consulted with a subordinate, gave answer in the affirmative.

"We can do it," said Mr. Calvin, and shut his mouth like a rat-trap. "What we'd like to know, and as soon as possible, is whether you want us to do it or not, Superintendent. You'll understand that we need a little time for preparation, and we shall need more time than we would normally if you want it done . . . well . . ." —Mr. Calvin shrugged—" quietly."

Pike said : "I'll let you know, if not this evening, before ten-thirty to-morrow morning."

Mr. Calvin nodded. "In case you do want it," he said, "I'll get the stuff down from our Lewisham depot right away. That won't hurt and I don't suppose the charge'll hurt the Government or whoever it is."

Again Pike nodded. "That's right, sir." He rose to go. He shook hands with Mr. Calvin, who, it seemed to him, was one of the few really decisive persons he had met since his arrival in Holmdale twelve days ago.

Outside The Electricity Supply Company's Office, the Blue Crossley was waiting, and the Crossley's nose was headed not back towards the interior of Holmdale, but straight for the open country.

Pike was suddenly seized with a wish, an imperative wish, to be alone.

He felt that curious, *bursting* feeling about the head, which comes to a man when his sub-conscious mind has developed a thought and it tries to compel that thought out of itself into the conscious mind, before it is really ready to deliver it up. He knew that if he went back to Jeffsons and Davises and Chief Constables, the only effect their society would have upon him, would be to thrust this half-born idea still further back into intangibility. He felt that there was a chance that if he were to get away into strange surroundings for an unstrained, uninterrupted two hours, he might, from the recesses of that inner mind, pull this idea.

He opened the door of the Crossley. He got into the car and shut the door behind him. He sat motionless in the driving seat for a full three minutes. At last he started the engine, slipped into gear and went slowly off, heading for the open country. . . .

3

When he got back to Holmdale, coming in this time by the Dale Road entrance, there was not upon his face a look of fulfilment or even satisfaction. He had not, though he had tried and tried, succeeded in bringing that idea—the idea which, he felt, had in it at least the beginnings of a solution to this foul problem—to his conscious mind. All he knew was, that somewhere within him there was a something which wanted to be known, but only wanted to be known in its own good time. . . .

Consequently he was, when he got out of the car to open the door of its garage in Fourtrees Road, pale and glum and preoccupied, with a frown creasing his forehead and closing his eyes to slits. The car housed, he came out into Fourtrees Road and hesitated upon the pavement. He looked first to his right at the

garden and pleasantly curtained windows of No. 14.
He looked then to his left and across the road, where
the lamp outside Jeffson's cottage showed a pale, sickly
radiance. He chose, his sense of the fit and proper
driving him to Jeffson's cottage. He walked there with
long quick strides and pushed open the door which was
ajar, and within a moment was inside what once had
been Mrs. Jeffson's parlour.

Jeffson was there and so were Davis and Farrow, but
the Chief Constable had gone.

Pike realised with a start that he should have known
by the absence of the Green Daimler that the Chief
Constable was no longer there. It showed him, this
little lack in observation, how preoccupied he was. He
stood just within the doorway of Jeffson's room and
looked at its occupants through the smoke. Jeffson
rose clumsily. Davis nodded with a curt nod, but
Farrow—the one-time inimical Farrow—came towards
him with a greeting.

" The Chief," Farrow said, " left a message for you.
He had to get back. Would you tell me, or Davis, what
it was you were going to tell him and we'll report when
we get back. We'll be leaving in about twenty minutes.
He's sending a car back for us." His tone was surly,
his face unsmiling and yet Pike warmed to him.

" I've been," Pike said, " to the Electricity Company.
I asked Calvin, the Manager, whether he could arrange
to supply power for searchlights for to-morrow night,
and as many nights as we might want them."

" Eh ! " said Farrow. And then suddenly his broad
heavy face became illuminated with a grin. " That's a
good one ! " he said. " Here, Davis."

" Calvin," said Pike, " told me it could be arranged
if we wanted it. Must say, I haven't quite made up
my mind, though. Anyhow they'll be ready if we
want 'em."

"How many?" said Farrow.

For a moment Pike's frown was smoothed away, for he was pleased with the result of his efforts.

"Twelve," he said. "Twelve doubles. That's to say, twenty-four lights altogether, in pairs, one pair at each important road junction or wherever we want 'em. Only, we've got to tell 'em the wiring points at least four hours before they're needed."

Farrow still smiled. It became borne in upon Pike that Farrow, in his own way, was a pleasant person. "That'll knock the old Butch," said Farrow, like a large school-boy. "Then if he don't want to operate down the lighted ways, the fact that the lights are there'll make him shy of the dark ways close to! That's good, Super."

Pike shook his head. "It's not good. It's just a sop as you might say, to Cerebos. But I think you've got it wrong, Inspector. My idea was not to have the lights all blazing away *all* the time. My idea was to have 'em switch on and off, sort of irregularly so that no one would either know when they were going on. . . ."

Farrow slapped fist against palm. "And that's a better one!" said Farrow. "All right, Super, I'll tell the Chief Constable as soon as we get back." He added, sotto-voce: "Not that it'll matter whether I tell him or not. . . . I'll tell you something; he's dead feared of you."

"That," said Pike, turning to go, "is a good job."

He went. He turned sharp left out of Jeffson's cottage gate and then, crossing the road, came to Number 12. He went in and in the hall met Molly Brade with her daughter Millicent.

Millicent made a rush at him. Millicent had a lot to tell him about Chuffers. First, she had seen the Flying Scotsman roar through Holmdale Station that morning.

Second, she had bought a small tin Chuffer with her bockey money. Third, she had evolved a new Chuffer game which, she seemed sure, could only properly be played with the participation of this friend.

Molly Brade intervened. She said, in the tone of one who means exactly the opposite: "You're being a nuisance again, Millicent."

Millicent stamped her foot. Her wide blue eyes blazed such wrath that even her mother quailed before them. Millicent stamped her foot again. She said:

" *Not* nuisance! Talkin' Chuffers." She looked up at Pike with a sudden melting. In an infinitesimal flash of time her whole frame had changed its expression from one of ire to one of almost amorous supplication. She said, the blue eyes fixed upon Pike's brown ones:

" *Do* play Chuffers! "

Pike, shyly but firmly turning down the half-hearted remonstrances of Millicent's mother, went, tealess, to play Chuffers.

CHAPTER THIRTEEN

THERE was another meeting in Jeffson's cottage at half-past ten upon the next morning. It was the morning of Friday, the 7th December, and the morning of the day during which the Butcher had stated that he would " do another job."

It occurred to Pike as he walked from Miss Marable's to the Police Cottage, to wonder whether the Butcher, if he could not, by killing someone before midnight, fulfil his promise to the police, would be so disgruntled as to kill himself. Pike both feared not and hoped not—an awkward state of mind, but a state of mind by no means uncommon to him.

This morning the Chief Constable was not in Jeffson's room, but Farrow and Davis were. And with Farrow and Davis, who had obviously spent much of last night with pen and paper, Pike went over the arrangements for the day.

He approved the scheme for tightening the patrol supervision and approved also the suggestion that the patrols should begin to function, not at 4.30 p.m. when the darkness was almost complete, but as early as 3.15 when the first signs of dusk would begin to evince themselves. He approved also the rearrangement of the patrol groups and control. . . . In short, he approved everything that had been done since the previous afternoon by Davis and Farrow. Farrow, having now got over his first reluctance to show his volte-face in regard to the Superintendent's merits, frankly beamed. Even Davis, though the points of his waxed moustache still showed tendency to bristle, was more affable than heretofore.

" And now," said Farrow. " What about these search-lights, Super ? "

There was quiet for a moment before Pike answered, and then he said, slowly :

" I've been thinking about these searchlights most of the night. In a way I want to have 'em put on. In a way I'd rather they weren't put on——"

" I know," said Farrow, interrupting. " You're think-ing, Super, that these searchlights, like the patrols and what not, are all what you might call ' preventatitive' measures like——"

" Exactly." Superintendent Pike smiled at Inspector Farrow. " That's just what they are, Farrow, and ' preventive ' measures are just, really, what I don't want. . . . But all the same, I believe that when the next hour's up I shall ring up Calvin and tell him that I want the lights. . . . You know what's the matter with Englishmen, don't you ? They're too blame soft-hearted. If we were sensible, if we were Germans or Frenchmen, or any of that sort of lot, we'd have the *real* humanity to let one or two or even five people die, in order that we could stop this business once and for all. . . . But shall we do it ? Shall we blink ! We wouldn't be allowed to act that way. The Government would step in or something." The emphasis on the word Government was withering.

" And you don't know yet," said Davis surlily, " whether you're going to ask for the lights or not ? "

Pike looked at him. " I don't know," he said curtly. " When I do, within an hour, I'll tell you. . . . Give you a ring if I don't come back." He turned towards the door.

" Ha ! " said Davis. " Where are you going ? "

Pike swung round on his heel, a very quick move-ment. Something in the way in which he looked at

Inspector Davis made Inspector Davis almost visibly shrink. There was a long pause.

" For a nice little walk in the fresh air," said Pike, and was gone.

This time he turned right-handed out of Jeffson's cottage-gate, walked down the length of Fourtrees Road, round the sweep of Fourtrees Crescent, down the hill by the Laurels Nursing Home, then left down the steeper hill, into Dale Road. In Dale Road he hesitated ; almost turned left to walk out of Holmdale altogether and down to Billsford ; changed his mind and turned right and walked up Dale Road towards the centre of Holmdale.

He walked slowly. His hands were thrust into his pockets and his chin rested upon his tie. His eyes were on the ground and his thoughts only just sufficiently with him to permit of his walking safely.

He came at last to the end of Dale Road and automatically turned right into Market Road. From the junction of Market Road and Dale Road to The Market itself, is perhaps a quarter of a mile. At his ordinary pace Pike would have covered this in something under five minutes. At his pace to-day he took ten.

He was walking upon the right-hand side of the road —the side, that is, upon which The Market itself lies. He would have passed The Market, not knowing that he had passed it, if it had not been for Mr. Percy Godly.

The time was past eleven o'clock and Mr. Godly was on his way from the Wooden Shack to the Carters, which lies at the top of Burrowbad Hill on the Main Road, Mr. Godly having, apparently, what he would have called, " taken a good load aboard " at the Wooden Shack, was none too steady in his walking. And Pike, as had been said, was walking with very little heed to his progress.

Pike and Mr. Godly met, chest to chest, outside the

first of The Market's swing doors. Mr. Godly, hiccoughing wildly, reeled. staggered, clutched at a lamp-post and finally fell. Pike picked him up and dusted him and looked rather hard at him.

Mr. Godly, waving a white hand, said indistinctly :

" Absolooly sharmed ! Very rare one meetsh genélum ! Only too sharmed to've been . . . to've been . . . to've been . . ." Mr. Godly stuck there.

Pike propped him against the lamp-post and left him. He put his hands back into his pockets and resumed his thoughtful walk. He passed along to the end of the easterly façade of The Market.

He would, no doubt, have crossed over the road, which runs between The Market and the post office, and passed down the rest of Market Road to Chaser's Bridge had not a large and puffing and gravel-filled lorry obstructed his way.

Taking, unconsciously, the line of least resistance, Pike swung to his right, keeping upon the pavement, and thus was walking along the southern frontage of The Market. He passed three-quarters of the length of this frontage, and so was abreast of the small sudden archway from out of which come at odd times The Market's messenger boys ; the archway which divides The Market proper from the offices of The Market's organisers and also the hair-dressing departments. Unconsciously Pike raised his head to look into this archway for he was accustomed to see here, when he passed—as upon a few occasions he had at this time— the very smart silver-grey and royal-blue perambulator of Miss Millicent Brade.

There again was the perambulator. Pike, alert now, looked round for Molly Brade. She was not in sight nor was, for just this moment, another soul. He crossed to the perambulator. He felt that perhaps a little light conversation about Chuffers would do him good. But

he was disappointed. For, instead of being wide-eyed
in her carriage, looking out with those far-sighted, large
blue eyes across the fields at the just visible railway line,
Millicent Brade was lying down, fast asleep.

She had upon her dark head a cap of blue velvet
cunningly edged with fur. Over her was a white woollen
coverlet across which there solemnly tramped a procession of blue elephants. One arm lay outside the coverlet and from the sleeve of the blue fur-cuffed coat
there peeped a hand from which the glove had slipped.
It was very cold this morning, and the hand looked
blue. Pike, gazing at his small and sleeping friend from
the end of her carriage, noticed this hand. He came
round to the side of the carriage and gently lifted the
hand. He thought that placed under the coverlet the
hand would grow warm against the warm little body.
With gentle fingers he lifted the hand.

And then, as suddenly as if it had burnt him, he
dropped it. He had seen that the middle one of the
seven elephants upon the coverlet was not wholly blue.

The blood drained away from his face. His hand came
straight out and hovered over the coverlet. It swooped
with a sudden decision and drew the coverlet away.

For a moment a blackness descended upon Pike's
world, and there was a roaring in his ears. . . . Slowly
he drew the coverlet back until now he drew it so that
it covered not only the small body but also the head.

CHAPTER FOURTEEN

I

THE grandfather clock on the landing of Number Twelve Fourtrees Road was striking noon as Pike came out of the room in which, with Dr. Jack and Miss Marable in attendance, lay Molly Brade. An hour before Molly Brade had been a charming and healthy and smiling young matron of something under thirty. Now, upon the bed in her darkened room, she was a dumb and shivering creature who might have been any age over forty-five. Since she had been put, outside The Market, into a car commandeered by Pike, no word— nor even any sound—had escaped her But she shook, she shook unceasingly. She shook so that her legs would not support her nor her hands obey her. Even as he came out of the room and closed the door softly behind him, Pike could hear the rattling of the frame of her bed as it knocked against the wall.

There was a man waiting for Pike downstairs. It was Curtis, who, having meant to speak so soon as he saw his chief, was, experienced though he might be, stricken for a moment into silence by the sight of his chief's face. Curtis said, after that pregnant instant :

" It's all right, sir, we've got him. Found him at The Carters up on Burrowbad Hill. He's very drunk ; leastways he's acting very drunk. Dunno which myself. . . ."

" Get a doctor ! " Pike's words came out like small, keen bullets.

" Got one, sir," said Curtis. " First thing I did. Dr. Seneschal. With him now——"

"What's he say?" Once more Pike's words cut across the other's talk like a sharp knife through soft material.

"Didn't wait, sir." Now Curtis was gathering something of his chief's urgency; his words were coming quicker and faster and clearer. "Came to report. Blaine went down to The Market with Jeffson and four men. Farrow and Davis are there, too. They're following your instructions and letting the catch out one by one and searching 'em." Curtis shrugged. "But somehow I don't fancy, sir, they'll get anything." He shifted his weight uncomfortably from foot to foot. It seemed to him that the eyes of Superintendent Pike were like red-hot gimlets boring right through him.

But Pike, for a long moment, said nothing. When he did speak it was in a voice subtly altered; a voice which showed at least its owner's effort for calmness and normality. He said:

"What's that row outside?"

Curtis seemed startled. "Row, sir?" He turned, craning his head to listen. He raised his eyebrows. "Did see one or two people sort of . . . sort of staring at the house as I come in just now. . . . Don't know what they were at, I'm sure."

Pike snatched his hat from the chair upon which it lay. "Come on!" he said. "Got the car out?"

Curtis nodded. "Ready waiting, sir. Where're we going?"

"Market," said Pike and in two strides was at the front door and had it open.

He left the house, Curtis on his heels, as if he would take the flagged path to Miss Marable's gate in four strides. And probably he would had he been able. But he was not able. There were obstructions between him and the car; obstructions even between him and the gate. And the obstructions were people. He had spoken to Curtis just now of a "noise outside," but his mind had been so busy that, once having asked the question, it had switched off even the continued and growing existence of the noise so that when, with the opening of the door and his appearance, a strange, snarling cry from perhaps thirty throats smote the air, he was as astonished as if he had had no warning. . . .

The crowd—for although there were well under fifty people in it, it seemed like a crowd—was unequally divided between the sexes. Fully four-fifths of it were women and it was this which made Pike halt. Before the gate and in the path, blocking his way, they were all women. Had they been men, his present mood and temper, added to experience, ability and a natural love of physical strife, would have taken him through them like a needle through sacking. But they were not men. . . .

He checked in his rush which had been almost a run, walked steadily but slowly. He saw their faces like uncouth, writhing gargoyles mouthing at him. He heard their cries like animal execrations. He halted. He said, and his tone was the tone of that young police constable Arnold Pike who, twenty years before, had *moved along* his first street crowd somewhere in Rotherhithe :

" Now, what's all this ! "

The screaming and shouting went on. The gargoyles mouthed ever louder but ever more incoherent. Behind the gate two of the few men brandished walking sticks and upon the inner side the gate one of the women waved a steel-ferruled umbrella and, detaching herself from her fellows, rushed at Pike—and the astonished Curtis behind him—with bony fingers hooked like claws. This one was gargoyle indeed. The mad stress of unusual and terrific emotion distorted what once had been a pleasant and even motherly face into that of a wry-mouthed and fanatical ghoul. . . .

She came straight for Pike. Her hands worked in the air, promising themselves his face. White crusting foam flaked at the corners of her mouth, whose lips were stretched back from yellow irregular teeth. Her shape-less hat had been pushed to the back of her head and from under its brim, which should have been down over her eyes, escaped four streaming strands of greyish, lack-lustre hair. . . .

Pike stood his ground. He waited, hands at his sides. With one half of his vision upon this advancing Fury he yet kept the other half upon the other momentarily less active furies behind. And now he saw that beside the waving sticks and the first waving umbrella were now arms being brandished and at the end of most of the arms were other sticks, other umbrellas, other rude and homely clubs. If he had not seen what he had just seen ; if he had not been through what he had just been through ; if what he had seen and been through during the past hour had not momentarily taken away his sense of humour, he would have smiled and the smile would soon have turned into a laugh. . . . But the Fury was upon him. He was forced to save his face from those itching, clawing fingers. He caught the bony wrist and twisted it just once and said : " Be quiet now. . . . What's all this ! "

She screamed at him, bellowing a thin, high, piercing bellow of which not a word was audible.

Seeing her in the clutch of the figurehead upon whom their temporary and utterly unusual rage had made them wish to vent their vengeance, many of the sup-porters moved up. Those upon the inner side of the gate pressed forward. Those upon the outside of the gate thrust the gate open and, jamming themselves in its narrow opening, began to pour through.

Pike stood his ground. Still calmly, but a great deal more fiercely than it seemed, he gripped the now helpless

Fury's wrist. From behind Pike Curtis came and stood
himself to face the oncoming rush.

" Now then ! " said Curtis. " Now—*then* ! What's
all this ! What's all this ! "

The onrush checked. One man alone came charging
forward. He brandished in his right hand a thick
walking stick of oak. Curtis, without even the slightest
hesitation, let fly. His fist, which was like the knee of
an ox, caught the attacker squarely upon the point of
the chin, and the attacker ·went backwards to crash
amongst the greenness of Miss Marable's neat box hedge.

" Now *then* ! " said Curtis again. " *Now then !* Any
more for any more ? "

Apparently there were not. Now sticks were lowered
and umbrellas and all those other club-like things which
had been waved. Once more the curious snarling sound
of the mob's voice filled the air. But now Pike and Curtis
were able to distinguish, if not the words, at least the
main purport. . . .

" You don't want," said Pike to the woman whose
wrist he was holding, " to be so silly ! "

" All right ! " said Curtis. " All right ! Stop your
shouting. Speak one at a time. All come along here if
there's any more for any more ! "

" At first," said Pike to the woman whose wrist he
was holding, " I didn't know what all of you were
driving at, but I've got it now. You don't want to be
so silly ! Everybody's doing their best—including
myself." His face took on suddenly an even leaner
aspect, harsh and fierce and somehow a little wild. He
said, after a pause :

" I know what's got you, all of you ! It's because it
was a child. . . . I knew that child. Understand that !
. . . I was doing my job and I'll do it still in the same
way, but if anything I'm going to do it harder and better
than I did before. Got that ? . . . What's the good of

you people coming and trying to put paid to me? Not a scrap! All you're doing is to make more trouble so that the police can't get on with the very work you're wanting them to do. . . ."

For the first time since he had begun talking the woman spoke. Her words were preceded by a strange, shrill laugh like a humourless neigh. She said, after this sound:

"*Work! Police!* Call yourself police? Call yourself *police!* And here you go letting these devils walk about murdering little children. . . ."

Pike's face went suddenly ash-white beneath its tan. His grip upon the wrist tightened suddenly and cruelly; tightened and twisted.

"A-ah!" said the woman.

"Be quiet!" said Pike. "Curtis! . . ."

"Sir," said Curtis turning, but yet, by the attitude of his body, conveying to the crowd behind him that still his challenge of "any more for any more" was open.

"Take this woman," said Pike. "Keep her in the back of the car while I drive. She's under arrest. Charges are obstructing the police in the execution of their duty and acting in a manner likely to cause a breach of the peace. Also assault. And Curtis, no bail. She'd better be kept in."

"Right, sir!" said Curtis. His round, red, shrewd-looking face gave no indication on its exterior of the smile which was breaking behind it. "Any of these too, sir?" He half turned as he spoke, nodding over his shoulder to the suddenly cooling little crowd of valiants. The man he had hit was now upon his hands and knees just by the box hedge into which he had fallen. He was being very sick.

Pike, some of the colour back in his tanned face, shook his head. "Not unless there's any more trouble. Tell them!"

Curtis raised his voice and told them. Curtis added that they had better move along quickly.

Like sheep they hesitated, staring, the faces now no longer gargoyles but merely and yet rather terribly ovine. And then, still like sheep, they followed the sudden movement of a new leader. One of the men it was this time. The man who had been behind the one whom Curtis had hit. This man left the garden, turned to his right and began, muttering to himself and swinging his stick, to walk down the road towards Marrowbone Lane and, therefore, the police station. Like sheep they shuffled after him and, perhaps even more imitative than sheep, they too muttered among themselves.

There was no further disorder. The way to the blue Crossley was clear. Curtis took the other wrist of Pike's prisoner and Pike, releasing his grip, went swiftly to the car and straight to the driving seat. The woman tried to hang back from Curtis's pull but she was now merely a bewildered and frightened and suddenly awakened lower-middle-class mother. She began to weep softly. Two tears rolled down her roughened, seamed face. She tried to speak but could not. Curtis got her to the car and threw the door open and thrust her inside. She went, not like a sheep, but like a lamb.

Curtis got in beside her, slamming the door behind him. Pike driving, the blue Crossley purred and was off, passing the now straggled flock who gazed some with angry, some with bewildered, some with terrified eyes at the prisoner within it. But no voice was raised and no movement was made towards the car, though, of Pike's set purpose, it moved past the flock at no more than ten miles an hour.

Pike turned left into Marrowbone Lane, accelerating suddenly and, taking the next turning to the right into Collingwood Road, brought the car to a standstill. He turned and spoke to Curtis behind him. " Let her get out," he said. Curtis, reaching across his prisoner, opened the door next to the left-hand pavement.

"Out you get!" said Curtis, jerking his thumb at the way of release.

The woman stared at him vacantly. Her face still worked and unshed tears stood in her tired eyes.

"Out you get!" said Curtis again.

But still she made no movement. Pike turned once more in his seat. He said, quietly:

"You don't want to go to prison, do you? If you don't, get out. I don't know your name; I haven't seen you before; so I can't come for you later—*if* you go now."

Then she went. As she stood upon the edge of pavement she looked at Pike and said something. They never knew what it was for Curtis's slamming of the door and Pike's rather noisy getting into gear drowned her words. She was left standing on the pavement staring after them.

2

When they reached it, all the doors of The Market were closed. And all around The Market was a thin, ever-swelling crowd which, having sensed drama from afar, was flocking to gaze with wildly speculating eyes at the blank, white walls and now shrouded windows.

There are five entrances to The Market and outside each of these entrances was now a uniformed constable. Patrolling the right-angled two sides of public frontage of The Market were two uniformed sergeants of police and these, every now and then, paused in their patrolling and bade the encroaching crowd to "move on there."

A hard, yellow winter sun was shining upon The Market. The air was crisp and cold and exhilarating like some pleasant, heady wine. The sky was a bright, hard,

cheerful blue and the railed-off lawns between The Market
and the Holmdale Theatre were green as pantomime
emeralds.

It was upon such days that the winter aspect of
Holmdale was at its best. Ordinarily, upon such days,
even its most bitter decriers were forced grudgingly to
admit that, for the purely temporary visitor, Holmdale
might hold a certain play-box charm. And yet, upon
this day, something had crept in which spoilt the sun-
light and the air and the grass and the cheerful red and
white buildings ; some intangible, invisible miasma
which sapped the beauty from these things and left
men with a cold, black cloak of horror and appre-
hension weighing upon their souls. It was as if all the
kindly, gay-seeming of things was staged to vent the
bitter mockery of an angry god.

Pike's face, as he walked across the pavement from
the car to The Market main entrance, was white and
grim and set. Even Curtis, that utterly unimaginative
person, seemed to walk with a heavier step.

The policeman guarding the doors saluted. They
passed him by. The swing doors rolled round for their
entrance. Just within the doors stood Inspector Farrow.
At the sight of Pike, his frowning, heavy face took on a
look of pleased relief. He touched his cap. Pike nodded.

" Any result ? " said Pike. " S'ppose not."

Farrow shook his head. " Not yet."

" How are you working it ? " Pike was crisp. " Didn't
have time to leave full instructions."

Farrow consulted the back of an envelope which he
held in his hand and upon which he had, apparently,
been scribbling in pencil. He said :

" There were a hundred and fifty-three customers in
when you had the doors closed ; fifty-one assistants and
eleven on the manager's staff, including the general
manager himself, Mr. Cuthbert Mellon. Blaine's split

the whole lot into two batches. One batch is in the
café with a couple of uniformed men watching 'em.
The other batch is in the Hairdressing, with the same.
Blaine got a couple of sisters from the hospital for
searching the women and two of my sergeants are
doing the men. As they're done they're giving their
names and getting passed out through the back way. . . .
All right, sir ? "

Pike nodded. " Very good. How many've they
done ? "

" I was round there a minute ago, sir, and they'd
done seventy-one, they told me."

" Any trouble ? "

Farrow shrugged. " Some of 'em were a bit upset
like. Some a bit scared. No real *trouble*. Shall I take
you across there, sir ? They're searching 'em in the
manager's suet."

Pike nodded. He fell into step beside Farrow and they
started to walk, Curtis following like a solid ghost,
through the echoing building, threading their way
between its now tenantless, well-stocked counters.

" Nothing yet, I suppose," said Pike, as they turned
out of the Haberdashery and round a corner, right-
handed, past *Books*.

Farrow shook his head. " Nothing, sir." He looked
curiously at his companion. " Would you say yourself
that we'll find anything ? "

Pike was silent. Suddenly, at the end of *Books*, he
halted. He said :

" Café's behind there, isn't it ? " He pointed back,
jerking a thumb over his shoulder.

Farrow nodded.

" And Hairdressing's there ? " Pike pointed to his
left front.

Again Farrow nodded.

" Where're they searching 'em ? "

" Just round here, sir." Farrow pointed to a door, at the far side of the department labelled " Refined Footwear," which bore upon it in red and black letters " Private—General Manager." " Blaine arranged that. There's a suite of rooms there—Mr. Mellon's—and the back way out's just behind them. There's one of the nursing sisters using one room and then my two sergeants in the next one, which is bigger."

" Right ! " Pike strode on ; edged his way behind the shoe counter and, reaching the door marked " Private " flung it open to find himself in a narrow, asbestos-sheeting-lined passage. Straight ahead of him two blue-clad backs. His long strides took him up the passage far ahead of Farrow.

He went into the room, and, with one of those dramatic coincidences which happen in cases more often in real life, than the critics would have us suppose, just as he stepped across the threshold there came a crisis in this affair which had promised so dully.

Upon the far side of the two broad-spreading, blue-uniformed backs he had seen from the passage, there stood, his arms upraised, a small and dark and, for the nonce at least, furtive-looking little man. One of the blue-uniformed figures was still bent in a slight rigid arc as he patted and probed in pockets upon the small figure's right-hand side. But the other—Jeffson—who had, apparently, been patting and probing upon the left-hand side, had suddenly straightened itself with an air almost comically blent of alarm and triumph. . . .

And in his right hand Jeffson held something aloft.

At the moment when Pike made his entry, no sound had, as yet, escaped the three actors in this small drama ; but there was in the air, already, a certain exciting and terrific tension. . . .

Pike leapt forward. He snatched at Jeffson's find. . . .

G

He found himself staring at a square, yellow envelope upon which was written in a curiously backward-sloping hand and in thick, shining black ink :

" The Chief Constable,
C/o Sergeant Jeffson,
13 Fourtrees Road,
Holmdale."

3

The small and furtive man from whose pocket Jeffson had extracted this envelope was Wilfrid Spring.

The two sergeants fell back. Pike looked at the envelope ; twisted it this way and that between his fingers but never held more of it than its extreme corners. He raised his eyes and met those of Sergeant Jeffson. He nodded his head towards the prisoner.

" Where ? " he said.

Jeffson stammered with astonishment. " I was just agoin' to pass 'im out, sir, like all the others before, when I puts me 'and once more into 'is left-hand pocket 'ere and pulls out that." Jeffson pointed with a trembling thumb at the envelope. " Dunno 'ow I come to miss it the first time 'cept that it must of been fixed against the wall of 'is pocket like.

Pike looked once more down at the envelope ; then up and into the eyes of the pale-faced Spring.

" Well," said Pike, lifting the envelope upwards and outwards perhaps two inches. " What've you got to say ? " His tons was non-committal and passionless, but there was behind it a strange vibration.

" What have I got to say ! " Spring, now that the opportunity for speech has been vouchsafed to him, shed much of his furtiveness. With his own words he seemed to swell. It was as if, with each of his sentences, he became more and more convinced that Wilfrid Spring, being a person of the very greatest importance, should not be thus mishandled by a parcel of policemen. . . . "What have I got to *say* !" said Wilfrid Spring and proceeded to say it. There was a great deal of it. It appeared that Mr. Spring had no notion whatsoever of how the strangely qualified envelope had found its way into his peculiarly perverted pocket. And Mr. Spring thought that it was carnally strange that some fool of an ensanguined policeman should have, even if the envelope was found in Mr. Spring's pocket, thought Mr. Spring could possibly be anything so revoltingly unimportant as the Holmdale Butcher. . . .

That, it seemed, was what really injured Mr. Spring's feelings, the thought that a Personage such as himself, one of the best known—if not the best known—Director in England (or anywhere else for that matter) should be considered as having either the time or inclination to go about murdering people.

"Good God, man !" said Mr. Spring, now fully himself again. "What the hell do you take me for ? "

Pike looked at him in silence. Pike's face showed nothing of the bewilderment which raged behind his brow. For Pike was puzzled. Was this bluff ? Or was it righteous innocence, however unpleasant ? Or was it that this man suffered from that peculiar form of amnesia which permitted a person to perform a deed quite foreign to his usual nature and then have it, by the grace of God or devil, completely expunged from his mind. And, anyhow, what about the weapon and its absence ?

"Besides," Mr. Spring was saying with vehemence, "I can easily prove that I didn't leave The Market from the time I came into it until the time when your blasted fellow shut the door."

Pike shrugged. " If you can do that, sir, of course . . ."
He left the sentence in mid-air.

Jeffson was still staring at the envelope in his superior's
hand. His eyes were wide and staring and his hair,
quite literally, seemed to be standing up. " Kor ! "
Jeffson was saying. " Kor ! Ooever would of believed it ! "

Spring, suddenly losing his small temper, exploded.
He pointed an irate finger at Jeffson. His horn-rimmed
spectacles slipped awry on his nose giving him a peculiarly
comic and inefficient look in direct contrast to his impassioned words. " That's the sort of bloody fellah,"
said Spring, " that makes this country the impossible
place to live in that it is——"

" That'll do, sir ! " Pike's tone was smooth enough
but very firm. " That'll do ! You'll quite realise that
I've got to detain you. . . . Jeffson, put this man on one
side." He swung round on the other sergeant. " And
you carry on with the job. Detective Officer Curtis
here'll help you. Carry on, Curtis."

<h2 style="text-align:center">4</h2>

It was three o'clock when, outside the white-fronted
Cottage Police Station, Wilfrid Spring entered the police
car and was driven away to the county gaol. There were
left in Jeffson's room, the Chief Constable, his satellites
Farrow and Davis, Detective Officers Curtis and Blaine
and Superintendent Arnold Pike. All these looked at
each other. The room seemed full of them as indeed it
nearly was.

The Chief Constable broke the silence. " *I* think,"
said the Chief Constable, " that that's our man." He
looked first at Farrow, then at Davis. He missed out
Curtis and Blaine and looked last at Pike.

Pike shook his head. " I'm sorry, sir, I can't agree.
In fact, if I may put in bluntly, I wouldn't have held

him. Not after those statements we've got from his wife and from The Market assistant."

Tempers were on edge this afternoon. The Chief Constable exploded. "But blast it, man, a fellah of your experience ought to know by this time—damn it, you ought to !—that a fellah's wife isn't evidence——"

Pike interrupted. The interruption was courteous-seeming, but interruption nevertheless. "I beg your pardon, sir," he said, "but we're not talking about evidence. This isn't a Court of Law, you know, it's a police station and because we've got extraordinary powers we've been able to put that man into gaol. . . . But *I* don't think he's the man. If I was a betting man, I'd lay you twenty to one that he isn't. I don't say that I'd actually oppose your holding him for the time being—though if I've read the gentleman correctly, there'll be a heavy claim for compensation when we let him go—but I *do* say, and mean it, that by this time to-morrow he'll be out. We've only got to collect these other witnesses he spoke of and we'll know he was speaking the truth because these others've got no interest in him whatever. Can't have. No, sir, you'll find he's not our man."

There was an uncomfortable silence. The Chief Constable, very red about heavy face and thick neck, seemed several times upon the verge of speech but, perhaps fortunately, restrained himself. . . .

5

It was four o'clock when a massed meeting of Holmdale. citizens, rapidly, and, as it were, almost spontaneously convened, took place on the wide, tree-lined grass plot opposite the northern aspect of The Market.

A wild meeting this and as foreign to Holmdale and

its ways as had been the demonstration to Pike which had taken place outside Miss Marable's house.

It was dusk and nearly dark when Inspector Farrow, with not only a posse of rather ineffectual specials but also no fewer than eight regular constables and two mounted policemen, dispersed this meeting.

There had been much talk by this person and that. There had been wild, fierce speeches against the police and their lack of training, method, initiative and morality. There had been, throughout these speeches, roared " Hear-hears." There had been a movement, put to the meeting by the most impassioned speaker—a part time socialist orator—and carried unanimously, to the effect that the citizens of Holmdale should take the law into their own hands. What, quite, they were going to do with the law when they had it, was left, as it generally is, in the thinnest of thin air. . . .

But they were all—and with some excuse—much moved. They were all, for the moment, fire-eating, fire-breathing hard cases. They were all, for the moment, ardent disciples of Judge Lynch. They were for some- body's blood, preferably, of course, the Butcher's, but if the Butcher's were not available, then for the blood of those responsible for this terrible delay in bringing the Butcher to book.

Arms were brandished. Voices were raised. Threats grew hoarse and eyes were fierce. Some of the more youthful components of the crowd—it must have numbered three hundred at least—procured from somewhere—in the way that such crowds magically will —fuel for a bonfire which, as Farrow and his men came up, was no longer belching clouds of white smoke but sending shooting tongues of red and yellow flame twenty feet into the air. . . .

An impressive scene. And, at least to the members of the crowd, a most meaning one.

On the outskirts of the crowd, Dr. Reade stopped his Chevrolet two-seater and listened to the crowd's uproar with a sardonic smile distorting his heavy face.

The Reverend Rockwall passed by quickly, shaking his head and muttering to himself.

Far away from the crowd, Mr. Wilfrid Spring was turning over in his mind, seated upon the edge of a government-issue truckle bed, the possibilities of a great publicity campaign when he should be free.

Separated from him by nine inches of stone wall, sat Mr. Percy Godly in an exactly similar position. . . . But Mr. Percy Godly was thinking only, with tears in his eyes, of the cruel devil in blue which so smoothly and so often refused his bribes and prayers and pleadings for " just one little one."

In the centre of the crowd stood Miss Ursula Finch, her umbrella clamped firmly beneath her left arm, shouting hoarsely with the rest, but with her keen little mind taking mental shorthand notes for a more startling issue of the *Clarion* than even she had ever conceived.

Behind the crowd, Mr. Israel Gompertz fed the bon-fire with boards from a heaven-sent packing case.

In the front ranks of the crowd, Mary Fillimore, her usually soft blue eyes hard and staring, found suddenly that she had no more voice left with which to shout.

In the centre of the crowd, Mr. Colby turned with excited gratification to his neighbour, saying : " Thank God ! Thank God ! . . . High time more sensible men took matters into their own hands."

Upon the first-floor balcony of his pleasant house, The Hospice, stood Sir Montague Flushing looking out with troubled face and rather frightened eyes at the leaping, starting glow of the bonfire. From where he stood the roaring snarls of the crowd smote his ears like a menace. . . .

" Terrible, terrible business ! " thought Mrs. Rudolph

Sharp as she tried to extricate herself from the fringes of the crowd, but could not.

. . . And then, as the thin jet from a fire extinguisher slays apparently unquenchable flame, the mere voices—throaty and assured and virile—of the maligned police plucked from this wild and bloodthirsty mob all their frightfulness. Among them, a few policemen moved solid and immovable and very, very permanent.

" Move along there. Move along ! " said the police. " Get along out of this. This has got to stop," said the police.

And the bonfire died down. And the crowd moved along. And the units of the crowd dispersed.

6

Pike, as he had been a few nights ago which seemed as many years, was kneeling on the window seat of his bedroom in Number Twelve Fourtrees Road. He was thinking about Wilfrid Spring. He was regretting that he had not been able, without open breach, to prevent the Chief Constable of the County from incarcerating Wilfrid Spring. He did not object, upon humanitarian grounds, to Mr. Wilfrid Spring's incarceration, because he thought that incarceration for eighteen hours or even as many months would do Mr. Wilfrid Spring a great deal of good, but he did object to the odium which must necessarily fall on to the police from the pens and mouths of the press and public. It all seemed so futile. Here they had, in gaol, a drunkard and a film director. What a pair, would press and public say alike, to pick upon. Could there be any two more unlikely to be this homicidal pervert than a man whose ambition was to crowd into his bladder as many drinks in a day as was possible and a man whose ambition in life was to produce as many flickering ghosts as possible? The one would be too busy with his alcohol; the other too busy with his ghosts. The one would be able to satisfy in his fuddled brain any latent impulse to horrid violence and the other equally able to do so (as indeed he seemed to have done) with his puppets. A drunkard, Pike thought . . . and a film director. . . .

'I wonder,' Pike thought, 'what sort of job that is . . . a film director's. Must feel like a sort of god making men and women do, not what they want to do, but what you want 'em to do. Funny things, pictures. Some people like 'em, others don't. Some would walk forty miles to see Lilian This and Percy That in *Love's Ashes*. Others shuddered at the very name of Lilian or Percy. . . . Great invention though . . . marvellous, when you came to think of it, to be able to show exactly what people did. Think of slow motion, for instance. Why, with a slow motion camera you could tell what a man did even if he didn't know he'd done it himself . . . and how useful it ought to be in the future—though it was doubtful whether any one could put it to this use— in teaching history. By Jing, if they took films of all the historic happenings—or happenings likely to be historic—which took place, and did 'em from now on, why, the kids in about a hundred years' time would know more about us than we knew about ourselves . . .'

Yes, odd things, films! Very useful in all sorts of ways —all sorts of ways—they'd even been useful to scientists. . . . No reason really why they shouldn't be useful to the police. . . .

"*Good Lord Almighty!*" said Pike aloud.

He leapt up and backwards from the window seat as if a bullet had narrowly missed him. Under the light he feverishly fumbled for the small notebook he always carried in a waistcoat pocket. He flicked over the leaves with an abandoned impatience utterly foreign to his nature. He found what he wanted—the address of Curtis's billet. . . .

Before he had knelt upon the window seat, he had taken off, as he was used to do in his Kennington flat at about this time of night—it was after eleven—his collar and tie. The boots with the very shiny toe-caps were no longer upon his feet, which were thrust into soft slippers of red brushed wool—a present to him by an elderly aunt one Christmas. A large calabash pipe had its stem clamped between his teeth and the bottom of its curve brushed against his long chin. But of collars and slippers and pipes he thought nothing. He made one stride of it to the door and five strides of it across the landing—past the door of the room where Molly Brade lay moaning, with a nurse in attendance, with an ice pack about her head. He went down the stairs in two silent leaps.

He slammed the front door behind him. He ran, having turned right, up to Marrowbone Lane and then turned right again. By sight he knew Curtis's billet and, having consulted his notebook, now its number. He found it without difficulty. There was a light in an upper window and at this window he threw a handful of gravel plucked with almost crazy fingers from the garden path. By chance the lighted window was Curtis's own and it was Curtis who leaned out gruffly demanding :
" What the 'ell ? "

" Pike here," said Curtis's superintendent. " Come down ! Urgent ! "

Curtis came down. Into the narrow passage Pike pushed his way.

" Where can we talk ? " he said.

Curtis threw open a door in the right-hand wall of the passage and snapped on a light.

Pike sat in an armchair of curious shape composed, apparently, of bentwood and turkey carpeting. He looked at his subordinate with pleasure, for Curtis, as yet, was completely clothed. Pike said :

" You're to come back with me, get out the car and take it straight back to the Yard. Drive like smoke. While you're starting I'll ring 'em and tell 'em you're coming. If necessary, ring Mr. Lucas and get authority, but I think I'll be able to fix that for you before you get there." He whipped the notebook again from his waistcoat, tore out a page from it and, as he went on speaking, wrote upon the small paper with a meticulous pencil. He said : " What you've got to do is to get down here before seven to-morrow morning, thirteen cinematograph cameras with an operator—two, if you like—to each. When I say you're to bring them down here, I don't mean it. I mean you're to take 'em to Batley and stow 'em away there somewhere quiet not showing their cameras and not talking and then ring me. By that time I'll have got the information I want and I'll come along and we'll post 'em. . . . And don't forget this, my lad : on no account whatsoever, if you value your job or even your bally life, are you to say a word about this stunt inside Holmdale nor are the men you bring down to say a word inside Batley. I don't care who it is, if it's the Chief Constable or the Archangel Gabriel, you know nothing. Mind you, I don't see how you can be asked because nobody knows there's anything to be asked about, still I'm telling you.   Get that ? "

Curtis nodded, once.

Pike jerked to his feet. " Right ! " he said. " Ready to start ? "

Again Curtis nodded. But this time he spoke. He said : " What's the stunt, air ? "

For an instant, Pike smiled ; such a smile as Curtis knew from the past, but had not seen all the time they had been in this place.

"It's good!" said Pike. "I want thirteen cinematograph cameras and operators, Curtis, because there are thirteen pillar boxes in this god-forsaken imitation suburb. Don't you see, Curtis, that the Butcher's bound to write to us again. And don't you see, Curtis, that if as from to-morrow, there's a secret twenty feet of film taken of every person that posts a letter everywhere, we shall be able to narrow down our field after we've got the next Butcher letter."

A wide replica of his chief's smile appeared upon Curtis's face, but only to fade almost as soon as it had come. Curtis shook his head. "I'm afraid, sir," he said, "I don't see it. I thought I did for a minute, but even if we did get pictures of every one who posts letters on a day when this 'ere Butcher posts a letter, I don't see how we're that much better off as you make out, because——"

Pike cut across this speech. "Don't," he said, "be a fool! Even if you didn't know it, you must've realised that by this time I've got an arrangement with the postmaster that the postmen making each collection from the boxes put each box's lot into a separate little bag so that instead of the letters being mixed up together, we know, after every collection, which letters have come out of which box."

Curtis raised thick, astonished brows. "I didn't know that, sir," he said.

Pike snapped at him. "Well, you ought to've guessed. The only thing that can go wrong with this is if it's the postmaster or one of the postmen who's the Butcher—then we're pipped, but it's a good move. It's an idea. It's the best idea I've had since I've been down here." He went to the door. "Now get a hat and coat and come along."

CHAPTER FIFTEEN

I

AT seven-thirty upon the next morning, which was that of Saturday, December 8th, the telephone in Miss Marable's hall rang shrill and impatient. It went on, at first intermittently and then without break, until—still rather sleepy-eyed, the elder of Miss Marable's two " dailies " stopped its ringing with her " 'Ullo ! "

The telephone was curt and official, and, to Janet, a thought alarming. It was, it said, speaking for the Chief Constable and wished to talk with Mr. Pike. Janet, stammering but ultimately clear, stated that she would call Mr. Pike.

But she did not call Mr. Pike because Mr. Pike was not there. Mr. Pike's bed had been slept in but Mr. Pike must have risen and gone out very, very early, because she had entered the house at six forty-five and she knew that, between then and now, no one had so much as moved within the house.

All this Janet, still stammering a little, eventually told the telephone. . . . The telephone, human anger destroying much of its officiality, would leave no message for Mr. Pike. The telephone, brusquely, cut itself off and Janet went once more about her work.

Mr. Pike, she noted, was not in to breakfast, which began at eight-fifteen—for what Miss Marable called her " town-birds "—and ended at ten for Miss Marable's " lazybones." But Mr. Pike came in at a quarter to eleven. He was smiling ever so pleased like and yet he didn't seem quite hisself like, for he took no notice of Janet at all when he brushed by her in the passage

although usually he was one who had a pleasant word
for every one. . . . It seemed to Janet as if Mr. Pike
was so pleased and sort of excited like that he couldn't
properly think about where he was going and what he
was doing. . . .

Janet was right. Pike was pleased indeed with his
morning's work. It had been a tough job to do in the
time, not only without help but also with the necessity
for secrecy making it the more difficult. But it had been
done and well done. . . . He went upstairs for a belated
shave whistling beneath his breath. And then he passed
the door behind which lay Molly Brade and the whistling
ceased and the half-smile faded and once more the colour
left his face and the harsh deep lines were graven upon
it again.

But he was all the more pleased with the morning's
work, for this seemed to him the first really powerful
move against this powerful devil. He set about his
shaving, and, while the razor worked, went over this
work in his mind.

There were thirteen pillar-boxes in Holmdale including that in the wall of the main post office. And
now, unknown to any one, each of these thirteen boxes
had trained upon it a cinematograph camera. It was
the secrecy which had made the work so hard and so
pardonably exhilarating. But fortune had been with
him to this extent—out of the thirteen boxes no less
than eight had untenanted houses near enough to them
and in such relative positions that the cameras, unseen,
could be worked from within them through the windows.
Getting the men and the machines into these houses
without being seen by patrols or neighbours had been
no small task for the short time they were forced to
allot to it. But Curtis had been invaluable. They had
had—successfully as it turned out—to chance the
neighbour problem, but the real danger of the patrols

Curtis, carrying out his own plan, had averted. Each time there was a likelihood of patrols seeing an entrance, Curtis had gone on ahead and, on pretence of being on a surprise inspection, delayed the patrol long enough for the entry to be made and the rest of the party to hide or pass along by another way.

Of the remaining five boxes, three had been covered—as late, these three, as nine o'clock—by a room to let in an adjoining house being taken with bona-fides supplied by Pike as guarantee. The cameras, not being of the very large, heavily-tripoded kind, had been skilfully camouflaged as ordinary baggage and thus, as it were, had helped themselves in by the very respectability of their seeming.

Two boxes only had it been impossible to cover from houses. . . . Pike, wiping the soap from his face, frowned again in memory as he had frowned in thought at the time ; smiled again in memory as he had grinned with relief when the idea had come to him. . . . Facing each of these two boxes, all day, would be a broken-down car, an ostensible mechanic busily tinkering beneath its bonnet or even chassis. And, sometimes in the car and sometimes beside it, would be its ostensible owner. . . . A good thing—a very good thing—that Curtis had brought more than one man to each machine ; and a better thing that, among the cameras, someone had had the foresight to include two newly-patented, no bigger than an ordinary snapshot-box and as simple to handle. . . .

Pike finished his shaving. Pike, having put on fresh linen, looked at his watch. His lips pursed themselves into a soundless whistle. He sat down at his table, reached for pen and paper, chewed for a moment at the penholder and began busily to write. He seemed in a hurry. The pen scratched and spluttered and ran on. Three sheets he covered with precise, angular script.

He threw down the pen at last, dabbed the last sheet upon the blotter and then, folding it with its fellows, thrust the small wad into a pocket and looked round the room for his hat. . . .

2

" God Almighty ! " said the Chief Constable. " Where in the Lord's name've you *been*, Superintendent ? Been lookin' for you and huntin' for you all over the blasted shop. Had to start without you. . . . What you been *at* ? "

Pike sat down. Facing him across Jeffson's table the Chief Constable looked like an overgrown and ill-tempered schoolboy. One at each side of him sat Farrow and Davis. In the background Jeffson hovered like a burly, solid ghost. . . .

Pike felt for the Chief Constable—a man out of his depth as they all, perhaps, were out of their depth ; but a man for whom the depths held strange and worried fears to mangle the fair smoothness of a life till now too placid.

" Sorry, Sir Gerald," said Pike smoothly. " I'd no intention of keeping you waiting. . . ."

" Where've you *been*, man ? "

" Nowhere, sir." Pike was gentle with the Chief Constable. " Only in my rooms. I've worked out a scheme." He pulled out the three sheets of paper.

The Chief Constable snatched them with a hand that shook so that the stiff sheets rattled against each other. He spread them out on the desk with little exasperated thumps. He grunted, and bent over them. He read in a silence broken only by the sound of his own laboured breathing. He looked up at last. Some of the tension had gone from his face. The frown between his brows was no longer so deep and, as he looked at Farrow and

David, his heavy-lipped mouth twitched to something like a smile. He said, breaking his speech with swings of his head and body as he turned from Davis to Farrow and Farrow to Davis:

"Dammit, that's *good*! . . . Damn good! . . . It's clever, that's what it is. Downright clever!"

"What's clever, sir?" Farrow was blunt.

Davis said nothing and sniffed over saying it.

"What's clever, sir?" Farrow said again.

"This," said the Chief Constable. "This." He tapped upon the sheets of paper covered with Pike's writing. "This, man. Briefly, the Superintendent's suggestion is that we should make . . ." He broke off. He looked at Pike. "Perhaps you'd put it shorter and quicker than I would, Superintendent. I won't pass these papers round, I think your talk'd be quicker. We can file your notes."

Pike nodded. "Thank you, sir." He looked at Davis, then at Farrow. He said: "Briefly, my plan was to advertise to Holmdale generally that those citizens wishing to assist the police in discovering the identity of the Butcher should send along a statement, witnessed by one or more of their friends, as to what they were doing at the time of the last murder. . . . Purely a voluntary measure, of course, but a useful and, as you might say, patriotic one."

Davis sniffed. "Don't see it. We'll only be snowed under with papers. That's what we'll be."

Farrow turned on him. "And what if there was hundreds of these alibis! Only wants a good clerk to deal with 'em and classify 'em like. . . . I see the Superintendent's idea." He looked at Pike with a certain warmth of admiration. "I see the Superintendent's idea," he said again. "He knows we'd get hundreds of these things—thousands of 'em—and he knows that when we get thousands of 'em we could discount all the thousands that bore reading and enquiry if necessary, thus, Davis me lad, what they call narrowin' our field."

Davis sniffed again. " Can't say," he said, " that I think much of it." He paused, and added : " With all due respect, of course."

" Any proposal," said the Chief Constable not without pomposity, " that narrows our field is a move which must at least be considered." . He looked at Pike, " Suppose, Superintendent, that you tell us really what you think of this scheme of yours yourself."

Pike shrugged. " Not much, sir. Not a great deal, that is. But I do think it's worth trying. As Inspector Farrow said just now, it narrows our field and while we're doing nothing we might just as well, you might say, do *something*."

" Ha ! " For the first time in forty-eight hours the. Chief Constable laughed ; or tried to laugh. " But I see," he said, " what you mean, Superintendent." Once more he looked from Farrow to Davis from Davis to Farrow. " What do you think ? "

Farrow was emphatic in assent. Davis, giving a little under the pressure of majority opinion, nodded noncommitally.

" How do you propose . . ." began the Chief Constable, looking at Pike ; and then stopped.

" What's that ? " said the Chief Constable.

The ten eyes in the room were fixed upon the window. The ten ears in the room had heard hurrying footsteps up the little flagged path. The ears went on hearing the footsteps and the eyes beheld a uniformed figure pass the window upon its way to the front door.

" Postman," said Farrow unnecessarily.

Jeffson started for the door. But although he had an advantage of several feet and also a clear path Pike was at it before him.

It was Pike who threw open the small front door and Pike who snatched from the breathless postman's hands a thick, official envelope, addressed, in an angular official hand, to the Police Officer in charge. . .

Pike went back to the room, pushing b' Jeffson's bulk. Jeffson entered after, closing the door behind him with an exaggerated and somehow ominous softness.

Pike walked to the table. As he walked he slit with his thumb the flap of the O.H.M.S. envelope. He reached the table. He shot out from the envelope, so that they lay fully exposed to the glaring eyes of the Chief Constable and his two satellites, three square yellow envelopes upon which were addresses written with a peculiarly backward-sloping hand and in a curiously black and shining ink.

" *Christ Almighty !* " said the Chief Constable.

There came a little hissing intake of breath from Farrow and a nervous half-strangled gasp from David. They bent over the envelopes. The first was addressed to The Chief Constable of the County, c/o Police Station, Holmd^le. The second was addressed to Sir Montague Flushing, The Hospice, Holmdale, and the third was addressed to Miss Ursula Finch, Editor of the *Holmdale Clarion*, Claypits Road, Holmdale. . . .

The contents of the three envelopes were identical. Each contained three single sheets of yellow notepaper. In each case, upon the first of these sheets, there appeared the following letter, differing only in its line of greeting :

" I must confess that I am regarding your efforts with a great deal of amusement. You have not got very far, have you ? I don't think it is for want of trying, but I must say, without in any way intending to give offence, that I consider that it *is* for want of brains.

" I am afraid the message by this little note of mine is going to cause you more trouble than ever, but it really cannot be helped !

"I am writing to tell you that I propose to take a little—and I hope you will agree well-earned—holiday. In other words, I am not going to carry out any further removals for quite a little while. When I really feel like it, of course, and when the time is propitious, I shall start again. You can hardly expect me to be so magnanimous as to give up altogether, can you?

"I hope this will not put you in a very awkward position though I fear it may.

"Very cordially yours,
"The Butcher."

"P.S.—I am so sorry that I have hitherto omitted to send you my little reference notes—which I hope will be useful for your files—in regard to the late Marjorie Williams and Millicent Brade. I now repair this omission and enclose them herewith."

The first enclosure was as follows:

"My Reference Five.
R.I.P.
Marjory Williams,
Died Friday, 30th November, 193...
The Butcher."

And the second:

"My Reference Six.
R.I.P.
Millicent Brade,
Died Friday, December 7th, 193..
The Butcher."

2

The sheets of yellow paper still lay open before the Chief Constable and now, for the first time during the ten minutes in which they had been there, the Chief

Constable was not looking at them. Instead he was looking, twisting round in his chair, at the door which had just slammed behind Superintendent Arnold Pike.

The Chief Constable straightened himself. He looked, like a bewildered infant, from one of his subordinates to the other. He said, in a tone curiously and almost comically blent of bewilderment and indignation :

" Where's he *gone* ? "

Farrow, frowning, was silent. But Davis sniffed one of his most expressive sniffs.

3

" Yes," said the postmaster. " They were taken from the box in Inniless Road by the second collection." He looked eagerly at Superintendent Pike who faced him across the table. " As you said, Superintendent, I didn't say anything to anybody and as I sorted the things myself I don't suppose there's anybody knows. *And* I didn't— bearing in mind your instructions, Superintendent— give that information in the covering note."

Pike cut him short. " Quite right. Quite right." He got suddenly to his feet, pushing back his chair with a squeaking sound across the postmaster's floor. He leant his palms on the table and looking down at the postmaster with eyes which seemed to bore through the postmaster's head, he said, speaking slowly and deliberately in great contrast to his previous curtness : " You know, Mr. Myers, you are carrying a great responsibility."

The postmaster shifted uneasily in his chair. "I realise that, Superintendent," he said nervously, " I realise that, I assure you. . . ." He laughed a small, restrained and yet almost hysterical laugh. " But how do *you* know, Superintendent, that I'm not the Butcher himself ? "

Pike's mouth twitched to the grim semblance of a

smile. " I know that," he said, " because I've taken the trouble to find out, Mr. Myers, without your knowing it, that on the occasions of these . . . these killings, you were conducting yourself ordinarily and properly somewhere else."

" Been doing things thoroughly, haven't you ? " said the postmaster, still leavening his words with nervous giggling sounds.

Pike nodded sombrely. " Got to," he said. " Now, Mr. Myers, you've been helping the police very considerably ; a good deal more considerably than you know . . ."

Mr. Myers swelled with importance. " Only too glad ! " he said. " Only too glad ! If I can be of any use——"

He was cut short. He was told how he could be of use.

4

Within five hours Mr. Myers, astonished and thrilled, yet intelligently dutiful, was sitting in the long barnlike tea-room of The Royal George in Batley. The time had gone fast for Mr. Myers. He had been whirled here and there in a closed car driven at a speed which he knew was illegal and felt was dangerous. He had been first to Number Nineteen Inniless Road and from the car had watched the curious and stealthy emergence from Number Nineteen,—which was an empty house !—of a man carrying a square, black and apparently very heavy box. This man had joined the party in the car, seating himself beside the Superintendent, who was driving. The car had then hurtled Mr. Myers and the rest of the party out of Holmdale by Dale Road and along the Main Road, by way of the new by-pass, to Batley.

Mr. Myers kept his eyes and ears open and, as befitted his new rôle of assistant to Scotland Yard. his mouth shut. Mr. Myers, arrived at The Royal George, witnessed

a curious transformation. Superintendent Pike seemed
to be no longer Superintendent Pike. His very speech
and gait—almost, if he had not known this to be
impossible, Mr. Myers would have said his clothes also
—had changed. He was now, it seemed, a Mr. Fortescue
and Mr. Fortescue was a gentleman who had something
to do with the film industry; something which he
appeared to wish to keep a very close trade secret;
something about which The Royal George had been
partially taken into confidence. . . . And the men who
composed the rest of the party—the strange man who
had emerged from the house in Inniless Road and the
two men who, at first, were called Curtis and Blaine by
Superintendent Pike and now were called Ashbridge and
Barney by Mr. Fortescue—all now seemed to have
changed not only their labels but their deportment. . . .

Mr. Myers's head had begun to reel. But now seated
uncomfortably upon an upright wooden chair gazing
through the dark, at a sheet upon which moving
pictures were being shown, Mr. Myers began to recover
a belief in the world's sanity. For Mr. Myers was
looking at the Inniless Road pillar box. . . . The
pictures were in jerky pieces and in a way were all the
same. . . . They shewed persons; persons whom, as
one of the oldest inhabitants of Holmdale, Mr. Myers
knew not only by sight but by name, walking up to the
Inniless Road pillar box and dropping letters and
packages into its maw. . . The pictures were shewn
through once in silence and then Mr. Fortescue—only
now Mr. Myers discovered with a shock that it was
Superintendent Pike again—now Superintendent Pike
came close to Mr. Myers's chair and spoke into Mr.
Myers's ear.

" I want you," said Superintendent Pike, " to tell
me, at the end of each bit, if you can, who the people
you see on this screen may be. . . . "

CHAPTER SIXTEEN

(Confidential memorandum by Superintendent Arnold Pike, C.I.D. to Assistant Commissioner E. Lucas, C.B., etc., C.I.D., dated Monday, December 10th, 193 . . .)

Have not sent you any word since Friday but have now to report that a scheme which I worked out on Friday has already been justified with results which I *think* may get us somewhere.

On Friday morning, as you were officially notified, there was another "Butcher" outrage, a small child named Millicent Brade being murdered in broad daylight outside the big shop here. On Friday evening I thought of the above-mentioned scheme which, in brief, was as follows :

In anticipation of the "Butcher" letter which, it seemed fairly certain, would follow this crime or precede the next, to take cinematographic pictures of all persons posting letters at all boxes. Result hoped for (as you already know, the post collections are made so that it can be told what box a letter came out of) to narrow down the field of enquiry by concentrating upon all people posting letters during the time the "Butcher" letter must have been posted. (N.B. I thought it highly improbable that the "Butcher" would repeat the trick of slipping in his letter with those of some one else, as he did in The Market once before. He is too clever to do this and therefore, I reasoned, would be most likely to post his next epistle himself.

I should at once inform you that as soon as I thought of the cinematograph scheme I made the decision not to inform *any one* down here in regard to it. I told Curtis and Blaine, of course, but I instructed them not to mention the matter. I have even kept the Chief Constable in the dark. I am sure you will appreciate that the situation here, as far as I am concerned, was one of complete ignorance. Any one—*any one at all*—might be the "Butcher." As my previous report shewed it was even more likely that the "Butcher" should be one with whom I come into frequent contact than one of the more ordinary residents.

I hope you will approve of my secrecy. If I am to continue working on this case, I do hope that this will be preserved. I am determined from now on to keep this secrecy even in regard to any other steps which I may take.

Am glad to report that the cinematograph scheme had immediate and satisfactory result. On Saturday morning, while I was at a meeting with the Chief Constable and others, the postmaster sent up three identical "Butcher" letters which had been found in the second collection. I got away from the meeting as soon as I could and immediately went to interview the postmaster (see note at foot of this letter). He informed me that the letters had been found in the Inniless Road pillar box. I cautioned him to keep quiet and immediately proceeded to Inniless Road (see separate report to follow as to how the cinematograph men were posted) took the film from the operator there and sent it by Curtis into Batley for private development. Later I collected the Postmaster (Myers) Curtis and Blaine, together with the Inniless Road operator, his camera and a projector and proceeded to Batley to a room for which I had arranged—under an alias—in which we could shew the film. When the film was ready, we ran it through and Myers was able, fortunately, to tell us who each of the twelve persons posting letters between the eight o'clock collection and the ten o'clock collection was.

You will appreciate that one of these twelve persons *must have posted the " Butcher" letters* and that, therefore, one of these twelve persons is, in all probability (see argument above) the "Butcher" himself. In other words, *we have reduced our " suspect-list" from approximately five thousand to twelve.*

I give a table in which I have set out the names of the twelve persons, their particulars, etc., and, most important, three columns shewing, first, whether they could properly account for the letters posted, second, whether subsequent enquiries proved them to have really indubitable alibis for the times of all the "Butcher" murders, and third, the reason they posted their letters in the Inniless Road pillar box:

The first question arising out of this table is, of course, the ability of *all* the twelve persons to account for the letters posted (*i.e.* to state to whom the letters were addressed and what the letters contained). The fact that they were all able to account for the letters did not worry me. I expected it because—as I foreshadowed in my last report—I thought the "Butcher," when posting a letter (in a disguised handwriting and on special paper, etc.), would be clever enough to post at the same time—in case he was asked—a genuine letter written on his paper in his own handwriting.

The next question is the large one of narrowing the field of twelve "possibles." I did this by examining the answers which I have classified under the sixth heading in the table. Analysis of the entries under this heading shows four entirely satisfactory persons— Claud Nickells, Mrs. Tildesley-Marshall, Mrs. Wills and Philip Matthews ; two partially satisfactory persons— Emily Potts and James Stelch ; two persons whose statements have not yet been checked (but whom, I

Name.	Address.	Age.	Occupation.	Whether able to account for letters posted.	Alibis for times of Outrages.	Reason for posting in Inniless Road Pillar-box.
Claud Nickells	30 Inniless Rd.	40	Clerk	Yes	Satisfactory	House by pillar-box.
Mrs. Tildesley-Marshall	14 Prester Avenue	37	Married woman	Yes	As above	On way to the Market.
Emily Potts	The Laurels Nursing Home, Minters Ave.	29	Nursing sister	Yes	Partly satisfactory. Two dates unsupported by evidence	On way to case.
James Stelch	3 Inniless Rd.	50	Commissionaire at Breakfast Barlies, Ltd.	Yes	Satisfactory as to three dates. Others unsupported by evidence	On way to work.
Ursula Finch	Flat over *Clarion* Offices, Claypits Rd.	35	Proprietor and Editor, Holmdale *Clarion*	Yes	Unable to give witnessed statements as on all occasions alone in *Clarion* office	Returning to office after seeking interview with Mrs. Brade.
Muriel Rowland	2 Fourtrees Rd.	19	Stenographer	Yes	Statements being checked	On way to station.
Sir Montague Flushing	The Hospice	56	Chairman to Holmdale Co.	Yes	Statements vague and unsatisfactory. Uncheckable	Passing in car.
Harry Formby	3 Batley Croft, Batley	30	Bricklayer	Yes	Impossible to check statements yet. Not resident in Holmdale	Opposite work.
Sydney Jeffson	Police Station	45	Sergeant of Police	Yes	No witnessed statements. On duty alone	Passing on round.
Mrs. Roger Wills	14 Inniless Rd.	27	Married woman	Yes	Satisfactory	Nearest post-box.
Philip Matthews	4 The New Approach	14	Schoolboy	Yes	Satisfactory	On way to school.
L. C. A. Rockwall	Vicarage, Church Rd.	61	Anglican minister	Yes	None actually, although many near times vouched for	Taking constitutional.

should add, seem to be almost certainly speaking the truth), Muriel Rowland and Harry Fornby; and four persons whose statements are unsatisfactory in themselves or uncheckable or both—Ursula Finch, Montague Flushing, Sydney Jeffson and Rockwall.

Nickells, Tildesley-Marshall, Wills and Matthews I am accordingly leaving out of consideration. Their statements have been carefully checked and there is no doubt that they could not have been, upon any of the occasions, anywhere near the scenes of the outrages.

In regard to the next two classes of partially cleared and checkable but unchecked—Potts and Stelch, Rowland and Fornby—I am having these people kept under surveyance until such times as their statements are completely checked up or not. For this purpose I shall use some of the extra men I applied to you for over the telephone for yesterday and who I met at Batley this morning. (I have sent D. O. Handley back as I am afraid he is not quite the type for the job, being too noticeably a Police Officer. I should like to get Richards if I can).

In regard to the last class—Finch, Flushing, Jeffson and Rockwall—I have put these under special watch, which I hope will be carried out skilfully enough for them not to notice it. There is, of course, the fact that the "Butcher," who *must* be one of these twelve, and, in my opinion, one of these last four, must be aware, by reason of the questioning, etc., that we are getting close to him. But any danger which this might have lead to of the "Butcher" "drawing in his horns" is neutralised by the fact that he had already decided to do this *vide* his last letter, copy of which was sent to you the day before yesterday.

I also propose to have carried out, as soon as practicable, a search of the houses of the four in the last class. In order to do this, if possible, without the knowledge

of the persons, I am proposing to hold interviews with
these persons, either at my rooms here or at the Police
Station, in which I shall probably apologise for any
inconvenience which the recent questioning, etc., may
have caused them. I hope that such interviews, if
I carry them out properly, will serve the double purpose
of keeping the suspect away while the search of his
house is being carried out and also lull him (for one of
them, in my opinion, in all probability is the " Butcher")
into a false sense of security and possibly decoy him into
making a step which would enable us to arrest him.

Following the unfortunate arrests of Reade, Spring
and Godly, all of whom had to be released following the
Brade murder, I am bearing in mind your instructions
that no other arrests shall be made until there is ample
evidence or unless the safety of the public seems to call
for it urgently.

I hope progress is satisfactory : I consider it so myself.
I have every hope that we are at last nearing some
definite conclusion. I hope, also, that my policy of
keeping from everyone down here, including the local
Police, all the recent steps I have taken (as reported
above) and any future steps whatsoever until the arrest
of the " Butcher," will be approved and respected, and
that any one from Headquarters will let even the Chief
Constable have any inkling. (Some justification for
this policy will be found on looking at the list of the four
main suspects).

From now I will send you memoranda daily, of course
telephoning any urgent or important developments.

(Signed) ARNOLD PIKE.

P.S.—In regard to the Postmaster Myers, whom I
had, over the pillar box scheme, to take into my confidence, I should report that I have persuaded Myers
to remain out of Holmdale until such time as I recall

him. He is at present staying in rooms which I found for him, in Penders Cross, a little village outside Batley. I have taken the responsibility of informing him that his expenses will be paid and also that some adequate honorarium will be paid to him at the end of the business. He seems trustworthy (of course before I took him into my confidence I found out that he had adequate alibis for all the outrage dates) but I didn't want him going back, after seeing the films, to Holmdale, and possibly being unable to keep what he knows to himself.

A.P.

CHAPTER SEVENTEEN

I

MR. EGBERT LUCAS was speaking on the telephone to Superintendent Arnold Pike.

" . . . . You said something last night, when we spoke, about it being all right to ring you on this line. D'you mean I can say anything ? "

" Yes, sir."

" How's that ? "

" Myers, sir—the postmaster. I made an arrangement with him to use a line here which can't be listened in to. Good job you rang up when you did. I was just going out. . . . Anything wrong, sir ? "

" Don't sound so anxious, man ! No. We're very pleased with you. You ought to've heard the Commissioner this morning. . . . No, there's nothing special. As a matter of fact, we're getting so worked up that we keep expecting you to make an arrest at any minute. . . . "

" 'Fraid you'll be disappointed, sir."

" Eh ? What's that ? Anything wrong at your end, then ? "

" Nothing exactly wrong, sir, except that the night before last Tuesday, we carried out the last of those searches—Rockwall's house and Flushing's. Flushing's was very difficult but Blaine and Curtis managed it between them very well with Stallard tricking the servant out of the way and me talking to Sir Montague in the Station. . . . "

" Are you trying to tell me, Pike, that you didn't find anything in *any* of these four houses ? "

" That's it, I'm afraid, sir. Not a thing that shouldn't be there. And nothing that would fit in with what the doctors say the weapon must be like. And no ' Butcher' paper and no ink. Nothing ! "

" That shake your faith at all, Pike ? In your own scheme, I mean."

" No, sir. It's only made me, as you might say, all the more determined to get at him some other way. I'm sure I'm right. . . . "

" Look here, Pike, what's your own idea about this ? Which one of the four do you plump for ? "

" . . . I don't think I'd like to say at the moment, sir."

" Go on, man. Go on ! As a matter of fact the Commissioner asked me to ask you that question himself. You're not bound to say, of course—anyway I don't expect you would if you didn't want to. But if you could give us a line on what you're thinking we should be glad. Purely for our own information, of course."

" I'm afraid, sir, that I'm as divided in mind as you are yourself. I can't say and that's all. I don't like Rockwall's attitude ; but then he's what you might call an eccentric and it may mean nothing. And I don't like . . . "

" Hold on a minute, Pike. You're going to say Jeffson. Am I right ? "

" Well . . . . I won't say you're wrong, sir. It's like what Colonel Gethryn's always saying. If it was Jeffson it would be so improbable that it might very probably be true. . . . But I'm not committing myself, you understand."

" Very cautious, Pike. But what are you going to *do* now ? Seems to be a bit of a deadlock. There's the ' Butcher ' having notified you that he's going to rest and there's you with four suspects that you can't narrow down to one. . . . Don't think I'm blaming you or anything like that. It's the devil of a job!"

"I've got an idea, sir. Had it just before you rang up, as a matter of fact. I was just going out to see whether I couldn't do something about it."

"Good man! What is it?"

"I'd rather not say at this stage, sir, in case I don't carry it out."

"All right, Pike. All right. Well, good-night and I hope we'll hear from you soon."

"Good-night, sir, and thank you."

2

The Chief Constable was astonished. Across his own study table he looked with bewilderment at Superintendent Pike.

"I don't understand!" said the Chief Constable. "I don't understand at all! . . . Damn it, I don't understand!"

Pike was apologetic. "I'm sorry, sir; perhaps you'll tell me what it is. . . . . ."

"But good God!" the Chief Constable exploded. "Good God, Pike! When the damn thing was at its height, when people were being slit up right and left and I and my men suggested this curfew, you put your foot on it. *Now*, when there's nothing doing and the damn lunatic's told us there's going to be nothing doing for a bit, you come here and calmly say that you agree at last to the curfew suggestion. Blast it, man. It's like Alice in Wonderland or a kids' pantomime, or something! It's not sense!"

Pike was still apologetic, but none the less firm for that. "I can't tell you how it is, sir, but I've got a feeling—I've got a sort of, well, I suppose you'd call it intuition—that that letter of the 'Butcher's' was

H

a trick. I seem to sort of *know* that there'll be another
outrage soon. It's *too* quiet now, that's what it is.
And I've been thinking over what you said—you and
the two Inspectors—and I've come round to the opinion
that a curfew is what we want."

The Chief Constable, slightly mollified by the deferen-
tial tone, was still bewildered.

" I don't see how I can *now*," said the Chief Constable. " When the thing was at its height I could've
enforced *any* measure. Now, it's all eased off and they're
all lax instead of tense, well, a thing like that'll take
a bit of enforcing. They'll all be wanting to go to the
pictures and out to the pub, and that sort of thing
every evening. Don't see how we *can* do it, Superintendent. Damned if I do ! And I'm not sure that we
ought to ! "

" I don't mean, sir," Pike explained, " that we ought
to make the curfew compulsory. What I meant was
that I'd like you to issue a Police request, as you might
say, asking people ' in view of certain knowledge which
has come into the hands of the Police '—or something
like that—asking people to help by not going out at all
after, say, eight o'clock at night. . . . "

The Chief Constable hummed. The Chief Constable hawed. The Chief Constable was most puzzled,
and almost epileptic by turns. But at last, under Pike's
urbane persistence, he gave way.

3

The ' voluntary curfew ' had been in operation for
two nights. And so it was that Curtis, driving much
too fast through the thick white mist which shrouded
the Main Road, was stopped at the junction of the Main
Road with the Dale Road entrance to Holmdale.

The Police car pulled up with a whining of brakes. The white mist eddied in smoky whorls about the black world. Curtis, rubbing the window with his sleeve, looked out. He saw the outline of a uniformed constable who held a bull's-eye lantern. Curtis, with two turns of his wrist, lowered the car's window and produced from his pocket, something which he shewed.

The constable, peering, looked first at this, and then, carefully, at its presenter. . . . The constable fell back, raising a hand to his helmet.

" Beg pardon," said the constable, " but we're gettin' very 'ot 'specially now the fogs're beginnin'."

Curtis nodded and slipped the car into gear and was off down Dale Road.

Ten minutes later—the fog in the valley of Holmdale was so dense that it took ten minutes to cover a distance usually killed in two—he pulled the car up outside Number Twelve Fourtrees Road.

As he got out of the car the fog caught him by the throat. He coughed and his eyes shed involuntary tears. He had to grope his way to the gate. The fog seemed, thicker, somehow, off the road. It seemed to Curtis that he took all of five minutes between the car and Miss Marable's front door. He rang the bell. He rang, not without diffidence because the hour was, he judged, long past that when Miss Marable and the most of her lodgers would be in bed. But the ring was answered with almost uncanny promptitude. The door was flung open and Curtis stepped across the threshold.

" Got it ? " said Pike.

Curtis nodded. He stood in the lamplight, blinking. His eyes still streamed with tears, and the fog still tickled his throat, so that it was some moments before he could get words out between coughs. " Yes," he said at last. " Think he's made a good job of it, too."

" Come up," said Pike. " Tread soft, though."

They sat before a blazing fire in Miss Marable's best front room. "Now," said Pike, and held out his hand.

Curtis rose, went to his heavy frieze overcoat which lay across a chair and from the pocket of the overcoat produced a square, foolscap-sized envelope, protected by thin sheets of cardboard and bound about with string. He took out a pocket-knife and cut the string. From the envelope he took, gingerly, something which he laid upon the little table which his superior had set down before the hearth.

Pike got to his feet and bent over the table and examined a square sheet of yellow paper upon which there were many lines of writing—peculiar writing in peculiar ink.

Pike grunted ; raised his head ; bent again to his examination.

" Not bad ! " he said. " Not bad at all ! " He took from his pocket a wallet and from the wallet another sheet, neatly folded, of the same coloured paper—the original of the first " Butcher " letter. He unfolded it and smoothed it out with careful hands and laid it beside the sheet already on the table.

Curtis came and stood beside him and now they both pored.

" It's good ! " said Pike at last. . . . " Who did you get to do it ?   Carruthers or Maxwell ? "

" In the end," said Curtis, " Mr. Maxwell did it. He didn't seem very satisfied with it himself, but *I* thought it was a real winner, sir."

" Got the envelope ? " said Pike.

Curtis nodded and produced from another pocket in the overcoat another and similar packet. " All three envelopes are here, sir," he said, " and the other two copies of the letter."

" Are they all as good as this ? " said Pike.

"Every bit," said Curtis, "no difference between 'em. Not that a man's eye could tell anyhow. . . . And I saw Mr. Lucas, sir, and he said to tell you that he thought your draft was very good. He only altered a couple of words."

Pike grunted. "Yes, I saw that. He's right. Just read it out, Curtis, and let's listen to it. . . . "

The telephone in Miss Marable's hall rang shrilly. Miss Marable went to it herself and within a moment was running up the stairs.

Miss Marable knocked at Pike's door and, most unusually, not awaiting reply, walked in.

Pike was in his favourite position upon the window seat. He turned and looked at the sound of the door opening and got to his feet. "Good-morning," he said.

"Oh, Mr. Pike!" said Miss Marable. "They've just telephoned from the Police Station. It was the Chief Constable himself speaking." Miss Marable was a little breathless. "He seemed very urgent. Would you go round at once, please. He said that three times." Miss Marable was a little pinker than usual in the cheeks. "He said that three times," she repeated, "and then rang off."

Miss Marable departed. Pike leisurely changed slippers for the boots with the very shiny toe-caps. He smiled to himself; a smile which was, at first, merely a twitching of the corners of his mouth, but which, by the time that the boots were on and he was descended Miss Marable's stairs, was almost a grin.

But there was no smile, nor hint of a smile, upon his brown, lean, lantern-shaped face as he went in to the room which, for weeks which seemed to Mrs. Jekson as many years, had been no use as a parlour at all.

The Chief Constable was there, and Davis and Farrow were there and, of course, Jeffson. They all, even Jeffson, were crowded round the deal table. So intent were they that Pike stood there for fully a minute before any one noticed his presence. It was the Chief Constable who saw him first.

" *There* you are ! " said the Chief Constable. He seemed changed. His heavy face was lean and sagging and now it had lost all of its colour. The pouches under his eyes were like black bruises. His voice, which trembled like his hands, seemed to be hiding fear under a mask of irritability. " Look at this, Superintendent. Look at *this* ! "

Pike came nearer to the table, halted suddenly and stared in excellent astonishment. " Another ' Butcher ' letter ! " he said.

The Chief Constable nodded. Brought round by hand about half an hour ago, he said.

Farrow, without a word, picked up the yellow sheet by its corner ; held it so that Pike could read. Pike read, half-aloud :

" DEAR POLICE,—I regret to say that I find this life of inactivity quite insupportable. You may or may not be glad to hear this. I fancy that you will be both. You will be sorry because you will doubt your ability to prevent my activities and glad because you will not be kept in this dreadful suspense.

" In order to make things really pleasantly easy for you I hereby announce my intention of carrying out the seventh of my—shall we call them removals ?— to-morrow (Monday, the 16th December).

" I am afraid that last time I gave you warning of a day my sense of humour got the better of me, and knowing that you would be expecting me to carry out my work at night, I carried it out in broad daylight, thus completely confounding you.

" This time, however, I will descend to no such mean tricks and I hereby give you full warning that the times between which my work will be executed (' executed ' is rather good, don't you think ?) will be 7 and 10 p.m.

" As usual I have sent copies of this letter to dear Sir Montague and to the *Holmdale Clarion.*

" Tolerantly yours,

" THE BUTCHER.

" P.S.—I find myself in an extraordinarily kind mood to-day. I cannot bear to think of you poor Police trying, in despair, to cover the whole of Holmdale for three hours on Monday night. So, in addition to telling you the date and time, I will tell you, approximately, the place. The job will be done between the junction of Market Road and Forest Road at the north-western end and the Wooden Shack at the southern end. Don't worry about your curfew. Nothing like this is going to stop me !

" THE BUTCHER."

" Well ! " said Pike. " I'll be *jiggered !* "

He thought for one horrid instant that the astonishment and concern in his voice had been overdone, but he looked round at the faces of the other men and found in them no suspicion. . . .

CHAPTER EIGHTEEN

On Monday the day was a clear day of bright, hard, frosty sunshine. But with evening, there came, with that frequent paradox of English climate, a drop in temperature. As early as four o'clock the mists began to gather again. By five, all Holmdale was shrouded in a fleecy blanket of white fog. By six o'clock, even in the brilliantly lighted patch before The Market, it was difficult for a man to see more than ten yards ahead of him : by seven o'clock it was impossible ; he could not see more than five.

At a quarter past seven at the junction of Collingwood Road with Market Road, Blaine, walking at a pace inconsistent with the visibility, ran into a living organism as solid as himself.

" *Uh !* " Blaine grunted ; then reached out a hand to grope, but even as he reached out his hand, another hand clutched its shoulder.

Detective Officers Frank Blaine and George Curtis recognised each other. They smiled ; then laughed softly.

" I thought," said Blaine, " that you were the Butcher."

Curtis laughed. They fell into step. They proceeded down Collingwood Road and turned, crossing the road until they were on the grass plot facing the northerly façade of The Market. The fog was very thick here ; so thick that barely could a man see his own hand at arm's length. They halted.

" About here, was it ? " said Curtis.

"Anywhere's along this side," said Blaine. He craned his head forward between his square shoulders and stared at the blurry blobs of light which were the lamps before The Market. "That's what he said."

"We'd better then"—Curtis coughed as the fog tickled his lungs—"stay put. That right?"

"May as well. . . . Yes, when you bumped your damn great hulking carcase into mine I thought you were the 'Butcher.' I was just goin' to tell you that anything you might say. . . ."

Through the fog Curtis peered curiously at his companion. "You don't mean," he said, "that you think this is a *reel* Butcher stunt we're on?"

There was sudden movement beside him as Blaine turned sharply round. "What the hell are you talkin' about? Real Butcher stunt? What d'you mean? Of course it is. . . ."

"'Tisn't I" Curtis, although with enough sense of duty to keep his ears alert, was yet delighted that for the first time for many months he was ahead of his colleague. He said:

"Mean to say A. P. hasn't told you?"

Blaine grew annoyed. "Told me *what?*" He tells me as much. . . ." He broke off coughing. The fog had got down his throat.

"He doesn't then I" Curtis was pleasantly triumphant. "'Course he would've done in time. But he hasn't had time."

Through the fog, brushing aside its white billows with black bulk, Curtis moved closer. His ham-like hand closed its sausage-like fingers upon Blaine's arm. He whispered into Blaine's ear:

"That Butcher letter—that last one, the one that come yesterday—that's a fake, boy I"

"Get out I" said Blaine.

"'Tis then I"

" Get out ! " said Blaine again, his tone incredulous. " Why, I was in the Station just after A. P.'d left and Jeffson shewed it to me. I've seen too many of those ' Butcher ' letters not to know one when I see it."

Curtis's fingers dropped the arm ; began to tap upon Blaine's shoulder. " That letter, I tell you," he said, " was written by Foxy Maxwell. I was there while he did it yesterday. If I'd seen you since I'd 've told you. So'd A. P., only he hasn't had a minute.

" Well, I'll be . . . . " Blaine said what he would be. And, when he had recovered from the first shock of astonishment, asked almost querulously :

" But w'y, *w'y* ? "

" My boy," said Curtis, " A. P.'s good. You and me know that. But this is the best he's ever done. It's pyschological."

" It's *what* ? " said Blaine. " You mean psychological."

" You know very well," said Curtis angrily, " what I mean. Anyway it's that. What A. P. reckons— he told me all about it last night—is this. We've got these what he calls possibles down to four : the old parson, Monty Flushing, Miss Finch of the *Clarion* and —and "—here Curtis dropped his voice still lower— " you know who ! "

" You mean Jeffson ? " Blaine's voice was the ghostliest of whispers.

Curtis coughed. " Blast this fog ! " he said. " Yes, that's right ! Well, that's something, isn't it ? We started with five or six thousand and we've got down to four. There's not many men at the Yard that would've done *that* in the time. In fact, no one would except A. P. . . . "

" Yes. Yes." Blaine was impatient. " But what about the letter ? What's the idea ?

" Can't you see ? " Curtis was all bland superiority.

" A. P. knew this letter'd be seen by all of 'em except Rockwall—and he'll get to *hear* of it. Now, any one of those four's the ' Butcher,' isn't it ? "

"Not," said Blaine the cautious, " *is*. *May* be ! "

"Well, I say *is*," said Curtis. " But I'll take your point. One of those four's most likely to be the " Butcher " isn't he ? "

"Yes," said Blaine.

"And all of those four've heard about this new Butcher letter, and mostly seen it. Well, the one that *is* the ' Butcher,' what does he think ? . . . Mind you, Blainey, this Butcher is a lunatic, don't forget that ! It's like what A. P. was saying to me last night. He's a loony in one patch like. Well, he gets to hear that some other fellah has been writing Butcher letters and bragging Butcher brags. . . . Got it ? "

"You mean," said Blaine in an eager whisper, "that he'll be—well, sort of puzzled and jealous all at the same time ? "

Curtis was approving. " They're almost A. P.'s own words. And as I said to A. P. when he told me about the scheme "—Curtis was very important—" That's *good*, I said, ' Good ! ' You've given the place, you've given the date, you've given the time and you've done the letter so that even if the ' Butcher ' sees it himself he won't know that he didn't write it. D'you. see it now ? "

"You mean," said Blaine slowly, still in a tense whisper which was so deadened by the fog that it reached Curtis's ear as a wraith of a sound. " You mean that A. P.'s expecting this *fake* letter to draw the *real* Butcher, because he'll want to go out and see what all this really is ? "

"*Exactly*," said Curtis. " Mind you, boy, A. P. hasn't told you, so you'd better not know. You and me aren't hardly even supposed to talk."

"I know that," said Blaine. "A. P.'s drummed it into me enough. I s'ppose it's because of this Jeffson possibility."

Curtis nodded. "May be, but I think A. P. 'd've made the same principle even if Jeffson hadn't come into it. By God, boy, s'ppose it *is* Jeffson!"

"My old mother," said Blaine, "used to say to me 'You never know!' And she was right. The more I live and the more I get about, the more I know I never do know."

"Bloody clever of A. P. whichever way you look at it! Jeffson told me there was the hell of a row between him and the C. C. when he suddenly said, the other day, that he wanted the curfew business after all. And here it's been on for three nights voluntary and it's taken on—well, you can see for yourself how it's taken!"

Blaine coughed. "Ah! Fog's helped it though."

"Never mind," Curtis said, "what's helped it! It's worked. And because it's worked A. P.'s scheme looks like coming off! There's no one out, but there may be. And if any one comes along the road mentioned in this fake letter—specially if it's one of the four— well, there you are! We'll know, metamphorically speakin', who the 'Butcher' is, and that's a good thing to know!"

"I should say," said Blaine in a hearty whisper, "it damn-well was!"

"Mind you," said Curtis, "except for *knowin'*, A. P.'s not sure that he'll be any better off for this stunt even if it does work. . . . "

Blaine interrupted. "You know," he grumbled, "you're like a book of crossword puzzles or something to-night. What're you talkin' about now?"

"He," said Curtis sententiously, "that has ears to 'ear, let him hear! A. P. says that although he may *find out* to-night he may not be able to *do* anything.

You see, Blainey, this Butcher's clever sort of a devil and although he may come down he won't come down without a proper excuse. A. P. said to me last night, he said : ' You see, Curtis, when he does come—if he does come—he'll have some boiling good reason, but that won't worry me. I daresay,' he said to me, Blainey, just like that, ' I daresay, in a manner of speaking, we shan't be any better off. But we shall, *really*, because we'll *know*. . . . ' "

Curtis's flow was cut short by a fit of coughing. The fog was thicker. It no longer swirled round them in now thickening, now thinning eddies, but pressed close about them like a malign and impalpable suffocation.

" Getting cold," Blaine growled, " let's walk."

They walked up and down, up and down, two large looming shapes in the white darkness. Every now and then they stopped to listen ; then resumed their walk. The warmth came back to their feet and, in some degree, to their bodies, but the fog did not lift. It got into their eyes and made them smart ; it got into their noses and made them feel as if they were breathing harsh wool ; it got down their lungs until they coughed ; they had to strangle their coughs for fear of noise.

Every now and then Blaine would ask Curtis, or Curtis would ask Blaine : " What's the time ? "

And this went on until with the last asking, Blaine said : " Nine-fifteen. I wonder. . . . "

" S'sh ! " said Curtis and gripped his arm with iron fingers.

They stood motionless. Not a sound came to them. Blaine shifted uneasily, but Curtis's fingers tightened their clamp ; held him quiet.

" Listen ! " said Curtis.

Suddenly, at first muffled by the deadening curtain of fog until they were only the phantoms of sound, but gradually growing until they were living and human and recognisable, there came the sound of rapid, crisp footsteps.

Blaine started forward.

"Wait!" Curtis whispered. "A.P.'s there. Over the other side. Wait!"

They waited. As the footsteps seemed to draw abreast of them, beating their way into the extra whiteness which shewed where The Market's lamps were placed, they heard other footsteps, coming, on an instant, out of nothing; footsteps which their trained ears recognised.

The first lot of footsteps ceased abruptly. The second ceased also. . . .

"Come on!" said Blaine, and went.

They guided themselves off the grass and on to the road and crossed the road by that lightening in the fog where it was thinned by the glow of The Market's lamps. As they drew near, they heard Pike's voice. They drew nearer, going cautiously and on tiptoe. The voices they could hear now that they were closer were cast in pleasant enough tones. But they knew. They were closer now, and not only their ears but their eyes told them that one of the figures was Arnold Pike. But they were looking at the other. . . .

They halted. Blaine stood, turning his head sharply to hiss into Curtis's right ear:

"Well, I'm . . . May God strike me dead!"

2

At half-past eleven that night, Curtis and Blaine sat, each upon the edge of his chair, in Miss Marable's lounge. Pike, his back to the crackling fire, surveyed them. He said, looking at Blaine:

"So Curtis put you wise, did he?"

Blaine nodded. " Yes, sir."

There was a moment's silence, then Pike spoke
again. He said: looking at Curtis this time:
" You saw ! "

Curtis grunted affirmation. He looked at his chief
with some anxiety. Pike's face seemed longer and
leaner and the lines of his frown seemed as if they
had been cut into his forehead with a graver's
chisel.

It was Blaine who broke the silence.

" What's going to happen, sir ? " he said. " What
can we do now that we do know ? "

Pike shrugged ; a gesture angry and bitter and more
than a little helpless. For the second time during this
case, he used an oath. " I'm damned," he said, " if
I know ! I hope I shall to-morrow. I'm going to
sleep on this, or to bed on it. You two get off now and
carry on with your ordinary duties, saying *nothing
to any one* to-morrow. If I'm not here, it means I'm
up in town. Good-night, now ! "

They rose and went out into the fog, two heavy men
who yet moved with a silence oddly at variance with
their action.

Pike was left staring at Miss Marable's fire. Presently, he dropped into a chair, put his elbows on his
knees and chin into his cupped hands. . . .

3

Upon the next day Pike did go to London. In
Holmdale, Curtis and Blaine, carrying on with stolid
faces their entirely unnecessary and most arduous
duties, awaited him.

They did not see him until half-past six upon that
evening which was the evening of Tuesday, the 17th

December. And when they did see him it was to receive news which flabbergasted them.

"*Leaving*, sir?" said Blaine, "without laying a finger on that. . . . "

Pike nodded. "We're going, to-morrow morning. I'll see the Chief Constable to-night. I'll also see you two again to-night."

Curtis and Blaine looked at him. They were used to moods and varying expressions. They had worked with him now for many years. Until now they had thought that they knew him; but now they found that they did not know him. They could read nothing from the long, blank face which he turned to them.

"Why can't we? . . . " began Blaine, forgetting position in agitation.

"Make an arrest!" said Pike quickly. "Is that what you were going to say?"

Blaine nodded, colouring.

"Because," said Pike grimly, "you poor dub, there's nothing to make the arrest on! We may *know*—we may know until we're black in the face as a lot of black sheep—we *do* know, but what have we got? We've searched the house, haven't we? And all the belongings. And we found nothing. Nothing! And then some more nothing. We've got no finger-prints, no connecting link at all except in our own mental knowledge. . . . How *can* we make an arrest? We'd be the laughing stock of the country in about five minutes. They were comic enough over Spring and that lot. . . . Of course we can't make an arrest. Don't be silly!"

Blaine hung his head like a chidden schoolboy. He muttered at the ground:

"No, sir, of course not. I see it."

"Well, cut off now," said Pike. "See you again." They cut off.

" Well," said the Chief Constable, " in a way I'm very
sorry. In a way I can see what he means." He tapped
the official letter at the foot of which Pike, pretending
not to look, could see Lucas's signature. " I mean I
can see Scotland Yard's point of view. And I must say,
Superintendent, that after your valuable advice . . .
er . . . er . . . " The Chief Constable got into
difficulties here and finished up with a weak " and all
that. I do feel that my own men can carry on. So
perhaps it's all for the best."

The Chief Constable rose, extending a podgy hand
which trembled. Pike shook it without warmth. He
also shook hands, displaying less warmth still, with Davis.
He turned and clasped the ham-like fist of Inspector
Farrow and gave this a hearty enough shake. He nodded
to Jeffson ; made a curious little ducking nod to the
Chief Constable and was gone.

Outside there waited the blue police Crossey. In it
were Curtis and Blaine. Pike took the wheel, and so the
only known members of Scotland Yard to have visited
Holmdale, left Holmdale.

They circled the town and many saw them go.

That was at noon on Wednesday, the 18th December.
By one o'clock all Holmdale knew of their going. There
were mutters in Holmdale. There were outcries in Holmdale against the leaving ; and also satisfaction in Holmdale on account of the leaving. Holmdale, as always
since the beginning of its curse, was divided into many
camps.

In the Police Station, the Chief Constable, Farrow at
one shoulder and Davis at the other, bent over the
letter signed by Egbert Lucas. In the corner Jeffson
stood erect, awaiting instructions. The Chief

Constable mouthed over to himself the letter's last paragraph :

"... The Commissioner, therefore, desires me to state that he feels it unnecessary that Superintendent Pike and his subordinates should remain any longer in Holmdale. While the Commissioner is willing and anxious to offer all the help he can in the most tragic and unusual circumstances, he is unable, owing to the scarcity of officers and men, to allow Superintendent Pike and his subordinates to remain with you indefinitely. Should any further developments or new turns to the situation arise, he will, of course, be only too glad to give you the benefit of any assistance which the Department might be able to provide. In the meanwhile, he hopes that you will agree to the withdrawal of his men.

"I am, sir,
"Your obedient servant,
"EGBERT LUCAS."

"And that," said the Chief Constable pettishly, " is that ! I can't say I think much of our Scotland Yard detectives. What've they done that we couldn't have done ? Eh ? Eh ? . . ."

Farrow grunted. But Davis said :

"Nothing, sir, and not near as much, if you were to ask me. And I reckon we've got this Butcher under and I reckon that it's our doing."

The Chief Constable shook his head, but a pleased smile creased his mouth. " I don't know about got him under," said the Chief Constable. " Certainly he didn't carry out the threat in his last letter and hasn't."

"Nor," said Davis confidently, " he never will."

Farrow grunted.

CHAPTER NINETEEN

I

THERE was fog again upon the Wednesday night and the Thursday night. But on Friday, in the afternoon, the wind changed and there started slashing, stinging north-easterly rain and hail. The hailstones rattled on Holmdale's little red roofs and the gutters of Holmdale ran turgid black-brown water.

It is queer how soon the human animal will accustom itself to changed circumstances. It had only required the failure of the last Butcher letter and the two days interval to make Holmdale, as a whole, slightly contemptuous of the Chief Constable's " voluntary curfew." The majority of Holmdale's citizens still roughly adhered to the curfew boundaries—but only roughly ; and there were many of the more hardy spirits in Holmdale who openly ignored it. The theatre and cinema were shut, but the Wooden Shack still was open. There were cinemas in Batley and dance halls in St. Raglands. And so once more there was life in the streets of Holmdale during night time, although people still went abroad in bunches and not singly. But the small stir did not last upon this Friday evening after a quarter to eleven. And yet upon this Friday evening there was abroad in Holmdale, between eleven-thirty and twelve, a solitary unauthorised traveller.

A small person this, dressed in a short and dirty frock of knitted wool which exposed lanky legs from ankle to mid-thigh. Over the frock, there was a short coat of threadbare black stuff, too big in the shoulders, and moth-eaten about its one-time astrakan collar and cuffs. There were thin and almost soleless shoes upon the little feet. She wore no hat and her hair, which was straight and sparse-seeming and parted in the middle and drawn back over her ears into two plaits with bedraggled tape bows at their ends, was saturated with the rain.

The water streamed down her face and the occasional hailstones stung her. She was in Collingwood Road, slinking along like some furtive animal in the shadow of the hedge. Footsteps came towards her; heavy, martial footsteps of one of the Chief Constable's recently doubled patrols. She slunk into the hedgeway and crouched behind the gate. She shivered as the rain came down upon her. The footsteps went by, slow and ponderous and stately. The little figure crept out again from the gateway and on to the pavement. Once more she slunk furtively along, casting terrified, wide-eyed glances this way and that. . . .

There was light in the offices of the *Holmdale Clarion* and also a light above, in the hall of the flat belonging to the *Holmdale Clarion*'s editor.

Miss Finch had come downstairs, from flat to office. Miss Finch was writing a letter. The sheet upon which she was writing lay square upon her blotter. It was covered with writing. Miss Finch, suddenly discovering the need for more paper, rose and went to the corner of the room in which there stood, in their magnificent, specially-presented, entirely free, book-case, the forty-seven volumes of the American *Cyclopædia*. She took out the volume marked Par–Pork; opened it; laid it flat upon the top of the book-case table and ran her finger and thumb lightly over its edges until she found

what she sought—some twenty-four pages whose outer
edges adhered one to the other. Into the centre of the
pocket made by these pages, Miss Finch slid her left hand
and brought it away bearing another sheet of notepaper
which she sought. There was a glove upon her left hand.

She went back to the desk. She dipped a strangely
nibbed pen into a small ink-pot and settled herself once
more to her task. She wrote :

" . . . and, therefore, I really do feel . .

But she got no further. Suddenly she raised her head.
Her large and beautiful eyes narrowed to slits as she
listened. Her neatly coiffed head was cocked to one side
like some small bird's. Miss Finch with a smooth, hasty
movement hid the two sheets of her letter beneath the
top sheet of her blotter. With another movement nearly
as smooth and even more silent, the ink bottle went into
the left-hand corner drawer of her desk. A key locked
this drawer and was slipped into one of the pockets of
Miss Finch's admirably cut tweed coat.

Yes. . . . She had been right. . . . There it came
again, a faint somehow timid-seeming rapping upon the
office door knocker. Miss Finch rose. She went through
the open glass door marked " Editor " and into the
passage. While she walked many expressions passed over
her face, but when she opened the door there was upon it
that smile which did so much towards enhancing her
charm. She threw open the door and stood upon its
threshold looking out into the wild darkness of driving,
beating rain and keen north-easterly wind. It was some
time before Miss Finch discovered what it was that had
knocked and then, shifting her glance downwards, she
saw at her feet a small, huddled, limpness half-sitting,
half-lying upon the bottom of the three steps which led
from the door down to the pavement.

Miss Finch, reaching out a hand, snapped on the passage light. Its effulgence bathed the steps. . . .

"Well, my little dear," said Miss Finch, "what's the matter?"

She did not go down the steps, but she bent a little as she stood on the top step. She peered downwards. From the limp, woebegone little bundle a small head was raised; a small head behind which there stuck out, ridiculously, two little plaits of hair tied tightly at their ends with dirty tape. The face which looked up at Miss Finch was a white oval in the yellow light. Out from it there stared huge dark eyes, black-rimmed with fatigue and terror.

"I'm afryde!" said a thin and trembling little voice. "Got lorst . . . and up there . . . and up there . . ." —a thin arm came out and made slight gestures behind its back—" up there, there was a man. 'E chysed me. . . . I'm afryde. Let me come in, Lydy!"

"You poor little dear," said Miss Finch slowly. "Yes, come in. Come in." She stood on one side. The small figure heaved painfully to its feet and made gasping way up the steps and over the threshold.

"Koo!" said the thin voice. "'Tain't 'alf luvly an' warm in 'ere"—thin fingers came out and touched Miss Finch suddenly and fiercely by the arm—" Lydy, that man 'e chysed me. 'E can't get in 'ere after me, can 'e?"

Miss Finch's hand came slowly out and patted the thin, sodden shoulder.

"Of course he can't, my dear. Of course, he can't. Poor little thing, you're drenched through and through. Come in. Come in."

Miss Finch, still with hand holding and caressing the thin shoulder whose bones she could feel beneath the shabby and drenched cloth, propelled her visitor gently towards the open door of the editorial office.

" There's a fire in here," said Miss Finch. " You can get warm, dear, and dry your wet clothes."

The waif, catching sight through the open door of the red glow of a large gas fire, dashed forward and crouched upon the hearth, shivering now so that her teeth chattered in her small head.

Miss Finch followed her more slowly. Miss Finch stood looking down at her visitor. There was a bright sheen, like unshed tears, over Miss Finch's fine eyes.

" Koo ! " said the visitor. " 'Tain't 'arf lovely and warm in 'ere ! 'Tain't 'alf bleedin' cold ahtside."

" My dear ! " Miss Finch was shocked. " My *dear* ! "

" Well 'tis," said the visitor. " Perishin' cold and wet. I sy, Lydy "—her voice had taken on now the professional whine—" cahn't I tyke me cowt orf ? "

" Of course, of course," said Miss Finch with something like a break in her voice. She knelt down beside the woebegone figure and with gentle hands took off the sodden garment. She stood back, the coat held unheeded between her hands while it dropped a little pool of black-stained water on to the grey carpet. Her visitor crouched over the fire like a tragic monkey, holding out long, slim-fingered hands to the glow.

Still holding the coat, Miss Finch spoke again. She seemed to have some difficulty with her voice. It was not the voice with which she had spoken when she had opened the outer door. It was a thicker voice, choked a little as if the words which she spoke were too big for her mouth. She said, getting these words out with slow difficulty :

" But what are you doing, dear ? Out alone at this time of night ! And what is your age ? . . . How old are you, dear ? "

" Firteen."

The waif looked with a soft, frightened movement over her shoulder and up at Miss Finch. Her great eyes

made Miss Finch's eyes flinch from them. She put up
her hand with a quick movement of her whole body as if
to guard herself from a blow.

" I ain't done nuffink wrong. I got lorst I told yer ! "

" My dear," said Miss Finch and moved forward a
little. The wet coat, now, was brushing against her legs,
but she didn't seem to notice it. " Of course you've
done nothing wrong." She seemed suddenly to become
aware of the wet coat. She hung it, with care, upon the
back of an office chair and turned again to walk to the
fireplace and stood, elbows leaning upon the mantelpiece, looking down at her guest.

" Tell me," said Miss Finch, still finding difficulty with
her words, " you poor little thing. How did you come
to get lost ? How is it that you, a child of thirteen, are
wandering about like this ? You don't live here, do
you ? "

" Don't live anywheres," said the guest. " Farver's
got a caravan and we go rahnd to fairs and when we
stopped to 'ave a bit o' dinner this mornin' I goes awye
for a walk and I'se very tired and I finds a hystack. I
lies dahn and goes to sleep and when I wakes up Dad
and Mum and the bleedin' caravan and Spot—he's my
dog—well the 'ole bleedin' lot's gorn, missus. Ever since
I've been walkin' abaht on me trotters to see if I could
find 'em, but they're gorn. Then it comes over reel dark
and I gets afryde like and lorst same as I tell ye. And
then I sees this 'ere plyce and I means to knock at
some door and arst for a doss or p'raps a bit o' bread to
put in me belly. And then that gryte man 'e chyses me—
Kor, Jesus ! 'e didn't 'arf frighten me . . ."

" My poor little girl," said Miss Finch. " So you're
only thirteen and your Daddy has a caravan and he's
gone away with the caravan and you don't know where
you are and your Daddy doesn't know where you
are ? "

"That's right, missus, that's right!" She sniffed; passed her hand across her eyes. "That's right. I dunno where I am and Dad, 'e doesn't know where I am—not that 'e'd care so bleedin' much if 'e never saw me agyne."

"You mustn't say that," said Miss Finch in a new and somehow crisper voice. "You mustn't say that!" She smiled down at her visitor who still seemed to cower away from her. Miss Finch began to bustle.

"I know what you'd like," she said. "You would like a nice hot cup of cocoa with lots of nice milk and sugar in it and some bread and butter? Now wouldn't you?"

"Not 'arf," said the visitor, "I wouldn't! You jest show 'em to me, missus."

Miss Finch bustled out. "I will. I will." Her voice came back through the open door.

And then the sound of her feet running up the carpeted stairs to her flat above.

The visitor cast a hunted glance about her; a fearful glance. She looked at the door. She looked at the gaily curtained windows. She looked round at the stern though comfortable furniture. She stood in the centre of the room by Miss Finch's table and gazed up at the great skylight window in the roof. Nervously she played first with an ink-pot, then with a pencil and lastly with Miss Finch's ebony ruler with the ivory tips.

Upstairs, Miss Finch, her breath so laboured that her breasts seemed at times to be going to burst the silk blouse which covered them, stood before the bentwood hatstand in the passage of her little flat. . . .

Lost . . . doesn't know where she is. . . . Father doesn't know where she is . . . just a small bit of human flotsam. . . . Miss Finch's hand went to her heart. Miss Finch's face was very pale. Her eyes looked, against their surrounding whiteness, almost as big as the great orbs of her visitor. Now her breath came hissing out between her clenched, white, admirable teeth. . . .

Lost. . . . Doesn't know where she is. . . . Father doesn't know where she is. . . . Just a small bit of human flotsam. . . .

Miss Finch went, half-pace by half-pace, towards the bent-wood stand. Her hand, crooked like a claw, came out until it grasped the handle of her dumpy umbrella . . .

Miss Finch stood upon the topmost of her steps and with her left hand, silently removed her shoes. Miss Finch, levering herself to her feet with a thrust of the umbrella, began slowly and very, very quietly to descend the stairs.

Lost. . . . Doesn't know where she is. . . . Father doesn't know where she is. . . . Just a small bit of human flotsam. . . .

Miss Finch reached the door of the Editor's room. She halted just before she was within the sight of any one inside that room. She seemed to have difficulty with her breath. She commanded herself. She moved the umbrella from the right hand to the left, her right hand hovering over the umbrella's handle. She took two steps forward upon her stockinged feet. Her face now was dead white; her eyes had a glassy, polished look like sea-washed pebbles. Her mouth worked and a thin line of white foam defined the junction of her close-clenched lips.

Lost. . . . Doesn't know where she is. . . . Father doesn't know where she is. . . . Just a small bit of human flotsam. . . .

Now she was squarely in the doorway. Crouched by the fire was her visitor staring with vacant, childlike eyes into the far corner, holding in her hands Miss Finch's ebony ruler, one of its ivory ends between her lips. Miss Finch's left hand holding the dumpy umbrella went behind her back. Miss Finch came brightly into the room. She spoke in a light, clear voice. She went near to her guest. She said :

" Your cocoa won't be a minute, my poor little girl. It's just on the boil. Stand up now and let's see what we can do about your wet clothes."

The eyes of the waif fixed their gaze upon her face. Slowly the small figure rose to its feet, gripping the ruler. " All right, missus," said a thin, high voice.

They stood facing each other and the yellow blaze from the electric lamp showed each the other's face.

Suddenly the waif backed. A little choked cry came from her. She took one step back, then two more ; then more, in a stumbling run which fetched her with a bang against the table of Miss Finch's assistant editor. The huge eyes roved wildly this way and that to the door ; to the window ; to the great skylight above her head.

" What's the matter, dear ? " said Miss Finch, coming forward slowly.

The eyes of the waif were wide and staring and the waif's mouth opened and a scream came from it.

Miss Finch came nearer. " What's the matter, dear ? " she said.

Lost. . . . doesn't know where she is. . . . Father doesn't know where she is. . . . Just a little bit of human flotsam . . .

Miss Finch was now very near. Again, with her eyes fixed upon Miss Finch, the waif screamed. Miss Finch's left hand came from behind her back. Her right hand clasped the handle of her dwarf umbrella. Her two hands came apart. . . . The umbrella, without the handle, fell to the floor with a soft clatter, but in Miss Finch's right hand there was a thin something which gleamed blue in the yellow light. . . .

Miss Finch drew in her breath with a little bubbling hiss. She moved her right hand.

Miss Finch's visitor raised, with a wild, ineffectual gesture, the ebony ruler.

Miss Finch laughed. . . .

With a sound which, in that small quiet room, was like the rending of heaven itself, the glass and frame of the skylight smashed inwards. From six feet above her, something dark and huge and heavy fell beside Miss Finch and clutched at her. . . .

Miss Finch rolled upon the floor. . . .

Outside there came another, different crash and the tinkling of more broken glass . . . and heavy running footsteps along the boarded passage.

The waif collapsed upon the table. The ebony ruler fell from her hands to the floor hitting the grey carpet with a little thud. . . .

There was a scuffling going on upon the floor.

The doorway suddenly framed two men, so that, with the man who rolled upon the floor with Miss Finch, there were three men now here.

The two newcomers bent over the struggling heap, but before they could put their hands on it, there was a click and a jingle and Pike got to his feet. There was a long bleeding scratch running down from the corner of his left eye to his jaw. His eyes were bright and fierce, but his mouth was wide in a smile of triumph.

On the Persian rug before the gas fire, Miss Finch struggled, despite the handcuffs, until she sat. Her eyes seemed to have changed colour; they were wide and staring. Her mouth worked but no sound came from it. . . . Her face was no longer chalk-white, but was duskily flushed.

Pike went forward. Behind him, the two men moved close. Pike stooped. He tapped his prisoner upon the shoulder. He began to murmur to her cautionary words. . . .

The woman's face remained expressionless. . . . Her mouth went on working. . . .

Pike came to the end of his rigmarole and then, even as he began to straighten himself, she flung back her head and spat into his face.

3

Two cars pulled up outside the headquarters of the County Police in St. Raglands. The hands of the clock over the town hall stood at one forty-five. The passengers of the two cars made a little procession which wound quick way through the swing doors. The uniformed sergeant saluted. Pike smiled at him.

" Get my message to Sir Gerald ? " he said.

The sergeant saluted again. " Yes, sir. He's in there waiting. If you'll follow me . . ." They followed him.

He threw open a door and the procession filed in. There was the Chief Constable and there, too, were Farrow, smiling all over his prizefighter's face, and Davis, looking like a glum fox.

The Chief Constable came to Pike, holding out his hand.

Pike shook it.

" My God ! " said the Chief Constable and could get out no more words. He looked over Pike's shoulder at those who had followed Pike. " But where is . . . where is she ? " he said.

Pike looked round too. " Just outside the door. She's not a pleasant sight."

The Chief Constable once more looked over Pike's shoulder. He saw Curtis whom he knew and Blaine whom he knew, but in between Blaine and Curtis was a small and shivering waif. The Chief Constable looked at Pike in bewilderment. " Who's this ? " he said.

Pike's smile grew wider yet. He turned to the waif. He said :

" You must pardon me. May I introduce Sir Gerald Mainwaring, the Chief Constable of the County. . . . Sir Gerald, this is Miss Barbara Fairley. I don't know whether you go to the theatre much, Sir Gerald, but you're sure to have heard . . ."

The Chief Constable was staring until his eyes seemed in danger of leaving his head. " Not," he said, " not Dinah in *The Golden Cup* ? "

" Quite right ! " said the waif, and then, looking from one escort to the other, " For God's sake has anybody got a gasper ? "